ORPHANS

Gerald Pearce

Walker and Company
New York

For Joan and Scott

Copyright © 1990 by Gerald Pearce
All rights reserved. No part of this book may be reproduced or
transmitted in any form or by any means, electronic or mechanical,
including photocopying, recording, or by any information storage and
retrieval system, without permission in writing from the Publisher.
All the characters and events portrayed in this work are fictitious.
First published in the United States of America in 1990
by Walker Publishing Company, Inc.
Published simultaneously in Canada by Thomas Allen & Son
Canada, Limited, Markham, Ontario
Library of Congress Cataloging-in-Publication Data
Pearce, Gerald
Orphans / Gerald Pearce
ISBN 0-8027-5764-2
I. Title.
PR6066.E15707   1990
823'.914—dc20   89-70692
CIP

Printed in the United States of America
2 4 6 8 10 9 7 5 3 1

▽

Chapter 1

IF I HADN'T COME back to leave the keys I wouldn't have been there when the call came through. At least I didn't heave the phone through the window. I just hung it up. It sat on the desk at the edge of a patch of sunlight as quiet as a headstone, while serenely busy dust motes danced in the afternoon brightness slanting through the window.

I dropped the keys beside the phone, and took a last look around. The office was just an anonymous room with some secondhand furniture and nothing to suggest anyone ever sat or leaned their elbows on it.

When I turned to the door the phone started up again. I ignored it and left the room. The phone kept ringing behind the frosted glass panel on which discreet black letters spelled out JAMES KELLER, ATTORNEY-AT-LAW, with smaller letters down in the corner saying "Enter." I checked the door to make sure it was locked and walked toward the head of the stairs, the ringing telephone fading behind me. It had to be Felicia this time. Anyone else would have given up long ago.

The rest of the building was quiet. I went down echoing stairs—the Barker Building had only two floors—across the empty lobby, and through the swing doors into a warm late afternoon that had a touch like a caress.

Courthouse Plaza deserved a more romantic name. A few graceful palms nodded over the central square and there were enough white-walled Spanish-style buildings to prompt travel writers to burble

1

about old-time charm. Unhurried and peaceful under skies un-dimmed by air pollution, it was confidently small-town. Usually. Today the plaza was a disaster area populated by women without makeup wearing jeans and T-shirts, and burly guys with clubbed hair and saws and hammers in their hands. Some were city workers erecting a couple of performance stages at opposite corners of the plaza. The rest were members of the Dos Cruces art colony who were setting up booths, pavilions, and displays for the festival opening the day after tomorrow. Dos Cruces had hosted the Lindero County Art Festival for more than thirty years. Tomorrow artists and craftspeo-ple from all over the West would be arriving and setting up, and the air of improvisation would get even more frantic.

Down toward Fourth Street, on the opposite side of the road, two men in work clothes were talking to a ramrod-straight old lady in a blue cotton dress who carried a clipboard. Half the world knew her as Katherine Cromwell, the artist, but to festival and art colony people she was Aunt Kate. She had to be around seventy, and had the white hair to prove it.

She finished her conversation and, seeing me, started across the street and waved. She didn't exactly jump around, but her step was energetic.

"Hi, Aunt Kate. What've they got you doing?"

She joined me on the sidewalk. The white hair was center-parted and drawn back into a no-nonsense little bun. The familiar rectan-gular reading glass hung from a ribbon around her neck, but today I thought she was wearing thicker prescription glasses than usual. They distorted her eyes. But her smile was as open and ready as ever.

"Oh, I'm in charge of geography, I guess." She gestured with the clipboard. "Who goes where. Unofficially I'm a sort of a den mother."

"Unofficially, how good's the work this year?"

"From what I've seen, there's a lot of self-conscious junk, a lot of serviceable craftsmanship, and a few pieces so good you want to cry." We strolled down toward Fourth. "Do you mind my asking—have you heard from Felicia?"

"Not directly. Just had a call from her lawyer. He's on her dad's legal staff. Nothing good."

"Is it true you're closing the office?"

"Just closed it. The lease is up tomorrow anyway, no sense in renewing. I've got job offers from two L.A. law firms that want answers by the fifteenth. Haven't done anything about selling the house, though. That's so final."

"Does there really have to be a custody fight?"

"She's trying to talk me into giving her full custody. I don't know whose idea that was—hers or her dad's. But we have a court date next week."

We reached the Fourth Street intersection. Fourth had been closed to traffic a block away. A pair of counterculture types perched on ladders at opposite sides of the street were lashing a fabric banner to the streetlight poles about twelve feet above the roadway. Red letters on the banner spelled out WELCOME and announced the 32nd Annual Lindero County Art Festival, Sept. 1–4.

A man, made conspicuous by his prim three-piece suit and dark tie, gave the sign a jaundiced look from the sidewalk opposite us. He shook his head. His voice was impatient, officious.

"That banner goes at the other end of the block where traffic is rerouted, to explain why. Not everyone knows what's going on here—or cares."

The man on the ladder near him looked doubtful.

"You sure, man?"

"Of course I'm sure. I'm Charles Cromwell, the mayor's executive assistant."

The man on our side had seen Aunt Kate. He wore an Australian bush hat and had an open beer can crammed in the hip pocket of his paint-spattered overalls.

"That right, Aunt Kate?"

"That's who he is, and I'm afraid he's right."

"Okay. Win a few, lose a few."

The banner came down as Charles Cromwell crossed the street toward us. He was tall and had probably once resembled his mother, but he had grown jowly and soft. He had discontented eyes and wore his three-piece suit like a proclamation of merit.

He gave me a nod before turning to Aunt Kate. "Are you really handling space assignments, Mother, or just running errands for someone?"

"I really am, Charlie."

"You're probably doing the whole thing by yourself—you invite everyone to take advantage of you. Why not simply exhibit your work?"

"Because my eyes aren't what they used to be and I can't produce much." Her voice was crisp and noncombative. "I like being useful, Charlie. If all I could do was run errands, why, then I'd run errands."

He sighed shortly. His disapproving eyes swiveled back and forth across the plaza. "The Chief's assigning extra patrolmen tonight."

Aunt Kate smiled gently. "Festival people are housebroken, Charlie."

"Damn it, Mother, don't call me Charlie. And you ought to stop letting everyone call you Aunt Kate. Times change. Most of this crowd are riffraff. What you call art is getting to be just something that interferes with the city's functioning."

"Art *is* the city's function."

He gave her a wintry smile.

"Dos Cruces is trying to grow up, Mother. Someday you're going to have to let it." His smile softened. For a moment he had sounded almost human. He gave me an abrupt nod. "Evening, Counselor."

He barged off toward city hall like a man harried by phantoms.

"What's he up to, Aunt Kate?"

"Oh, you know Charlie. He wants to turn Dos Cruces into the new Palm Springs," Aunt Kate said, watching him leave. "I think he's planning to run for mayor. He'd better get himself a new wardrobe—we're still a pretty unbuttoned community. Poor Charlie."

I caught the echo of deep sorrow in her voice; but she gave me a warm smile and extended a thin strong hand and squeezed my arm.

"I'd say buy me a drink, young man, only I have to get back to work. You take care."

My old Hornet station wagon was in the lot two blocks down Fourth. I retrieved it, drove it to the gym, and swam ten two-hundred-yard freestyle repeats in respectable time. Then I had something to eat at a truck stop and got home just before dark.

Home was fifteen minutes from Courthouse Plaza in what was going to be a residential suburb in a few years. I drove out the Pollock Highway to Fox Hollow Road, turned left into low desert hills, then took the unfinished track leading off to the right. They'd been going to pave it "any day now" for the last three years. So far there was only one house on it, ours—mine: an ordinary two-bedroom-and-den overlooking a stretch of lawn and the desert hillside sloping back to the highway. It had been going cheap because it was a bit before its time and hard to sell this far out in the boonies, though it was actually just inside the city limits and there were nice homes farther up Fox Hollow, before it descended into the suburban developments.

The air in the house was hot and still. In spite of my stuff strung around, the place had that unlived-in look. I opened the windows in the bedroom and the French doors from the living room out onto the lawn.

The evening was still, reasonable. A car went by on the highway but failed to disturb the early stars. The Fox Hollow shopping center might have been fifty miles away instead of only one. On an evening like this the desert smelled the way it must have smelled to the Indians. I turned on the lawn sprinklers, got a beer from the refrigerator. Maybe no one lived here, but it would be a lot to give up. I had to, though. It was either that or give up my daughter. Some choices don't need weighing.

I turned on the stereo. I was deciding between early Jefferson Airplane and Alfred Brendel playing Mozart when a sound like small firecrackers exploding came from over the hill in the direction of Carver Canyon. A man named Clinton Farrell lived there. I'd never met him but I'd heard of his boozing and heard the noise of his .22 when he climaxed a serious drunk by blazing away at empty cans and bottles and, presumably, private phantoms looming out of his alcoholic fog.

I spindled the Brendel and started the turntable.

At 8:30 the phone rang.

I turned down the music before answering, giving my name in a tone that was supposed to invite people to tell me their troubles.

"Mr. Keller." A familiar male voice, cool as the edge of a filing cabinet but not so chummy. "This is Mr. Engle again, representing the former Mrs. Keller."

"You're sure you're not representing her father?"

"As you know, I'm a member of the law firm of Hamner, Engle and Belden, which represents Hammond Industries and Mr. Hammond personally; but no, in this matter, I assure you that I'm representing Mrs. Keller, as I did in her recent divorce."

"All right."

"Mr. Keller, the, ah, offer I submitted to you this afternoon was incorrect. I don't know how I could have misunderstood my instructions. My apologies."

"So they changed the rules on you," I said.

"As I said," he insisted coldly, "it was my error."

"Don't you think it's outrageous, offering a man thirty thousand dollars to renounce all rights to his daughter, even visitation rights?"

"My error. The correct figure is sixty thousand."

"If she has that much money, it's because her father gave it to her."

"The money is available—in cash, the day the custody decision is handed down, or payable in whatever increments you choose over the next five years, whichever suits your tax purposes."

"Why is Ed Hammond trying to avoid a custody battle?"

"Mr. Keller, I refuse to engage in that kind of conversation—"

"Mr. Engle, I appreciate your reluctance to discuss the character and motivation of the people you represent, okay? But realize that if I were the kind of man who'd sell his three-year-old kid I might've done it for a lot less than thirty grand. But when I don't jump at the offer it gets doubled. Why?"

The sigh that came over the phone was that of a reasonable man having his patience unfairly tested.

"Mr. Hammond," he said carefully, "wishes to resolve this matter as equitably as possible. What he and his daughter have determined is right for his granddaughter involves your surrendering your rights as a parent, whatever value you place on them. What he has offered is his suggestion of a reasonable price."

"He has a defective idea of parenthood, which may explain why his own daughter is a narcissistic, destructive, emotional cripple."

He had raised her alone, too. At age forty Ed Hammond had become a single parent when his wife, who was a decade younger, had walked out on him, the marriage, and their only child. Age three. Katy's age . . .

I thought something relaxed at the other end of the line. Engle laughed gently.

"Is that to be your line of attack, Mr. Keller? It'll do you no good, you know. She is charming, intelligent—"

"And therefore all the more dangerous. You've made your pitch, I've turned it down, so let's call it a night, okay?"

"I would urgently suggest, however, that in the interests of all concerned—"

"You're no judge of anyone's interests except Ed Hammond's, and possibly Felicia's. Good night, Mr. Engle."

I hung up and got another beer.

So the Hammonds had launched an all-out campaign, which meant that things would get worse before they got better. I would have to hang on to a dispassionate, analytical attitude.

Trying it gave me the shakes.

The record came to an end, the tone arm moved back onto its rest, and the turntable clicked off. In the oddly fragile silence that followed, someone knocked on the front door.

Puzzled, I opened it. Standing there was a guy I'd never seen before. He was in his late twenties, with a sinewy look and lean, strong-looking hands. His dark skin and thick black hair suggested Mexican ancestry. He wore a beat-up blue shirt, a small silver and turquoise ankh on a chain around his neck, and a pair of worked-in jeans. His moccasins were the kind that come up over the ankle and have a couple of abalone-shell buttons. There was a watch on a handsome tooled leather strap around one wrist and a rather fine silver ID bracelet around the other. He looked like an off-duty cowboy with a nice taste in personal jewelry, only none of the cowboys I knew ever went anywhere without those high-heeled boots on.

He said in an unaccented Anglo voice, "I hate to bother you, but my car died on the highway. Could I use your phone to call the auto club?"

I invited him in. "What's the trouble?"

"Overheating, starting to seize up. Turned out I threw a fanbelt—which I just had installed in April, so it was either defective or the installation was, I don't know."

I showed him into the den. There was an extension phone on the desk. He looked up the number and dialed, then turned around and noticed the framed painting on the opposite wall, a barren desert landscape after rain, with retreating clouds piled up in the distance. He grinned suddenly.

"That's a Katherine Cromwell! You know her?"

"Yes. She says it's a very minor piece but I like it, so she let me have it on long-term loan."

"Nice lady. I met her at last year's festival." He pointed to his bracelet. "Silversmith. Mike Garcia."

"Jim Keller. Like a beer?"

Before he could answer, someone at the other end picked up the phone. Suddenly, from outside, at the intersection of the highway and Fox Hollow, came a brief squeal of brakes, then the sound of a crunching impact. A heartbeat later there was a more confused crash, as though a loaded vehicle had tipped over. It sounded like a bad one.

Garcia's face went gray.

He said, "Jesus. Fran." He dropped the phone and ran for the door.

I said, "I can drive there faster than you can run."

Moments later we were in the station wagon accelerating off my part of the hillside.

▽

Chapter 2

WHEN I TURNED ONTO the highway toward town my headlights showed a tan Mercury Cougar blocking the citybound lane.
Ahead of it, at an angle following the curve of the road where it
began looping around a swelling in the land, an imaginatively
decorated van lay tilted against the pale rocky earth of the desert
hill. Its emergency flashers were blinking dutifully and someone
with long straight hair, in blue jeans and a denim jacket, was
climbing out of the driver's window. Before I had braked to a stop
Mike Garcia was out of the car and running to help her, wrapping
her in a bear hug as her feet touched the ground.

I got a ring binder notebook and a felt-tipped pen from the glove
compartment and got out of the car, leaving the motor running and
the headlights on.

"She okay?"

The girl's face swiveled off his chest. It was drawn and shocked.
She looked like a high school kid.

Mike nodded.

The Cougar was only a couple of years old. Its headlights were
out. What I could see of its front end was crumpled up like tin foil
and I heard water dripping. I didn't know why the car looked oddly
familiar until I went around the driver's side and saw who was at
the wheel. I'd seen him drive it into the city hall parking lot often
enough. He was staring straight ahead, still in the three-piece suit
and narrow tie, his hands in his lap.

"Hi, Charles. You all right?"

No response. He didn't even seem to breathe. I was about to reach in through the open window to see if he was still alive when he slowly moved his head and looked at me. His face had the lively color of a lump of lard and about as much expression.

He summoned a remote half-smile.

"I see you're on the job, Counselor."

"I live here."

His voice was bodiless, unemphatic. "How'd you like to represent me when I sue the incompetent driving that wreck? Probably an artist here for the festival with a skinful of dope."

"Easy, Charles. You hit a stationary vehicle with its emergency flashers on."

"It was illegally parked."

"The cops will look into that. Now come and meet the people—and for God's sake don't argue. Can you manage that?"

He shrugged without interest and unbuckled his shoulder harness.

"I wish I knew who was driving that oncoming car."

"What oncoming car?"

He gave me a look of dawning suspicion.

"Jesus Christ!" His voice was regaining its waspishness. "You don't think I'd do something like this through sheer native talent, do you? *What* oncoming car? The one coming from town! It took the turn too fast, fifty to sixty, lights on high beam. It blinded me. I took a jog to the right to avoid being hit, and before I could see again I ran into that stupid van. Satisfied?"

"See what kind of car it was?"

"If I could've seen anything, would I be sitting here now?"

He unlocked the door and got out—carefully, as though testing for injuries. Mike Garcia was lighting the last of three emergency flares, which he placed in a diagonal that cut off the citybound lane. The dark-haired girl had the back door of the van open and was checking inside with the help of a flashlight.

I put the ring binder and the pen on the Cougar's trunk in the glare of my car's headlights. Charles walked to the front of the Cougar like a man with glass knees. He looked bleakly at the damage, then at the van. Buckling had centered behind the van driver's door and was bad enough to suggest frame damage. Mike Garcia came over then, and Charles got his first good look at him. His mouth twisted as though he tasted something bad. Mike started to speak but Charles overrode him.

"Were you driving that piece of garbage?"

Mike stopped, gave Charles a surprised look, then clenched his teeth and went straight to my notebook on the Cougar's trunk and began writing, digging out his billfold to get his driver's license.

The back door of the van closed and the girl joined us. In the light she looked a little older—nineteen, maybe twenty. She was small. The long dark hair framed an appealing angular face with a generous mouth and wide-spaced eyes that flashed vivid blue in the headlight glare. Eyes need help to flash like that. Hers were wet.

She palmed moisture off her cheeks.

"Garbage is probably all it's got in it now, Mr. Loudmouth. Before you hit us it was carrying over six thousand dollars' worth of pottery and at least that much again in jewelry."

Charles gave a barking laugh.

"Do you smell extortion in the air, Counselor?"

The girl said, "Jesus, Mike. These guys know each other."

Mike put down the pen. She tucked her pale hand into his brown one.

"We're not exactly drinking buddies," I told them. "I'm a lawyer and he's Charles Cromwell, executive assistant to the mayor of Dos Cruces."

Mike said, "Cromwell?"

The girl made a strangled sound. "What'll I tell Aunt Kate?"

A film of sweat covered the gray pallor of Charles' face, but he managed to stand an inch taller.

"If you mean Katherine Cromwell, the artist, you're talking about my mother." He took two cards from his wallet, dropped them contemptuously on the Cougar's trunk, then grabbed the ring binder and read what Mike had written. "This is incomplete." He picked up the pen, stabbed it at the girl. "Who're you?"

"Fran Rowan. Frances Mary Rowan."

Charles hesitated. For seconds his mouth hung open. A long way off a police siren began howling.

". . . Rowan?"

"R-o-w-a-n. Frances Mary Rowan. Same address."

He wrote, then looked at her bleakly.

"Same address as . . . ?"

"As mine," Mike said.

"Of course." He wrote, tore the sheet out, and fumbled it into an inside pocket. Suddenly he staggered, turned, and blundered away along the shoulder beyond the station wagon.

He stopped and we heard him retching.

"Serves him right," Fran said with conviction.

I asked, "Got any contraband in the van? Grass, cocaine? If you have any, lose it. Charles is Aunt Kate's son but the relationship is only physical. He doesn't like the festival, or artists, or people with different last names living together. The first thing he's going to do when the cops get here is say you were acting weird so they'd better search the van for dope."

Fran said, "Can they do that, just on his say-so?"

"They might, because he's part of the city administration."

Mike shook his head.

"The van's clean."

"When you looked in the van, did you find a lot of damage?"

"The cases I moved sounded bad. Good thing jewelry's not that fragile."

"What else is in there?"

"Lumber and flats to build our booth, a picnic cooler, a couple of pieces of luggage with clothes and stuff. You don't travel light in this business."

The siren was louder, closer. I wondered who had called them, and why the siren.

"What were those dollar figures based on?"

"The retail value of the stuff we brought," Fran said. "We've got inventory lists on every crate. Are you his lawyer?"

"God, no!"

Beyond the station wagon Charles cleared his throat, spitting noisily. I asked Fran if there was other traffic at the time of the crash.

"Well, sure. I'd just taken my bandana off my head and was combing my hair, so I wasn't paying much attention, but I know one car came around that bend. Then a second after it went by—crash, the van tipped over and I couldn't see anything. All I could think was, 'Oh, God, Mike'—I was afraid something had happened to Mike."

Her face screwed up suddenly. She turned into Mike's chest and began to cry, awkwardly, without release.

Approaching footsteps crunched heavily.

"What's going on?" Charles demanded, coming into the light.

I said, "For Christ's sake, Charles. What d'you think's going on?"

"She's got some crying to do from before," Mike said.

Charles jerked his head toward the approaching siren.

"Who called them?"

I said I hadn't, and got him to write his car and driver's license numbers on the back of his insurance card. The other card he had thrown onto the Cougar's trunk was his own business card. I gave both to Mike as the siren screamed and two squad cars careened around the bend.

They shot by, turning up Fox Hollow. The trailing car stopped and backed up a few feet while the leader shifted gear and roared up the hill. A spotlight hit us.

A man's voice called, "Mr. Cromwell? Anyone hurt?"

"No."

"Have you called the station?"

"You're here, aren't you?"

"Not on a traffic call." The spotlight went out. "You know who lives in the house opposite Carver Canyon Road?"

"No. Counselor?"

"No."

Charles approached the squad car. "Why?"

"Have you seen anyone? Any traffic?"

"Just us. One car earlier, coming from town. What's this about?"

"I can tell you, I guess. We got a report of a shooting. We'll call the accident in for you."

There was a squeal of tires and the cop car went chasing its bounding headlight beams up Fox Hollow. I remembered the fire-cracker popping of Clint Farrell's .22. Or what had sounded like someone's .22.

I reached into the station wagon, turned off the lights and the motor, turned on the emergency flashers.

"They'll be a while," Charles said. "You needn't wait."

"I'll wait."

Charles went over to his car and felt around on the front seat. Beyond the range of the flares and the yellow blink of the emergencies, the night was very dark. And quiet. A long way off a dog barked in someone's backyard, but that was all.

Fran Rowan and Mike Garcia sat close together a few feet above the tilted roof of their van. I propped myself against the front of the station wagon as Charles wandered back from his car. In the flashing yellows he still looked badly shaken.

He had brought back a pipe and a leather roll-up tobacco pouch. He began filling the pipe.

"Soon there won't be any Anglos left in this part of the country." At least he kept his voice down.

"You're just pissed about the accident," I told him. "Don't take it out on those kids."

He flicked a lighter into action, applied it to the pipe. He sucked noisily for a few seconds, then blew smoke at the stars.

"I don't plan to stand around with my thumb up my nose being Mr. Nice Guy while my insurance rates go up like a rocket. Want a new client?"

"Come on, Charles. First, I can't. Second, it would cost you more than any increase in your car insurance."

"Why? I didn't ask to get blinded by that other car."

"Any accident that costs your insurance company more than three hundred dollars is chargeable, which means your premiums go up. Your insurers won't be able to collect from theirs because you hit a stationary vehicle. You did a lot more than three hundred dollars damage to your car alone. Add the damage—"

"All right! Look, at least do this. As a favor. Check a few details, advise me if I'm getting screwed."

I agreed, more to shut him up than anything. He sucked awkwardly on his pipe, as though he were new to it. I knew he'd smoked a pipe for years. Maybe it was more a matter of image than enjoyment.

After a while another cop car and a tow truck arrived and parked. The two guys in the tow truck were blond and chunky and wore grubby overalls. One looked like a high school kid and the other like his big brother. They moved with an air of impatient physical competence as they checked both vehicles and said they'd have to tow the Cougar in. The van might not have tipped if the right wheels hadn't slid broadside into a sandy depression when it was hit. They'd have to unload it to avoid more damage to the fragile cargo when they hauled it upright, then they'd unjam the driver's door and install a new fanbelt. They began unloading boxes through the back door.

The cops were just cops nobody knew, in their thirties, with stone indifference underlying their surface politeness. The blond was Hardy and the dark one Vasquez. They set out more flares and got everyone's name straight. I gave them my business card, but when I explained that I wasn't a witness they decided to ignore me. Hardy took Charles into the squad car to take his statement while Vasquez took measurements of skid marks and distances and made notes.

An ambulance came tearing around the corner from town and turned up Fox Hollow. Charles got out of the squad car, then first Fran and then Mike got in.

Charles reloaded and lit his pipe.

"If the damn festival didn't mean so much extra work," he complained, "I'd've been home at a reasonable hour and wouldn't have decided on the Steak House for dinner."

"It's Wednesday. The Steak House is closed Wednesdays."

"Have you ever had a day that made you forget your own name? So I forgot what day it was. Most restaurants close Monday or Tuesday. Why does the Steak House have to be different?"

Mike got out of the squad car and Officer Hardy invited me in. Maybe I'd become a witness after all.

"Just a couple of questions," he said from the front seat. "Did you see either Miss Rowan or Mr. Garcia enter their vehicle, or possibly remove anything from it?"

"Miss Rowan looked into the back of the van with a flashlight. They were bringing merchandise to the art festival—hand-thrown pottery and jewelry with considerable retail value."

"How much is considerable, Mr. Keller?"

"They said about twelve thousand dollars."

"Did you at any time see either of them throw anything away?"

"No. Did I have them under observation at all times? No. And no, I saw no sign of intoxication induced by alcohol or other drugs. Mr. Garcia was frightened for Miss Rowan's safety when he heard the crash from my house, but has always been very much in command of himself. Miss Rowan was shaken by the collision but nothing inappropriate. I asked them if they had any controlled substance in the van. They said no."

There was a long moment of silence from the front seat. Then Hardy said in a carefully casual voice, "Why did you ask that, Mr. Keller?"

"Because I thought Charles Cromwell would try to make trouble for them any way he could. If he can show they're users, then anything he wants to accuse them of is going to carry more weight, and he won't look so bad."

"Are you acquainted with either Miss Rowan or Mr. Garcia?"

"Never met either of them before."

"Are you representing them?"

"You think they need representation?"

He retracted the tip of his ballpoint.

"Okay. Thank you, Mr. Keller."

But I still had two bits' worth to contribute.

"You'll have trouble justifying a search of the van," I told him. "You can ask Mr. Garcia and he may give his permission, but then you'd have to ask Mr. Cromwell's permission to search his car, too. You'd want to avoid any suspicion of conducting a biased investigation. You never asked me if Mr. Cromwell showed signs of intoxication, Officer."

Another of those silences.

He said tightly, "I was getting to it."

"Good. Since you ask: no, he didn't."

He half-turned and stared at me.

"Then why make such a big thing out of it, Mr. Keller?"

"The answer's no big thing. That you didn't ask the question was."

He kept me skewered to the back seat with that stare. It was probably a standard bit from *Miami Vice*. He said abruptly, "I told you I was getting to it. Okay, Mr. Keller. Thank you."

As I got out of the car, the ambulance, followed by one of the cop cars, pulled to a rolling stop at the bottom of Fox Hollow. The ambulance punched its siren and sped toward town. The squad car proceeded more sedately, the officers in the front seat trading solemn recognition signals with Hardy and Vasquez. There was someone huddled in the back seat.

The two mechanics had already moved the Cougar out of the way. Now they hooked the tow truck's winch to the raised frame of the van's tilted chassis. Hardy and Vasquez had a consultation while Mike and Fran held hands and watched the winch power their van back upright. It crunched noisily onto all four wheels.

The officers aproached Mike and Fran.

"Mr. Garcia," Hardy said, "we'd like permission to conduct a search of your vehicle."

"What for, for God's sake?"

Hardy and Vasquez traded glances. I drifted over. Hardy looked at me stonily.

Vasquez had a gentler voice than Hardy, though not enough gentler to make anyone cry.

"There's a suspicion that you got drugs in there."

"Sure there's drugs," Fran said. "Birth control pills and an unopened bottle of Excedrin."

"Not those kinds of drugs," Vasquez said.

"What aroused this suspicion?" I asked him.

"You're not in a courtroom, Mr. Keller," Hardy said. "You got no standing here. You're interfering."

"If Mr. Garcia retained me as his attorney I'd have standing enough to protest your hassling him, and to advise . . ."

"No one's hassling him," Vasquez said.

"If we arrest him we'll give him his rights," Hardy said.

"He has rights even if you don't arrest him."

Mike said, "What'll it cost to retain you?"

"How about a buck?"

He handed me a dollar bill.

Hardy said, "I guess our report will have to show that Mr. Garcia objected to having his vehicle searched."

"I don't object to having the van searched," Mike said, "just to being harassed."

Vasquez said slowly, "Then we have your permission?"

"Why not? Just don't do it here if you want to go through all the cases. The insurance man's going to want to see all the pieces."

Hardy chewed his back teeth. Vasquez took him aside for another conference. I gave Mike back his dollar and the two cops went over to Charles. No one was happy. I heard Vasquez murmur, "Yeah, but we got no real reason to search the van either . . ." Charles finally threw up his hands.

"Okay, okay, if my say-so isn't enough, forget it." He came barging over, looking both exhausted and ready to fight. "What the hell are you trying to do, Keller?"

"Save your butt. If it ever came out that you had the cops harass innocent civilians out of concern for your future election chances . . ."

"I'm concerned about the quality of life in Dos Cruces."

"Save it for the campaign, and stop making things worse than they are already."

The mechanics finished installing the new fanbelt. The young one told Mike to fire her up while his partner wiped his hands on an oily rag. Mike climbed in. The starter cranked, and the motor caught and shook a little then began running smoothly. The older guy unhooked his worklight and shut the hood. He gave the worklight to the kid, who carried it to the tow truck, coiling cable as he went. The older guy got in on the passenger's side of the van. Mike eased it into the citybound lane and drove off around the bend on a test run.

Charles followed me to where the kid was packing tools away.

I asked, "What about the old fanbelt?"

The kid shrugged.

"Back on the highway somewhere. Half a mile, two miles, depending on how fast the van was going, how hot it runs—a few things like that."

"Was the van roadworthy?"

"Oh, sure. There's a highway patrol inspection sticker on the windshield." He stowed the toolbox in the truck.

"You don't know it was roadworthy," Charles said frostily, "until you check the condition of the old fanbelt."

"It was in a condition to get thrown. It mighta been old and worn or it might not. But that's a motor that's had a lot of care. It sounds like it just had a tune-up, the battery's nearly new, the fuel pump's nearly new, and if the belt was worn his mechanic woulda got him to change it."

"You don't know that," Charles yelped. "Maybe he's his own mechanic and just didn't bother."

The kid gave Charles a sad smile. "Maybe." He started writing up the work on a printed form held on a metal clipboard.

The van came back around the bend, halting near the stuff that had been unloaded. There was no more talk of searching it.

Vasquez said to Charles, "They know where to tow your car, Mr. Cromwell?"

"I told them Ortega's."

"We can give you a lift in the squad car."

Charles threw me an empty look.

"Provided the counselor here doesn't go into cardiac arrest at such a blatant example of police prejudice."

I said I'd try not to. Charles said that a ride in a squad car would be a perfect end to a lousy evening and climbed in.

Mike Garcia signed for the work done on the van, then gave me a business card. It said Craft Design Studio, gave an address in Santa Barbara, and had both their names on it.

"Is Mr. Cromwell always like this?" Mike asked.

"Pretty much, but I guess he's real sensitive about his image right now. Rumor says he's planning to run for mayor. I think he'll run for anything he can catch."

"Whatever he catches," Fran said with an urchin grin that made her look like a kid again, "I hope it's serious."

Mike bundled her into the van like an indulgent parent, then stuck out his hand and said thanks, he owed me a dinner. I said that he didn't owe me anything, but I'd take him up on a cold beer. He said they had a room at the Ramada Inn, and to give him a call next time I got thirsty. Fran wiggled her fingertips at me as he pulled the van back onto the road.

I wasn't ready to go back to that empty house, so I U-turned the station wagon around the two cops, who were kicking flares off the road, and drove out the Pollock Highway.

What I knew about fanbelts you could lose under your thumbnail, but the thing I picked up 1.7 miles from the Fox Hollow intersection certainly looked like one. Holding it close to my headlights, I saw a lot of reddish color showing through superficial grime. Whatever it was made of was brittle; at one point the laminations were separating and elsewhere tiny cracks scarred the surface. One of these had sheared clean through. The belt might be from the van and it might not. Even if it was, there would be no way to prove it against determined opposition. I kept it anyway, tossing it behind the front seat.

$\triangledown$

Chapter 3

W HEN I FINALLY GOT home, I turned on the light in the garage, raised the hood, and looked at my own fanbelt.

It was a uniform gray. I had replaced the old one more than three years ago on the advice of a mechanic at the Mobil station at the Fox Hollow shopping center. "Might be good for years," he'd told me, "or it might go tomorrow." He had grinned. "You wouldn't want it to happen right when you're taking that nice-looking lady down to Maternity on the big day, would you?" So I'd had him install the new one, and three weeks later I drove Felicia down to Maternity without incident. The baby weighed in at six pounds eight ounces. Katherine Elizabeth Keller. Katy. And then, very subtly at first, something had begun happening to Felicia . . .

I closed the hood and the garage door and went inside. The indoor air had cooled a little. I went outside through the living room and turned off the lawn sprinklers—and the goddam phone rang. It stood on a table next to the easiest chair in California. I went back inside and picked it up dutifully.

"James Keller."

Felicia said in a voice like tinkling icicles, "It's about time you got back."

"There was an accident down at the corner. I was being useful."

"And finding yourself a rich client, for a change? That *would* be a change."

Patience, Keller. "We were never broke, Felicia. I've got rich clients and poor ones. No, Charles Cromwell was the only offer I got and he's not rich, not yet anyway. Had to say no. Business out of town."

She gave a little sigh. I could see the faint smile that went with it—rueful, a little sad.

"Oh, that." Now she sounded sweetly reasonable. "You know you're being very silly about that, Jim. You know it's just to spite me. You never cared about being a father . . ."

"Where'd you get that one? Same place you got the one about my being a sex fiend sadist?"

"But it's true! What do you know about parent-child relationships? You were teaching her to read, for heaven's sake. Do you think the child is some kind of freak?"

I hadn't heard that one before.

"She wanted to learn so I was teaching her. She'd be reading third grade stuff by now if you hadn't taken her away."

"Do you think it would do her good, this precocious accomplishment? Don't you think a little girl of three has more important things to learn? Things her father can't teach her?"

"Probably. There are things I can't teach her, and there are things you shouldn't be allowed to teach her."

She said instantly, with soft menace, "Such as?"

"How to dissemble. How to manipulate. Things that don't have to be consciously taught—or consciously learned."

A light laugh. The menace was forgotten.

"Oh dear, aren't we being spiteful! And you used to say you loved me. Well, I'm the same person."

"You couldn't prove it by me."

"Perhaps you never knew me. How like you that would be! I used to think that what you never wanted to know was my father's money. How silly, how adolescent! Why couldn't you have let Daddy give you a job and make us comfortable?"

"It would've meant becoming a corporate lapdog."

"And you're counselor to the poor and downtrodden, right? Bullshit, buster. You just like to pose that way. You were so drawn to all that money that you had to prove it was beneath you. You had to avoid the suspicion it was what you had married me for. Well, now you've got your chance to get your hands on some of it, without having to go on a payroll or take orders or anything, and you can go on being counsel to vagabonds and dopers and prostitutes for the rest of your life. All in exchange for stopping this spiteful custody thing."

"Go play with your paper dolls, Felicia."

"Jesus Christ, you pervert, what do you want?"

There wasn't much point in going on with this. I said, "You wouldn't understand," and hung up.

When she called back I kept her waiting four rings before answering.

"James Keller."

"Don't ever hang up on me."

"Don't be silly. You can call me all the names you like, but nothing says I've got to sit around and listen. After all, this time I'm thinking of Katy's good and my own. I'll see you in court."

"Do you think you're good enough, Counselor, to give the Hammond attorneys any trouble?"

"Nothing says I've got to represent myself."

"You know lawyers don't give freebies. Good lawyers cost money. *Real* money."

"I'll sell the house."

"That house is half mine!"

"According to the property settlement, I have six months to raise the cash to pay you for your half. If I want to sell to raise the money, that's up to me. What I do with my half is also up to me. Meantime I get to live here."

"You're a malicious, spiteful son of a bitch. You had me fooled once, but you don't fool me now one bit."

"What was it you called to say, Felicia?"

"I've changed my mind."

The phone clicked in my ear.

Talking to Felicia was like arguing with smoke. I had been married to her for more than six years and was beginning to suspect that the personality I had known had never been more than a beautifully realized performance.

A red light reminded me that the stereo was still on. I turned it off and had a quick shower and went to bed. I might as well have stayed up and watched used car commercials on TV. When I finally got to sleep, it was to flail around in anxious dreams in which the identities of my daughter Katy and Frances Mary Rowan were hopelessly confused. I woke up around six, baffled and shaken, with a sense of irremediable loss.

$\triangledown$

Chapter 4

WHEN IT BECAME OBVIOUS I wouldn't be getting back to sleep, I fumbled into the day and got it started. While the coffee perked I showered again and shaved, then climbed into a blue T-shirt and jeans worn as soft as old suede. I had breakfast looking out the window at a sky of inexpressible serenity arching over pale bleached desert to the horizon.

No office today. No court dates. Just some practical chores and housekeeping. I paid a few bills and picked up around the house. I didn't have the patience to fool with a load of wet wash, so I crammed the laundry into a duffel bag and threw it into the station wagon.

Fox Hollow wound through low hills for half a mile before the houses began. These were low and weathered and looked as though they had grown naturally from the hillsides. Then the hills became hillocks and an unpaved road gave access to Carver Canyon, where Clint Farrell practiced drunken target shooting out of sight to the right. Then the cross streets began and you were in suburbia, with green lawns and kids on bikes and basketball hoops over garage doors, and suddenly there was the shopping center, fresh and optimistic in the bright morning.

Dropping the duffel bag off at the quick-service laundry, I took West Eleventh Street through the suburbs into town, parked in my usual lot on Fourth, and hiked to Courthouse Plaza.

A few trucks and vans with participant stickers for the art festival were being unloaded around the plaza, and directly across from the Barker Building two guys were hanging a sign up to identify a completed booth. The sign read CANYON CONCEPTS POTTERY. One of the guys, a rangy teenager with sunbleached hair and eyebrows, was perched halfway up a folding stepladder. The other guy could have been his dad. He stood on a metal folding chair and had a big curly square beard hiding most of his face. His color and waistline made you think more of beer and late nights than of sand and surfboards. When I went up to them, two pairs of gem-hard light blue eyes turned on me.

"Which one of you's the potter?"

"Mostly me," the burly one said. He jerked a thumb at the teenager. "He's going to college. Business administration. To make the family business pay enough to send him to college." A broad grin twitched the beard and flowing mustache. He dropped off the chair, sending a ripple from his belly to his beard. "What can I sell you, friend?"

"How much should a hand-thrown coffee mug bring?"

"How long's a piece of string? You buying 'em by the carload?"

"I'm taking an informal survey." I took Fran Rowan's card out. "Ever hear of the Craft Design Studio in Santa Barbara?"

"Oh, sure." He lifted his beard to show me a silver and turquoise cross hanging from his neck by a silver chain. "The folks I got this from. Mike Garcia's the jeweler. His old lady's the potter. Fran Rowan, Kate Cromwell's protégé."

"She any good?"

"That's what I'd like to find out," the kid said, coming down the ladder.

The older man said equably, "Hey, was it really that bad, being eighteen—all the time horny as a billygoat? How'd we ever survive?"

"It wasn't easy."

"Sure ain't," the kid said.

The potter made sympathetic noises.

"Couldn't find any pretty bones to jump before breakfast. Stands to ruin his whole day and mine, too. Yeah, Fran's good. What she does I couldn't do without pricing myself outa the market, and I ain't no slouch. What's this all about, friend?"

I gave him my business card, explaining about the office number not being good anymore.

"I'm trying to clear up some facts about a damage claim. Someone smacked into Fran and Mike's van last night and wrecked some pottery. I'm trying to find out what constitutes a fair price."

Both pairs of blue eyes became frosty and still.

"Who're you representing?" the bearded man asked.

"Nobody. The other driver asked me to look into it for him."

"I take it this 'other party' is a friend of yours."

"God forbid."

"You're doing it for someone who's *not* a friend?"

"I don't know if I'm doing it for him or to him. He'd like to dispute the damage claim, and I'm trying to talk him out of it."

"Gonna tell us who it is?"

"Hell, it's probably made the local news already. Charles Cromwell, the mayor's executive assistant."

"Why so concerned about this nonfriend, friend?"

"Just guarding my rear."

"Yeah, well, maybe. Okay, the prices vary. Five ninety-five, seven ninety-five, depending." He didn't say on what. "Now, if you'll excuse us, friend."

They went about their business. Suddenly I just wasn't there anymore, for either of them. I said thank you and good-bye. They were much too busy to answer.

The Ramada Inn was three blocks beyond the plaza, a sunny two-story building with a small dining room, a coffee shop, a swimming pool, and no pretensions. The coffee shop was a long, rectangular room filled with people and talk and the rattle of dishes and silverware. While I was standing behind a sign that asked me to wait for a hostess to seat me, I saw Fran Rowan and Mike Garcia being shown to a booth halfway down the room. The hostess, distributing menus the size of the *National Enquirer*, was too far off to waylay me.

Fran saw me and waved. She had lost some of her waiflike look; she was still petite, but if you hugged her she wouldn't break. She had on a white blouse and jeans, and she clearly wasn't wearing a bra. Her face, with its short nose and angular jaw, was softer than it had looked in the glare of the headlights, and her eyes were the biggest and darkest blue I had ever seen. Her unpainted mouth was gentle and humorous and sexy.

She slid deeper into the booth, moving her place setting, and patted the seat beside her.

"Have breakfast with us, Mr. Keller," Fran said.

"Just a coffee, if I may." I sat down with them. "Jim is easier."

"Okay."

"I picked up your fanbelt last night," I told Mike. "At least I guess it's yours."

"You went *looking* for it?"

Mike looked much the same as he had last night. Rested and unpressured, he had an air of relaxed vitality and competence.

"Nothing else to do. Less than two miles from the accident. Some color showing, so it can't have been too old. Maybe it got old on the shelf before you bought it."

"I'm gonna chew someone out about that," Mike said.

"I just got through talking to a bearded potter under a sign that said Canyon Concepts Pottery."

"That's Hank Cronjager," Fran said. "From Laguna Beach."

"He says you're very good at your trade. How'd you get so good so young?"

"I started early." No coyness or modest disclaimers. "Real early—in grade school. That's when I met Aunt Kate. She came to judge a little craft fair we had and to talk to us about art. She kept encouraging me from then on, and we got to be friends."

Mike Garcia laughed softly.

"Wow, talk about evading the question." He folded his menu and set it aside. "Okay, she's skillful because she's had a lot of practice, but that doesn't explain the important part—the talent. It's like blue eyes. Either you have them or you haven't. If you haven't, all the hard work in the world won't get 'em for you."

"All right," she said tartly. "Explain talent to the man."

"I just did. You're good because you can't help it."

Her left hand curled around his right and held it tightly. She smiled at me a little shyly.

"It's nice, having a fan."

"I know a good thing when I see it," Mike said.

An ample waitress with straw-colored hair and flushed skin gyrated our way with a half-full glass coffee pot. She left us with steaming cups. A little later she came back without the pot to take our orders.

Mike said over his cup, "We lucked out on the insurance. I looked up the local agent in the yellow pages and called him at home first thing this morning. He took pity on us, I guess. He said if I would bring the van to Ortega's Body Shop he would make sure an adjuster got to it by 9:30. Adjusters are independent, so I don't know how he could make a promise like that."

"Who's the agent?"

He pulled a half-sheet of notepaper from his pocket.

"Marcus Fox," he read. "Southwest Bonding and Insurance, 835 Ocotillo Drive."

"He's probably the only man in town who could. Ever hear of the Gang of Three? The three Fox brothers. He's the oldest. The middle brother is Lincoln Fox, District Attorney of Lindero County. The youngest is State Senator Harlan Fox—Handsome Harlan, wind-up doll for the real estate interests. Marcus is the one with the money. Insurance agent is only what he started out as. He's diversified."

"Why would he bother with us?" Fran wondered.

"Partly because it's good business to give good service, I guess, and partly because he wants to be seen being helpful to festival people because he's one of the guys behind some development plans the Dos Cruces art community's unhappy about. He's never run for office, but that doesn't mean he isn't in politics."

Mike grinned. "Good thing I didn't know any of this. I wouldn't have had the nerve to call him. Incidentally, I mentioned your name. He said he knew you."

"We've met, that's all."

"I told him you might be inquiring about how much damage there was. He was a bit suspicious, but he said he'd cooperate."

"Does Aunt Kate know you're in town?" I asked.

"Yes. We called her last night." Fran's nose wrinkled. "Poor Aunt Kate. I told her about the accident, and she was pretty shook up. Pretty mad at Mr. Cromwell, too. She's never talked much about him. They're not close, huh?"

"I don't think so, though you'll never hear her say a word against him. I think he respects her accomplishments but doesn't really approve of her. He thinks the art colony has outlived its usefulness."

"No family of his own?"

"No. I always think of him as a lost dog who can't quite remember where he buried that bone."

We all agreed that Charles was a sad case, and for a while his graceless, unappealing figure was an invisible fourth in the booth with us. I finished my coffee, envying Mike and Fran the palpable bond between them. Mike said the coffee was on them. I got up and said good-bye and went out through the lobby to the sun-drenched sidewalk.

$\triangledown$

Chapter 5

IT WAS GETTING BUSY, as Dos Cruces understands the word.
The natural Dos Cruces pace was a gentle amble, which I liked. It
drove Charles up the wall. He was part of the Marcus Fox group
negotiating to attract the money to turn Dos Cruces into a resort
and develop the surrounding desert until Lindero County was
mostly tract housing, gas stations, and fast-food joints.

I hiked back to the plaza and was starting up the city hall steps
when Arthur MacAndie came through the plate glass doors. He
called my name and came angling toward me.

Everyone called MacAndie Mac. Tall and slatty, a pale blond going
gray and sparse on top, he had a wide forehead and a pointed chin,
with a worn middle-aged face between. Blue-gray eyes peered from
behind wide bifocals—restless, dissatisfied, editorial eyes. As associate editor of the *Lindero County Chronicle*, he was a gangling
crusader in a faded plaid shirt and frontier pants. I didn't know if he
could tell a Norman Rockwell from a Picasso, but his paper was a
selfappointed watchdog over city and county government and a
staunch defender of the old Dos Cruces, the art colony, and whatever
encouraged the creative spirit.

He said breezily, "Looking for Charles?"

"Isn't he in?"

"Oh, sure." He gave me a quick close-mouthed grin. "Didn't
know your affairs were common knowledge, did you?"

"Are they?"

"Did you know the widow Pavlik?"

30

I shook my head, moving toward the glass doors. He stayed with me.

"Lived at 3029 Fox Hollow. Mrs. Eugene Pavlik? First name Helen? Kind of handsome, fortyish, medium brown hair tinted to hide a little gray?"

"What's this all about, Mac?"

"She was shot last night. At home. Discovered by Clint Farrell, boozed out of his brain. He called the cops on her phone. They found him asleep in a flowerbed and booked him. Suspicion of murder. He was carrying a .22 Armalite rifle, and Helen Pavlik was killed with a small calibre gun."

I said, "Okay."

"Not really." His voice held an imperfectly disguised hint of glee. "Farrell tied one on yesterday. When he does that at home he usually sets up a couple of hurricane lamps out in back of his place and whiles away the happy hours plinking away at empty bottles and beer cans—until the booze is all gone or he passes out. Two years ago he did it in the dead of winter and almost died of pneumonia."

"Teach him a lesson?"

"If I know Clint, he switched to a higher octane whiskey."

"Can't they charge him with unlawful use of a firearm?"

"Not in the county. His house is in the city but most of his property isn't. Oh yes, he owns all Carver Canyon, thanks to his great granddad. Ever since he got out of the army, all Clint's wanted to do is sit in that old house and eat cheap and drink rich, and once in a while sell off a chunk of the property for grocery money. Carver Canyon's what's left. He says he didn't know Helen Pavlik."

"Believe him?"

"Why not? She only just moved in, rented the Osterreichers' house for the summer while they're off in Europe or somewhere. Of course, he might have known her twenty, twenty-two years ago. She was Helen Fairland back then. Worked as a waitress at the Lindero Grill, where the Ramada Inn is now. Handsome, strapping, bouncy girl—who got bounced by half the blades in town."

"How was she?"

"*Half* the blades in town." He smiled thinly. "Until one of them, fresh out of college, oozing enthusiasm and sex appeal, froze the others out. Who would believe he was ever the romantic type?"

"Who?"

"Everyone's friend and your client, Charlie Cromwell. Until one day she just up and left town. For good."

"Charles isn't my client. Who says he is?"

"He isn't?" He looked disappointed. Then something kindled behind the broad bifocals. He smiled. "Sorry. Drew the logical conclusion without making sure it was also the right conclusion. I'll explain. I heard there'd been a murder and went over to ask Police Chief Hostetler how come this happens the night he assigns extra patrolmen to protect us. He told me who the victim was. I thought Charlie might have something interesting to contribute. As you know, the *Chronicle* opposes this whole development scheme Charlie's a part of, and frankly I hoped to dig up some dirt. Sometimes what you can't print is every bit as useful as what you can. I told him Helen Fairland was back in town and had been murdered last night, and he just sat there behind that big desk like an overdressed tailor's dummy and said, 'Jesus God' two or three times. You figure he was really surprised?"

"I wasn't there."

"Hell, he's played everything so close to his vest for so long that he has second thoughts first. Anyhow he gave me that fish-eye stare and asked if I thought he'd committed the crime, and was that behind my visit. I said of course not, which wasn't entirely true, and he said that before I jumped to any slanderous conclusions I should check with James Keller, who was looking into a possibly fraudulent damage claim that was going to be filed as a result of an auto accident he was in last night—at about the time of the murder. Is that part true?"

"I don't know when the murder was. The accident happened around 8:45. Mostly to shut Charles up I agreed to look into the claim without signing him up as a client. I'm not looking for clients."

"Where was the accident?"

"Pollock Highway at Fox Hollow."

He became very still. The blue-gray eyes glittered.

"He was in the vicinity, then."

"Sure. So were a lot of people. Careful what you say or Charles will sue your ass off."

Mac's lower teeth sawed reflectively at his upper lip.

"You know the first thing's gonna come into a lot of minds when they hear this?"

I didn't.

"Bet you've never seen Charlie's den." He looked hungry. "One wall is mostly medals and trophies from when he was in college. He was a free pistol shooting hotshot of national standing, a real champ with a .22. Got a small arsenal of them."

"Okay, but let's postpone the crucifixion. Let's be sure Mrs. Pavlik was killed with a .22 and not some other small gun. Let's be sure she wasn't killed with Clint Farrell's Armalite. I know it's a lot to ask, but our philosophical differences with Charles and the fact that he is or was a skilled marksman and has a gun collection just aren't enough to go on."

He replaced the hungry look with a disarming smile.

"Not gonna let us stage a nice vindictive witch-hunt?"

"I just hate the thought of being maneuvered onto Charles' side."

Mac hooted with laughter, conceding that that would be pretty embarrassing. He waved a hand and took off at an unhurried lope in the direction of the *Chronicle* building. I pushed my way through a glass door into city hall.

After the bright morning outside, the lobby was as dim as a cave. When your eyes got used to that, you found yourself looking at a rare example of civic pride manifested with imagination and restraint. The lobby didn't pretend to be the Roman forum. Instead of the usual stiff murals showing Hammurabi and Solon and George Washington looking self-important, muted mosaics swept around the walls showing the desert and some of its inhabitants: a lonely coyote, a dove nesting in a cholla cactus, a mother skunk with her young, a prowling bobcat.

A security guard was leaning against the curving information counter, shooting the breeze with the clerk on duty behind it. The clerk was an olive-skinned woman of middle years with thick raven-black hair and the trace of an accent. Elena Valdez had held the job nearly thirty years, ever since the building had opened. Beyond the information desk was a newsstand, and opposite the newsstand were two self-service elevators, one of them actually waiting. I took it to the fourth floor, where the mayor and his staff had their offices. In one of them, unless Mac hadexaggerated,I expected to find the mayor's executive assistant going catatonic.

Instead he came boiling out of the men's room by the elevators just as I stepped out onto the landing. He took one look at my jeans and T-shirt and snarled, "Jesus Christ, Counselor, d'you always wear those clothes when you're conducting business?"

I gave him a polite nod.

"And a good morning to you too. I'm not conducting business, remember? I'm doing you a favor."

He was wearing another summer-weight suit this morning, another severe tie. This one was midnight blue with a compulsively regular pattern of tiny white polka dots. Charles looked as though he needed sunshine, exercise, and a good night's sleep.

"I need more than a favor." There was a sharp *ping!* and the other elevator opened. Two well-dressed men got out. They nodded to Charles as they turned down the hall. Charles bit hard on his molars and dragged me in the other direction, finally letting go somewhere between the double doors of the mayoral suite and what looked like a janitorial broom closet. "I'm not kidding, Counselor. I need you to represent me.

Something was really bugging him. The murder of a long-ago girlfriend? Surely he was overreacting. Anyway, it was none of my business.

"I can't represent you," I said reasonably. Sounding reasonable is a practiced professional skill. Sometimes it takes more effort than it's worth. "Personal business out of town."

"Yeah, well listen, I heard about your custody thing. I guess that's rough. But if you represent me, I'll put half the city's legal business in your lap. That'll give you a plus in the custody suit. It'll turn you into an acknowledged pillar of the community."

"I might have to wear a suit all the time. Thanks, but I can't, okay?"

He took a long, slow breath.

"The legal profession," he finally ground out between pale lips, "is the biggest goddam hoax that ever victimized this country. You've got us brainwashed to where we can't take a piss without your sanction. But where are you when we need you? Do you know how many lawyers in this town are political enemies, or personal enemies? How many aren't qualified to write a will for a skid row bum? God damn it, I need a *lawyer*."

"What for?"

His face was clenched, his eyes mottled and fearful.

"What for?" he said in a strangled voice. "Because I'm facing a malicious accusation, a *murder* accusation. Because our public-spirited police chief Dave Hostetler won't push a case against his old buddy Clint Farrell, and because that son of a bitch MacAndie and the *Chronicle* are after my blood."

"Who's accused you? Be reasonable, Charles. You're part of City Hall, you know how to pressure Hostetler if he isn't doing his job. And MacAndie doesn't run the *Chronicle*, for God's sake—"

"So what? His boss is editor and publisher and answerable to nobody. She's the same half-assed sentimentalist he is. You think she won't jump at a chance to make me look bad? I've seen the old bitch operate." He took a gulp of air and glanced around furtively. "Remember last night? Two squad cars looking into a shooting?"

"Sure. Mrs. Eugene Pavlik, who used to be Helen Fairland. Did you know she was back in town?"

"What? . . . Of *course* I didn't know! Who've you been listening to? Watch it or you're going to be ass-deep in sewage!"

"But I'm supposed to listen to you slander the police chief and the *Chronicle*? Come on, Charles. How do you know Farrell's guilty?"

"I don't *know* Farrell's guilty. I just don't want people bending over backwards to ignore the evidence, especially people who'd be only too happy to stick a knife in my back."

"Why would Chief Hostetler want to stick a knife in your back?"

Charles started to speak but caught himself. For a moment something like a smile warmed his bleak eyes and his face was smug with remembered triumph.

He said abruptly, "That's neither here nor there. The point is he would. I need protection—legal protection. And that's your job."

"Why? Because I'm an outsider? One who wasn't around when whatever it was was happening many years ago? There's got to be someone in the Establishment who'll take you on as a client."

"The Establishment," he said in a bitter near-whisper, "is *peo-*

ple—with interests to protect. Right now it's split down the middle. There's a lot of delicate maneuvering going on—"

"Bottom line, Charles. I can't. I'm leaving town."

His face closed up stubbornly. Spitefully.

"I hope you're of more use to your other clients."

"You're not my client."

"Thank you," he snapped. "You've been a great help."

He stood to his full height, which gave him about a half-inch on me, sneered down his nose, and turned to the mayoral suite door, pausing to adjust his tie before snatching at the handle and opening it. I heard the brief murmur of a woman's voice and the remote rattle of an electric typewriter before the door closed behind him, leaving me in a swamp of irritation.

$\triangledown$

Chapter 6

IN THE LOBBY, A few people were wandering around looking at the mosaic mural. The security guard stood at parade rest, looking official, and Elena Valdez was on the phone behind her information counter. I went to one of the public phones and placed a credit card call to Andy Feldberg in Westwood.

Andy was one of those big city boys who manage to sound impatient even when they're telling you what a great lay they had last night.

"Hi, Jim."

"New wrinkle. Yesterday Felicia's attorney called to offer thirty grand to relinquish all rights to Katy. I said no. Later he called again to offer sixty. I'm sure she hasn't got that kind of money, so her father must be providing it."

"Why?"

"Anything for his little girl? Or is he scared of what will come out if I contest?"

"To find out we might have to put Felicia under twenty-four hour surveillance. Know what that would cost?"

"I can raise money on the house. Going to sell it anyway."

"Your equity wouldn't go far. Twenty-four hour surveillance means three operatives—call it five hundred a day. Been a while since you could hire Philip Marlowe for twenty-five a day and expenses."

"Even so, I think we have to go for full custody."

"Yeah. I don't know how yet. Forget the surveillance for now. What's the guy's name who called you?"

"Engle. Of Hamner, Engle and Benden. He got her divorce. First name's John, though he'd like you to think it was Mister. After I talked to him the second time I got a call from Felicia—I don't know what about. She tried to get me to admit I'd never had any interest in being a father, so why pretend now?"

"Got witnesses to the contrary?"

"I guess so. Kate Cromwell?"

"Talk to her about it. Otherwise, keep your head down. I'll talk to Ed Hammond and this guy Engle. Call me tonight."

"Thanks Andy."

"No sweat, man."

He hung up abruptly. I stepped out of the phone booth. Arthur MacAndie was leaning against the information counter looking comfortable as a cat, grinning at me.

"Elena told me you were still here. How's our friend?"

I grunted. He unfolded his long body off the counter and came with me toward the glass doors.

"No great revelations, huh? Well, maybe they'll come. Meanwhile, Dave Hostetler wants to see you."

"The Chief? What about?"

"Maybe he wants you to represent Farrell."

"That's silly. Farrell can get his own lawyer."

I pushed a glass door open. He followed me outside.

"Farrell's an old high school buddy of Dave's."

"That's what I keep hearing."

"Charlie brought that up, did he? I'll bet he wants people to think Dave's trying to bury the evidence against Farrell."

"Is there any?"

"Ask Dave." He shrugged narrow square shoulders. "Clint was there, drunk, with a gun. Ballistics will tell us if the gun's guilty."

"And if it doesn't, there's nothing against him?"

"Nothing I've been able to sniff out."

The blue-gray eyes behind their bifocals were flat and empty. Perhaps I was supposed to start wondering what Charles might say if Farrell's gun proved innocent.

I started down the city hall steps. He kept up with me.

"You talked to Chief Hostetler after talking to me?"

"That's right," he said. "Got this bright idea and called him to say you'd be a good man to represent Clint if it—"

"God damn it, Mac. You know I'm leaving town."

He grinned the pointed grin that showed no teeth. It made his chin look longer, his face unreliable.

"I forgot," he said airily.

We turned away from the plaza and went up Courthouse Avenue half the length of the city hall to where low brick pillars interrupted a neat sweep of lawn; between the pillars steps started down to a concrete walk and the basement entrance to police headquarters.

"Stop meddling, Mac."

No lip this time. His aging triangular face took on the inflexible integrity of sculpted bone.

"Not a chance, Counselor. I'm going to make this thing come out right. It won't, unless someone works on it."

"Don't trust people much, do you?"

"Not much."

He followed me down the steps toward the double doors under the sign that read DOS CRUCES POLICE DEPARTMENT.

I had been in the copshop often enough. There was a high counter with a gate in it and a built-in desk with a young-looking cop I didn't know sitting at it. He had thinning hair and a lot of muscles in his jaw. He gave me the automatic blank challenging stare they always do until he saw Mac behind me and became almost human.

"This is Jim Keller," Mac said. "The Chief wants to see him."

That made the cop suspicious all over again. He swiveled his eyes at me, brown and blank as a pair of shoe-buttons. The name tag over his breast pocket said he was R. Hamill.

"Yeah?" He put a meaty protective hand on the telephone.

"He hasn't done anything," Mac said. "Dave just wants to talk to him."

Officer Hamill picked up the phone. He dialed a four-digit number, and talked in a confidential murmur. Maybe my jeans and T-shirt made me look like an aging adolescent picked up for boosting hubcaps.

I said to Mac, "Are you going to sit in my lap while I talk to the Chief?"

"If I'm invited."

I said he wasn't. Officer Hamill put down the phone but kept the protective hand on it while his other hand gave me a plastic tag. It bore the Dos Cruces PD logo and the word VISITOR, and had a metal clip for fastening to my lapel. My T-shirt didn't have lapels.

"Wear this at all times. Through the gate and through that door, turn left and it's the last door on the right."

I thanked him and clipped the tag to my sleeve. He assured me stiffly that I was welcome, but the beady brown eyes stayed blank and watchful. He wasn't taken in. He had my number. He wouldn't be accused of having misread me when I was hauled in for arson or spitting on the sidewalk.

He touched the invisible buzzer that opened the gate. I went through it, threaded my way between desks with cops at them, and went through the door he'd indicated into a wide hallway. On the right the detective division was blocked by swinging doors. Straight ahead a narrower hall ran deeper into the building. I turned left. Voices came from behind closed doors and somewhere nearby a typewriter made choppy bursts of sound. Police headquarters was about as intimidating as a suburban grade school.

The last door on the right was open. I saw a cramped but neat secretarial office in which a woman in civilian clothes sat behind a desk with a phone to her ear, making notes on a steno pad.

She looked up before I could tap on the door frame. Her hair was crisp and short and wavy. Her face was all right, but her eyes were superb: big, dark, intelligent, rimmed with heavy black lashes. She might have been thirty-six or -seven. I liked her at once. She excused herself to whoever it was on the phone.

"Mr. Keller?"

I confessed it. She indicated an open door behind her and told me to go right on in.

The inner office was bigger, with a line of windows high in one wall. The usual office furniture could have been bought at a fire sale, but there was also an old imitation leather-covered sofa that looked as comfortable as a glove. It must have been hauled here when it got too beat up for someone's living room.

A stocky middle-aged man stood behind the desk reading the contents of a manila folder through heavy black-framed glasses. He took these off when I came in, dropped them on the blotter, and stuck out a hand.

"Hi, I'm Dave Hostetler."

I shook his hand and said I was Jim Keller. I had met him once at some municipal function, but didn't try to remind him. He had receding dark hair that was graying at the sides. He didn't look happy, but his tanned, muscular face wasn't that of a man at war with himself either. His desk was cluttered enough to suggest that work got done at it; besides the usual correspondence trays and office junk there was a circular pipe rack, a glass tobacco jar, two photographs in standing frames turned toward him, an intercom unit, a heavy glass ashtray, and what looked like an old-fashioned cigarette box.

He waved me to a seat on the old sofa. It was easy on the bones, just as I'd suspected.

"Arthur MacAndie said you wanted to see me."

"Yeah, thanks for getting here so fast." He lowered himself onto the swivel chair behind the desk, took the lid off the cigarette box, tilted it toward me. I said no thanks. He put the lid back on and chose a short dark pipe with a curved stem from the rack and opened the tobacco jar. The lines around his eyes deepened, but he didn't quite smile. "Mac tried to feed me some b.s. about what a great lawyer you'd be to represent Clint Farrell, who's in the lockup. Maybe so, but I heard you aren't going to be around."

"That's right."

"So what d'you suppose he had in mind?"

"No idea."

"Me neither." He filled the pipe with workmanlike fingers and put the lid back on the tobacco jar. "More opportunity in the big city?"

"Scoring points in my custody fight with my ex, who lives in Beverly Hills. It's supposed to improve my position if I'm nearby and working for an established law firm, as well as making it easier on the kid."

"Boy or girl?"

"Girl of three, named Katy for Katherine Cromwell."

He grunted sympathetically and leaned back in the swivel chair, which creaked faintly, to dig an old Zippo lighter out of his pants pocket.

"Anyway, what I wanted to talk to you about was yesterday's busy evening out your way. Are you representing those young people, Frances Rowan and what's-his-name Garcia—Michael Garcia?" I said no. He went on, "Vasquez and Hardy weren't sure. What got them mad at you?"

"They were being too accommodating to the mayor's executive assistant. I got on my soapbox and made a few speeches."

"I figured it was something like that. I was here when they came in—the festival's got everyone working extra hours. Their report didn't say much about you, but when I talked to them I could hear teeth grinding every time your name came up." He tucked the pipestem between his teeth, spun the lighter, and sucked flame into the tobacco. "You know there was a homicide farther up the street?"

"So I heard."

"Hear anything unusual last night? Cries, gunshots?"

The pipe hadn't caught. He lit it again. When the fire was going well he drew in a mouthful of smoke and sucked it clear down to his ankles.

"What I took to be gunshots, yes," I said. "Small calibre, coming from the direction of Carver Canyon. They began a little after eight. I turned on my stereo and drowned them out. At 8:30 I got a call from L.A. I wasn't aware of any then. After I hung up, Mike Garcia knocked on my door and wanted to call the auto club because his van had broken down. We heard the crash when the van was knocked over a couple of minutes later."

"Around when?"

"Don't know exactly. Maybe 8:45 or a little earlier."

"Any more gunshots?"

"Not that I heard."

"Hear any cars go by?"

"No. It would be hard to, with the stereo on." Then, simply because I was curious: "How much of a case is there against Mr. Farrell?"

He looked noncommittal. "Why?"

"I know it's none of my business, but I keep hearing things from unreliable sources. I understand the victim was Helen Fairland Pavlik, who used to live here twenty years ago and was generous with her favors until Charles Cromwell froze the other guys out. Then she left town. She came back just recently and rented the house on Fox Hollow in the owners' absence. Charles says he didn't know she was back. Someone shot her with a small calibre gun. Clint Farrell reported the shooting from the scene and was found drunk and in possession of a .22 Armalite."

His face had tightened at something I said. For several seconds he stared at me through a wreath of smoke.

Then he said, "That's about it."

"Did you find the spent shell?"

Chief Hostetler shook his head.

"Isn't the Armalite a semi-automatic?" I asked. "If that's what was used, there'd be a spent shell case at the scene."

"There'd be an ejected case if any semi-automatic was used, unless the killer was smart enough to remove it." The swivel chair creaked as he shifted position. "The officers found Helen lying on the living room floor in her bathrobe with a bullet wound in her temple. Some powder burns—not many. Powder burns are funny. No burns means the shot was fired at least six feet away, or at least fifteen, depending on the type of weapon, the type of cartridge, atmospheric conditions, maybe phases of the moon for all I know. We don't know where the shot came from. The French doors were open, so it could have been from outside. I got men looking for the spent shell all over. Who told you Charlie didn't know she was back in town?"

"He did. He's one of the unreliable sources I mentioned. The other was MacAndie."

"What makes you think they're unreliable?"

"I thought I heard axes being ground."

He smiled faintly, but his eyes remained watchful.

"Wouldn't surprise me. That's one of the reasons this investigation's going to be tricky."

"You handling it yourself?"

"Nobody on the force has any experience with homicide. At least I used to know the victim and a lot of her friends. Which may not be important. Sure hope it isn't. I mean, she could've been killed by some passing freak, or by someone out of her last twenty years. Until we know, I'm gonna have to make myself unpopular raking over cold ashes."

"So you don't think Farrell's guilty."

"Hell, we're old friends. Don't see much of him anymore, but so what? Being in the service messed him up, I guess—he drinks too much. No, I don't think he did it, but he's a drunk and drunks can surprise you. At least ballistics will tell us if his Armalite's the weapon. If the gun's clean, the trouble starts. Know when we last had a murder?"

"No idea."

"I was a patrolman." He puffed on his pipe, looking nostalgic about the untroubled intervening years, then shook his shoulders. "Is Charlie real shook up?"

I said carefully, "He's not happy. I think he's hearing those axes being sharpened."

"How about last night?"

"Jumpy, bad-tempered. He went behind my car and threw up."

"Like a man with a bad conscience?"

"Or like a man suffering from the shock and embarrassment of ramming a stationary vehicle and doing a lot of damage."

"Yeah, who's to say? Hell, suspecting Charlie would be politically awkward. We're both members of the city administration, and I'm committed to support him for mayor. That's politics. I guess it would be a damn sight worse, though, if I did suspect him and he was a political enemy. Until I got more to go on I guess I'll have to suspect just about everyone. Probably even you."

"Fair enough. All the alibi I've got is that phone call from L.A. Phone company records will give you the time and a lawyer named Engle will testify that it was me he talked to. Then a few minutes later Michael Garcia knocked on the door. Maybe he knows what time it was."

"You got a gun?"

"No. You got a time of death?"

"Yep." He grinned. "Ten-nineteen in County General." The grin vanished. "You thought we had a time frame for the shooting. Well, we don't."

"So the responding officers found her alive."

"Vital signs so faint they almost missed them." He put his pipe down in the heavy glass ashtray. "We don't even know how long she was lying there. Son of a bitch." He said it wonderingly and shook his head, for a moment not a cop at all, then put his hands flat on the desk as though about to stand. "Well, Counselor—"

I said, "Did Mrs. Pavlik rent that house through a local real estate agent?"

And that, for some reason, brought the cop back. The lines around his eyes became stiff as stress lines in concrete, the eyes themselves just cop's eyes, empty of everything but the knowledge of iniquity.

He snapped, "Who wants to know?"

"I do."

"Who else?"

Maybe I'd missed something. Or asked too many questions. Or asked them without the deference expected of the innocent. Maybe he thought I had a client with an interest in the investigation's progress—or its derailment. That struck me as pretty dumb, but nothing says a cop has to be smart. Most are just working stiffs like everyone else. And Dave Hostetler might have been a good cop, but as chief of police he was a political appointee of the city council. He could already be under some kind of political pressure.

"Nobody else," I said cheerfully. "I only asked because I've got real estate on my mind. Got a house to sell."

He kept the stony stare going a bit longer, then ducked out of it with a knowing half-smile that suggested he knew something I didn't. Like Officer Hamill, he had the goods on me.

He pushed himself up from the desk.

"Then talk to Margaret, my secretary. Her sister runs Sunrise Realty. It's no secret that Jennifer handled the lease or rental or whatever it was."

He followed me into the outer office. The secretary with the marvelous eyes was crossing from an open file cabinet to her desk. Walking she looked even better than sitting, tall and deep-breasted and sleek as a swimmer in her white blouse and tan skirt. I wondered what she did for fun, and would she welcome company doing it.

"Mrs. Radek, Mr. Keller," the Chief grunted, torpedoing that line of thought. "He's a possible client for Jen, Maggie."

She must have heard us talking, but diplomatically pretended otherwise.

"Oh, good." She dipped into a drawer and gave me a buff-colored card with lively brown printing on it. I recognized the rising sun logo.

Below it the name "Jennifer Kendall" appeared in very large clear type, of which the lowercase letters were just smaller capitals. Was Jennifer anything like her sister? Was Kendall another married name? "My sister's card, with her business and home phone numbers. If you don't call her, she'll call you."

I thanked her. The Chief said abruptly, "Thanks for coming in, Mr. Keller. I won't take up any more of your time."

He started easing me toward the door. I resisted being eased until I had caught Mrs. Radek's eye, promised to call her sister, and said it was nice meeting her. She responded appropriately and the Chief followed me out into the hall.

He said in a low, satisfied voice, "You like Maggie, don't you?"

"Did it show?"

"Stuck out a mile." A door closed, echoing. The muffled sounds of the copshop reasserted themselves. "You're what, thirty, thirty-one?"

"Thirty-three in December."

"You like 'em a little older."

"No preference for older."

"Maggie's thirty-seven. Helen Pavlik was thirty-nine. Did you like her too?"

"I never met her, as far as I know. Show me a picture."

"Don't worry, Counselor." A faint, flinty smile stretched his mouth. "I don't think you killed her. You wouldn't have used a gun. You like using your hands too much."

I stopped dead. He gave me a knowing stare. It was supposed to make my blood run cold. What he had said had already done that. He must have heard some of Felicia's wilder accusations. I had a moment's disorientation in which all I could think to say was, "I *what*?" I guess I didn't yell, because my voice didn't echo. Then in my head a gear shifted awkwardly.

I gave him the curled lip, the offhand manner.

"If you believe that you'll believe anything. And your tough cop acts stinks."

I headed for the exit. Behind me he chuckled softly.

"Don't go away mad, Mr. Keller."

I kept going and opened the door back into Officer Hamill's turf. Arthur MacAndie unfolded his slatty frame off a chair and followed me through the gate. Officer Hamill took my visitor's tag while doing isometric exercises with his jaw muscles.

I turned to face Mac at the foot of the steps outside.

"Why did you suggest me to represent Farrell, Mac?"

He was wearing his cryptic triangular smile.

"To bring your name up. To involve you. I told you this thing wasn't going to come out right all by itself. Was Charlie scared when you talked to him?"

"Why should he be?"

"Because he can't prove he was coming back from the Steak House when he ran into that van."

"Can you prove he wasn't?"

His bifocals glinted in the sunlight. His lips parted enough to show he actually had teeth in there.

"Come on, Jim. Have you no room in your soul for a little old-fashioned intuition?"

A woman in a soft yellow cotton dress paused at the top of the steps, then started down toward us. Mac interrupted himself to greet her.

"Hi, June. The festival didn't actually give you time off!"

"Of course not—I'm playing hooky. Have you seen Dave?"

"A while back," Mac said. "Jim was just talking to him. June Hostetler, the Chief's wife. Jim Keller, who looks like a vagrant but is actually a lawyer."

I said, "Hello, Mrs. Hostetler."

She was perhaps a shade too slender, with straight short hair that had once been brown but now showed a lot of silver-gray, brushed forward onto her ears and down across her forehead. Tiny diamond studs flashed from her earlobes and she wore fashionably tinted glasses in elaborate frames. Her face was thin, calm, even serene, but the serenity was at odds with the passionate intensity of the eyes behind the tinted lenses. Her skin was clear and practically unlined, but her mouth was ungenerous.

She seemed to have heard my name and was about to say something conventional—but then the penny dropped. She looked at me sideways. The corners of her mouth tilted upward in the most distant imitation of a smile I had seen since Felicia left town.

"Of course—Mr. Keller, the lawyer. I know your wife. It's ex-wife now, isn't it? You must miss her."

"I'll be seeing her next week," I said, avoiding combat.

"How lovely for you."

Her eyes, which had been carving up my face, flicked away. She almost turned her back on me to say something terribly warm and friendly about having to hurry if she hoped to catch her husband, and when was Mac coming over for a drink?

"As soon as the present fuss is settled," Mac said.

"Oh, is there really going to be a fuss? Well, I'm sorry to hear that, but as soon as it's settled then!"

She swept gaily past him and through the copshop doors.

Mac gave me a jaundiced look.

"What was that all about?" he asked.

"Why, aren't you on drinking terms with them?"

"Sure I am. But she's no fan of yours—"

"A friend of Felicia's, I guess."

I started up the steps. A friend of Felicia's who'd been regaled with accounts of how Felicia had to lock herself in the kid's room every night while the sadist husband prowled beyond the door, a story June Hostetler of course passed on to her husband, giving him something to threaten me with—

"Next stop?" Mac asked brightly at the sidewalk.

"Go find somewhere to wait for the ballistics report. Unless you plan to report it in advance by sheer intuition."

"I'd like to wait in your company. I'm a newsman, remember, and things happen around you."

"Not today."

"Okay, be boring." He grinned his quick sly V-shaped grin. "But remember. This one won't come out right unless someone works on it."

He turned and hurried back toward the plaza.

$\triangledown$

Chapter 7

Bert FOWLER WAS THE lawyer who would be taking over my practice. I spent a few minutes in his office wrapping up loose ends. Bert was tall, with a high forehead and hair that began halfway back on his skull and fell to his shoulders. He also had gentle brown eyes, Victorian sideburns, and a flowing rich red-brown mustache. His brain was part computer and part SWAT team. Most of what I had turned over to him was fairly routine, but he already had it so well in hand that I felt unnecessary, like something instantly replaceable from a box of mass-produced facsimiles. I told him this. He grinned and shook my hand and said we were all just dust in the wind anyway. I told him his philosophy made me feel very secure, and went to Ortega's.

The insurance adjuster was still there, finishing his paperwork. He pouted over my business card and grudgingly admitted that Marc Fox had told him to expect me—another imposition on his good nature. He'd had to mangle his schedule to shoehorn this job in this morning; he was going to stop doing favors for people, you just wound up with more work than you could handle, and exactly what was it I wanted? I said raw figures on the damages. He provided them. I thanked him very much and left him muttering under his breath.

I called Charles from a pay phone. A woman's voice told me he was busy, would I care to leave a number where he could reach me after lunch? I gave her my name and said that if she would mention it to Mr. Cromwell I was sure he would talk to me, but if he wouldn't, to hell with him, I wouldn't be reachable.

She gasped. Five seconds later Charles's voice barked, "Yes?"

"Raw figures on the damage are as follows: thirteen hundred and twenty to the van, thirty-eight eighty-five to the pottery based on retail value, plus an as yet uncomputed amount for damage to jewelry that will need repair, plus another two hundred for damage to display cases."

"What about the other matter we talked about?"

"I'm still unavailable."

He hung up. I hiked to Courthouse Plaza and went to lunch at Bernie's.

I usually did, when I was working. It was a basement restaurant and bar in the corner of the block opposite city hall: wide, uncarpeted, low-ceilinged. The tables had red-and-white checkered oilcloth tops, and the chairs looked like an odd-lot consignment remaindered in 1920. I went through the cafeteria line and took a French dip sandwich and a Health Food Salad Bowl and a beer to a table against the windowless red brick wall that paralleled Fourth Street. I was enjoying lunch in pleasant solitude when Arthur MacAndie's voice said at my shoulder, "I knew I'd find you here."

He moved into my line of vision, already unloading his lunch tray onto my table. Someone came from behind him. "Jim Keller—Clint Farrell."

Farrell placed his tray on the back of the chair opposite mine. He asked tentatively, "You sure this is okay?"

"Sure, why not?"

Moving with great care, Clint Farrell transferred his lunch and a beer from his tray to my table. He was a fairly big man with faded light-brown hair and faded eyebrows over wide eyes embedded in pouched and wrinkled skin. The whites of his eyes were the color of weak tea, the irises a washed-out blue in which the pupils were almost invisible, but the rest of his face was tanned and weathered. His nose must have been badly broken at some time.

Mac dragged over an empty chair from a nearby table and sat down. Farrell cautiously put his tray on a folding stand behind his chair and sat down too, looking fragile. Mac began spooning vegetable soup into his mouth. Clint sighed deeply, reached for his mug, and sat down with both hands on the frosted glass, communing with the contents. Then he picked it up by the handle, using his other hand as a guide, and brought it reverentially to his lips.

With that much buildup I expected him to swallow the whole thing in one gulp; but he took only two modest swallows before putting the mug down and closing his eyes.

"Vitamins." He sighed, then gave me a look of mild surprise. "They let me out."

Mac said, "He passed his ballistics test."

"Yeah." Clint lowered his beer another notch. "Worse'n waiting for the results on a Wasserman."

Cautiously, he began cutting his rare roast beef.

"You didn't know?" I asked.

Mac said, "He didn't remember doing it, but he didn't remember *not* doing it either. Clint's Armalite takes .22 long rifle ammunition and the slug they took out of Helen was a .22 short. The Armalite will fire a .22 short if it's hand loaded into the firing chamber, but then it won't work as a semi-automatic. His gun had two long rifle cartridges in the clip and one in firing position. He was too drunk to have faked that. Anyway, the slug that killed Helen was fired from a different gun."

I asked Clint, "How much do you remember?"

His eating had gained confidence. He sat straighter. The pinpoint pupils had grown to the size of pinheads.

"I got sauced." He grinned crookedly, drained his mug. Mac put his untouched mug in front of Clint.

"More vitamins." Mac smiled his sharp triangular smile.

"Gotta take my vitamins," Clint said prayerfully, and inhaled a few. "Like I said, sauced. I took my rifle and some ammo and a pint of Ancient Age out to the target range behind the house. Killed the pint, went to take a leak against a eucalyptus that had been giving me some backtalk, and bang, this shot from up the hill. So I climbed up to the road and crossed it and there were lights on in the Osterreicher house. I can remember it seemed mighty unfriendly that someone was up there shooting off a gun—disturbing the neighbors—and mighty suspicious that those lights were on. Guess I'd forgotten that someone had rented the place. Anyway, I found the front door and rang. No answer. So I went around the front to where the French doors were open at the corner of the living room, and I went in and found her. Didn't recognize her. I mean, I was so shitfaced I wouldn't have known her if she still looked like twenty years ago. I put the gun down and called the cops. At least I guess I did. Remember talking to somebody. Then I thought, that poor dead lady, the noisy creep who fired that shot did this—I better go find him. But I passed out. The cops tell me they found me outside under a rosebush."

"What time was it when you heard the shot?" Mac asked him.

"Last time yesterday I knew what time it was I was listening to the noon news on the radio." Clint scraped the last mouthful of baked potato off the dark, dried skin. "I been answering questions all day. Thanks for the lunch, but enough, okay?"

"Don't thank me," Mac said expansively. "You're on the expense account. Speaking of which—"

He got up and rejoined the service line.

I finished eating. Clint just sat there waiting for something to happen, or for someone to tell him what to do next, as though he had nothing to do except wait until he died.

"For a guy who says he can't remember," I said, "seems to me you remember pretty clearly."

"Yeah, well, that's what I remember when I string it all together. But I stopped a few times. Either went to sleep or blacked out. Once was before I crossed the road. Another was when I was waiting for someone to answer the doorbell." He picked up his second mug one-handed and upended it over his mouth. "If I'd had any idea how long I blacked out for it'd be different. Anything coulda happened during those times."

"Except we know you didn't shoot her."

"Yeah, yeah, but I wish I could remember it."

A fleeting worry, or maybe a distant dread, darkened his big face. He sighed, a sound like dying dreams. His gaze wandered, then caught something behind me and became a riveting stare. I looked. A young woman in a sleeveless red-and-white striped blouse and denim shorts stood with her back to us, talking to a couple two tables away. Her legs were tanned and tapered, sleek of thigh, and there was a fetching plumpness to the contours of her bottom; but the shorts were hiked up too far, so twin curves of buttock sagged below the denim.

I turned back to Farrell.

"Anything bad ever happen when you were having a blackout?"

"Huh? . . . What?" His gaze came back my way. Not fast, but at least he didn't have to move his whole head. "Oh . . . No. I guess not. But there's always a first time."

Mac showed up with a full beer mug in each hand. He gave Clint one, me the other.

"I saw what you two horny young studs were looking at." He sat down. "Disappointing from the front. Tits the size of peach pits. Any bright ideas while I was gone?"

Clint sucked up half his fresh beer in a single pull. "I told him about my blackouts."

I said, "What time did Clint's call come in?"

"Eighty forty-eight," Mac said. "Who knows how long after he heard that shot. What about the ejected shell case?"

"What he means," I explained to Clint, "is that they haven't found one. He's trying to get people to jump to conclusions. Maybe there's no spent shell because she wasn't shot with a semi-automatic. A revolver or a single-shot target gun wouldn't eject a spent shell, and who does target shooting make you think of?"

"Charlie Cromwell? You suggesting Charlie did it?"

I waved at Mac. "He is."

"He's full of it. Anyway, not all target guns are singles."

"Conceded." Mac smiled. "Drink up, men. You heading out to Fox Hollow, Jim? Can you give our friend here a ride?"

I said I could and Clint finished his beer. I left most of mine. As we started up the steps to street level, we met Bert Fowler coming in. He said hello, smoothing one side of his flowing red-brown mustache with a thumbnail.

"Message, Jim. Call your ex at home, wherever that is."

I thanked him and apologized if the phone referral system was turning his office into an answering service. He smiled, said he'd do the same for me one day, and went on in to lunch.

Chapter 8

THE STATION WAGON LOOKED a bit the worse for wear, but its chrome glinted bravely.

"I'll come with you," Mac said. "You can drop me off at the Osterreicher house."

We loaded Clint into the back seat, then got on the Pollock Highway. Halfway to Fox Hollow I began hearing the deep, regular, constricted sound a man with a broken nose makes when he falls asleep and breathes with his mouth shut.

"Sounds like his nose walked into a healthy swing from a baseball bat."

"Or something," Mac said. "It happened when he was in the army."

"Was he in action somewhere?"

"No, nothing like that. I heard he was in some kind of fight. The personal kind."

"Boozed up?"

"Dunno. Wasn't there. I was four-F, asthma, though it hasn't bothered me for years. Clint was a macho high school jock, but he never had a drinking problem before he went into the service."

"Was he one of Helen Pavlik's boyfriends?"

"Don't think so. No, I'm sure he wasn't."

"How about Chief Hostetler?"

"Dave? He was already married to June—their twenty-fifth anniversary's this fall. But I guess I wouldn't put it past him."

Which sounded too discreet to mean anything less than a strong maybe. Or maybe he really didn't know. I was only gossiping anyway.

We drove through the last of the sparsely built-up area. The sidewalk ended and the real desert began.

"Dave and June have any kids?"

"They couldn't. June kept miscarrying." I thought erratically of Katy. Mac went on, "A lot of people thought she had married beneath her because her dad ran a bank and his worked in a hardware store. Besides, June went off to college and Dave went straight into a patrolman's uniform. But it's worked. She's a neat lady in many ways. Too bad you wound up on her shit list."

Low dry hills rose on the left. The sky was pale with heat. The desert threw a painful glare back at the sun. Soon the highway bowed out into the curve that preceded Fox Hollow. Remembering last night, I took the turn at a sedate twenty- five.

Two men stood beside a squad car parked off the roadway at the scene of last night's accident. One wore the uniform and helmet of a motorcycle cop. The other had on a pale brown Western-style shirt and sunshades and was smoking a pipe.

"That's Dave," Mac said. "Let's see what he's up to."

I stopped across the highway from the squad car. Mac sensed my reluctance.

"Where's your sense of adventure?"

I said I'd lost it, but switched off the ignition and looked in the back seat. Clint was sprawled across it like an ungainly kid, breathing noisily but looking peaceful.

Mac was already out of the car. I got out too and followed him across the road to the cop car. The early afternoon air was thin and hot, like the air inside an oven.

The Chief looked unwelcoming. The uniformed cop had the obligatory stone-blank watchful eyes that mark the nemesis of purse snatchers and similar big time crooks. His name tag read H. Hoffman.

The Chief said, "What did you do with Clint?"

"He's in the car, sound asleep," Mac said. "Did you find the weapon?"

Hostetler tapped his pipe empty against the heel of his boot, reached into the squad car, and put it on the dash.

"Not yet."

"It could've been tossed from a moving car, or shoved back under someone's mattress."

"That's right."

"What made you suspect Charlie?"

"Who said I did?" The Chief's lips quirked up at the corners. With no eyes visible behind the reflecting sunshades, the effect was menacing. "He wasn't the only one here last night."

"Frances Rowan and Michael Garcia?" Mac said brightly.

"To name two." The Chief looked at me briefly. I saw myself, reduced and irritable, reflected in the black lenses. "Look, Mac. Charlie and Rowan and Garcia all say they got to this intersection driving toward town along the Pollock. But there's no proof. Charlie could've come barreling down Fox Hollow, made the turn too fast, and plowed into the van. Or the van could've lost its fanbelt anywhere up Fox Hollow, started to seize up and just made it around the corner—then got hit by Charlie coming in from the Steak House. Two scenarios. How you gonna choose between them?"

I said, "I picked up a fanbelt one point seven miles up the highway from here last night."

The Chief's face went slack, came around slowly. His mouth hung open. Then something behind the shades pulled the strings. His lips closed tightly and his nose grew pale and pinched.

"You what?" He jabbed a forefinger at me. "You found *what*? You got some explaining to do, mister."

"Nothing to it. Charles had been insisting the van wasn't roadworthy. Mike Garcia said the fanbelt had to be defective or improperly installed because it was almost new. I went looking for it, because if Charles got snotty enough Mike might have to prove his case."

"Never thought to tell me about it this morning, did you?"

"I didn't know it might be evidence in a homicide."

"You didn't know it was evidence!" Hostetler exploded. "You just got in your car and measured one point seven miles and found a dropped fanbelt on a moonless night because you had nothing better to do."

"Almost," I said.

"*Almost* nothing better to do—so you drive out of your way to fuck around with the evidence!" He snorted. "You covering up for someone?"

"I picked up the ball Hardy and Vasquez dropped."

"Can you prove the belt you found came off Garcia's van?"

"Of course not. If it's the right size and about the right age, that'll create a strong probability, but that's about all."

That made him happier. His mouth twitched, as though to suppress a grin. "Hell, even if you could prove anything, so what? It would only mean that the van drove in on the Pollock, turned up Fox Hollow, and drove back after the shooting."

"Not that it did. Only that it could have—*if* the motor could have lasted that long."

"Where's the fanbelt now?"

"On the floor of my car."

"Get it. I'll need a deposition about how you found it."

I walked over to my car and heard Mac ask if the cops had found any link between Helen and either Rowan or Garcia. The Chief said they were working on it, and Mac invited himself up to the Osterreicher house.

When I was getting the fanbelt from under Clint's feet, three cars drove up and stopped. A small crowd was converging on the Chief as I recrossed the road. There were a couple of uniformed officers, a plainclothesman, and what looked like a Boy Scout troop in civvies. I gathered that they were there to comb the desert looking for the weapon. The plainclothesman took charge and the Chief climbed into his squad car.

I handed the fanbelt through the window. Mac was sitting beside him.

"Remember the deposition. How's Sleeping Beauty?"

"Sleeping."

"You know Carver Canyon Road? Doesn't go much of anywhere except Clint's place."

"I'll get him home."

He nodded abruptly and they drove off, swinging up Fox Hollow. I followed more slowly.

Street lighting was scarce along Fox Hollow, but there was a tall gray light pole in front of one of the houses on the left—and several police cars. Across the road, the featureless desert hill Fox Hollow had been snaking around gave way to a depression into which Carver Canyon made an unobtrusive descent. Less than a hundred yards along the Canyon road an old low sprawling house baked quietly under the summer sky. A few palmettos grew nearby. In front of the house a date palm made stately shadows like Arabian latticework on the dusty ground, and I could see the tops of a couple of eucalyptus trees poking up over the roof. Beyond these, sand-colored stony hills cleft by Carver Canyon made a backdrop as romantically involving as a cloud of dust.

I parked in front of the house, got out, and opened the back door. Clint Farrell came suddenly awake, his eyes red-rimmed and bewildered.

"Jesus. I'm home." His voice was blurred. "Jesus . . . Sorry I crapped out like that. Thought I was shutting out the glare. Is that glare, or is it me?"

"It's glare. But you could be extra sensitive today."

He got out of the car, moving like a touchy invalid who has to show he doesn't need help. Sweat beading on his face caught the sunlight.

"Come in for a beer, or I'll make coffee."

"Sorry, I can't. I'll take a raincheck, though. I live just over the hill."

"Okay." He eyed the front of the house. "Place is gonna fall down if I don't give it a coat of paint." I wondered what a loner like him did with a house that big. "It's not the first time, you know."

"That you tied one on?"

"Naah. Blacked out. And couldn't remember if anything bad had happened."

He dug a key out of his pants pocket and started for his front door like a robot in need of a tune-up.

I said, "Any reason to think anything bad *did* happen?"

He turned to give me a lopsided smile.

"I got evidence that says it couldn't've, but I don't *know.*"

"As a lawyer I'd say go with the evidence."

"Yeah. Easy to say." He unlocked the door and stepped inside. "Thanks for the ride, man."

He closed the door. I got into the station wagon and headed back up Carver Canyon Road, where I found a big, young- looking cop with his hands hooked into his gunbelt blocking access to Fox Hollow.

He didn't move until I stopped the car about four inches short of his knees. Then he unhooked one thumb and moved around to my window with the provocative insulting slowness that's supposed to accentuate the majesty of the law or something. His face was thin and handsome in a 1930s sort of way, with a slender mustache and a chin like a granite monument. He must have stood six feet five in his socks.

"Mr. Keller?" His voice was too bodiless for his face and frame. His name tag read M. Vurpillat.

"Yes?"

"Chief of Police Hostetler wants to see you immediately."

"What about? I was talking to him ten minutes ago."

"I wouldn't know, sir. He's at the scene of the crime. Turn into the Osterreicher driveway and park behind the police vehicle."

I did as I was told while he followed, watching me as though expecting me to make a break for the border. He was only two feet away when I got out onto the ragged asphalt of the Osterreicher house.

The driveway was a semicircle of which part of Fox Hollow Drive was the diameter, enclosing a patch of living desert where another house might have had a lawn. The front door opened from a verandah that ran all the way along one side of the house. It stood open. Mac waited in it, wearing a savage grin.

"You're looking pleased with yourself," I said.

Behind his glasses, the editorial eyes did a berserk dance. He jerked his head for me to follow him. With Vurpillat behind me, I went into a rather dark entrance hall with an old-fashioned coatrack. On the left an open arch showed me part of a living room with an easy chair upholstered in a sunny tweed, a console model radio-phonograph, and an overweight plainclothes cop named Scanlon squatting in front of a bookcase going through the books. Opposite the arch was a door Mac opened. It led into the dining room.

The dining table and a handsome sideboard were nicely polished and a little old-fashioned—sort of homey. Three dining chairs were pushed neatly under the table. Chief Hostetler sat at the fourth with his glasses on his nose and a fireproof lockbox in front of him with a magazine under it to protect the table's veneer. The box was open, showing what looked like householder's papers. A few of these, along with three bankbooks, were spread out on the table. He was holding a wallet-sized document in a plastic envelope, the kind detectives put evidence in.

The Chief turned the envelope facedown before I could see what was in it.

"Okay, Mo. Ray could use you outside."

"Yes, sir," Officer Vurpillat said. I heard him leave.

Hostetler took the reading glasses off and almost threw them onto the table.

"You too, Mac."

"Me too what?" Mac said.

"Get lost."

"Mac stays," I said.

"Is he your lawyer or something?"

"He's my witness."

He stopped himself before asking what I needed a witness for. I needed one in case he tried to intimidate me again. After a moment's hesitation he stabbed a finger at my chest.

"You holding out on me, Keller?"

"Of course not."

He gave me a bleak stare. I pulled out one of the other chairs and sat down. It surprised him a little, but the surprise didn't last long. He demanded unpleasantly, "What do you know about *this*?"

He turned the plastic envelope over and slid it across to me.

I picked it up.

It contained what looked like a photostat of a California birth certificate. It said that on March 23, 1970, at 8:23 A.M., a baby girl named Frances Mary Rowan Fairland had been born to Helen Marie Fairland, of San Bernadino, and Charles Everett Cromwell, of Dos Cruces, California.

Chapter 9

I PUSHED THE ENVELOPE back to the Chief.

"News to me."

"It's also privileged information. You too, Mac." The Chief picked up the envelope. "Charlie never mentioned this?"

"Not to me. It'll have to be authenticated."

"How about Rowan and Garcia?"

"Not to me. I think it'll come as a nasty surprise to Fran."

One of the detectives came through the door to the kitchen, knocking briefly on the frame.

I knew him slightly. His name was Ray Gallardo. He wore a thick mustache trimmed short and shaped down around his mouth.

"Yeah?" Hostetler snapped.

"We found something. Out in back."

"Okay."

The Chief gathered up the papers, the bankbooks, and the plastic envelope and put them in the lockbox. He locked it with a small key that he crammed in his pocket. No one was going to mess with the contents of that box. He got up and headed out through the kitchen without a word.

I got up too. "Three bankbooks?"

"She wasn't broke," Mac said. "Whoever Eugene Pavlik was, he made sure she'd be okay. Savings, investments. She owned an apartment building in West L.A."

I followed him through the kitchen and across a screened-in service porch. The door to the outside was on a long loose spring but had been propped open with a kitchen mop. A single wooden step led down into the backyard, where three pieces of weathered patio furniture crowded a strip of lawn.

The Chief and Gallardo were looking at something on the stone barbecue that stood at the back of the property. With his hands behind him and his booted feet planted firmly in the "at ease" position, Office Vurpillat towered like an imposing guardian god, junior grade. A charred smell hung on the still air—and something else.

"Someone barbecued a pillow," Mac quipped brightly.

"They used a weird sauce," Gallardo said. "Paint thinner?"

What they were talking about was some twenty inches by sixteen and lay on the barbecue grill. It was burned black, except for a little patch of colored fabric visible in one corner.

"Sort of oatmeal colored," Gallardo said. "Looks like a match for the pillow on the davenport in the living room."

The Chief said, "Where'd you find this?"

"Seventy or eight feet up that way, sir." Vurpillat pointed to a narrow gully that opened up almost at the edge of the Osterreicher property and showed a way into, and maybe through, the low hills that were already beginning to sink into the suburban flatlands. "Detective Gallardo ordered me to search the vicinity. I investigated the gully because I smelled something, maybe turpentine, and something burned. I found the remains of a pillow behind some rocks, sir. Or maybe it's a cushion."

"Whatever," the Chief said. "You got a good nose."

"Thank you," Vurpillat said, looking fussed and forgetting to say "sir."

Hostetler noticed me for the first time.

"You want something, Counselor?"

"I was wondering if that cushion had a bullet hole through it."

"We'll find out."

"If it has," MacAndie said, "then maybe whoever shot Helen didn't leave by way of Fox Hollow."

The Chief grunted.

"Does it really work?" I asked. "Shooting through a pillow to muffle the sound of a shot?"

"Bound to, some. With a .22 it might cut out the muzzle velocity pretty bad. Best thing would be to wrap the pillow around the gun, leaving a tunnel for the slug to travel through."

"If the shot went through the pillow, wouldn't there be fibers in the wound?"

"There were fibres," the Chief said shortly. "Okay—police business. Ray, want to show Mr. Keller out?"

"About that privileged information," I said. "I hope you're not planning to spring that birth certificate on Fran Rowan before it's been authenticated?"

"This is a homicide, for Christ's sake! I got to pry people open with whatever I can get my hands on. Half this job's legwork and the other half's leverage."

"So you're just going to walk up to her and say, 'Here's proof you're a bastard, your dad's a shit, and your mother's a whore, did you kill her, where'd you hide the gun?' "

He said instantly, in a voice so restrained it was almost bodiless, "She wasn't a whore."

That didn't surprise me much. I grinned.

"Sorry," I said in a knowing voice.

Hostetler became deadly still. The blood drained from his face until his lips were pale as candlewax and the skin under his eyes was the color of dirty snow. Then two spots of red began to burn high on his cheekbones.

"I said get rid of this guy, Ray."

"Sure, Chief," Gallardo said.

He gave me a warning look. I couldn't think of an exit line that wasn't inflammatory so I said mildly, "Okay," and headed back to the house.

Gallardo followed me up the single step and through the service porch and the kitchen into the dining room. The lockbox squatted in assertive solitude where the Chief had left it. I stopped and looked at it.

Gallardo said, with a gesture that included the house and everything that had happened in it last night and since, "You make anything of all this?"

"Nope."

"What's your involvement?"

"Nothing, except your boss is trying to dump on some people I like. What's with him, anyway?"

"He's in a bind. The Pavlik woman had some boyfriends who became bigtime. He doesn't want to embarrass the innocent, but he doesn't want to be accused of covering up for VIPs."

"Was he going through the lockbox looking for anything that might tie him to Pavlik?"

He gave me a sharp look. "Do you know something, or are you just making noise?"

"Making noise. He keeps sending for me and then getting mad because I'm around so much."

Gallardo saw me out the front door. My steering wheel was almost too hot to touch, but I managed to get home.

The garage was hot as a sauna. I checked the mailbox but found only an ad for a stereo set I could buy on time with a gasoline credit card. I dropped it in the trash and went in the house.

It was blessedly dark. On this side of the hill a tiny breeze made itself felt. Drifting across the baked desert flat and crossing the highway, it rose with the land, entering the living room like a welcome guest through the one window I'd left uncurtained. I kicked off my shoes and stood in that gentle breath of air, enjoying the silence, not thinking, until the sweat sticking my T-shirt to my ribs began to evaporate, sending tiny chills up my back. But this delicious sensation couldn't last. I returned to the real world and switched on the air conditioner that was set into the wall and got a beer from the refrigerator. I tried to think—first about Dave Hostetler.

The Chief seemed so used to leaning on people who couldn't lean back that he lost his cool when someone did. But he did have a legitimate claim to my cooperation. Which meant that I couldn't warn Fran Rowan about that birth certificate. Or even Charles. Not that I was anxious to save Charles from embarrassment, but I did my best to find a colorably legitimate excuse to call and warn both him and Fran. When I couldn't, I picked up the phone and dialed Felicia's father's house in Bel Air.

The maid who answered the phone took a while to remember who Mrs. Keller was. Then the penny dropped and she apologized and said she would fetch *Mrs. Keller* right away. Felicia came on the line sounding crisp and bright and not to be trifled with.

"Hello?"

"Hi," I said. "Gone back to your old name?"

"It's no business of yours. I'll do as I please."

"Next time I'll just ask for Felicia. You called me."

"I just wondered whether you'd come to your senses, or were determined to extort more money from me. Next time, if there is a next time, ask for Miss Hammond. I have trouble believing I ever had any other name."

"I'd have trouble, too, if it weren't for Katy. How is she?"

"My daughter is well."

"Can I speak to her?"

"Certainly not. You would be quite disturbed to learn how little she even remembers you."

"No doubt," I said. "I've been getting the fallout recently from some of the lies you told about me here."

She gave a light, silvery laugh, then said with quiet venom, "You sexual cipher!"

"You're the one who took to sleeping behind locked doors."

"You should have done something manly about it. But that would be too much to expect, wouldn't it?"

"Keep trying new explanations; maybe one day you'll find one you can believe."

"Was this phone call supposed to be about something?"

"Just returning yours."

"I shouldn't have wasted my time. Oh, there was one thing I wanted to ask you. Are you really going to sell the house?"

"Of course."

"You really are vile. A vile, mean, despicable man."

"Good-bye, Felicia," I said, and dropped the phone onto its cradle.

There was no satisfaction in it. I sat there and quivered like an autumn leaf while my brain fibrillated.

I peeled off my clothes and got under the shower with my beer can perched on the top level of the three-tiered plastic soap caddy stuck to the wall. For all I knew or cared the phone rang continuously for ten or twelve minutes. When I turned off the shower I was squeaky clean, the beer was gone, and the shakes were under control. I went into the bedroom, and the extension phone beside the bed began ringing.

I grabbed it.

"Yes?" I said impatiently.

Instead of chilly and crystalline, the woman's voice that answered was warm and fuzzy, soft as doeskin, almost tentative.

"Mr. Keller?"

"Yes."

"This is Jennifer Kendall. Maggie Radek in Chief Hostetler's office suggested I call you. Maggie's my sister. She says you have a house to sell."

If it had been Felicia, I would probably have said something dumb. So I ought to have thanked Jennifer Kendall for not being someone she wasn't, but I was in no mood to talk to a real estate agent. All the same, I was forming the conviction that not getting to know the owner of that soft voice might be a mistake.

So I fumbled my mouth into the right gear and said, "Oh, hi. Sorry I sounded like the start of World War Three. I thought you were someone else. I didn't mean to yell at you."

"That's all right. You didn't, really."

"Maggie said you might call. You don't sound anything like a real estate agent."

"Oh, well, we try not to. We're struggling for a new image at Sunrise Realty: early birds and optimists but no polyester suits and no voices that are all elbows." Words flowed easily past something still tentative in her voice. If it was a sales trick to gain sympathy it was working fine. "Your house is 4344 Fox Hollow Road, is that right?"

"That's the mailing address. The house is on a block-long un-paved track that turns off Fox Hollow just up the hill from the Pollock Highway."

"Yes. Did you know that your little street's getting a name? Fawn Lane. I guess someone's interested in developing out there."

"Charles Cromwell's friends?"

"I don't know yet. If the area's being developed, would it make any difference in your decision to sell?"

"No. If it doesn't sell, maybe you could lease it."

"Not many people looking to lease these days."

"You found someone to lease the Osterreicher house."

"Oh, goodness, is that all over town? . . . But you would have gotten it from Maggie or Dave Hostetler, wouldn't you?" I said from the Chief. She went on, "I'd almost given up on the Osterreicher place. Do you know them?"

"No."

"A nice couple in their sixties. They have family in England and Hawaii, and last spring they took off for a year of traveling and visiting. The house went on the market in April. Not even a nibble until I got this phone call from someone who said she was Helen Pavlik. Of course, the name didn't mean anything, and then she told me who she used to be."

"You knew her?"

"Oh, sure. Not well—she was Maggie's friend and Maggie's three years older than I am. I guess they met in junior high. Helen was a couple of years older than Maggie, but only a year ahead in school. She dropped out after her junior year. I guess she was nineteen when she left town. She didn't come back until that quick visit last month. She called Maggie, and Maggie referred her to me to find her a place to live. Helen didn't know I was in real estate till Maggie told her, or what my name had changed to either."

"How did she contact Maggie? Her name must've changed too."

"Oh, yes. Helen sent Maggie a Christmas card the year after she left. Then Maggie married Carl Radek and sent Helen an announcement to the return address on the card. She must've got it. Anyway, that's all ancient history. The point is Helen got hold of me, I showed her the house, and she signed the lease the same day. I wish I'd never heard of any of them. I don't suppose there's any chance Helen wasn't murdered after all?"

"Afraid not."

"I just hate the idea of its having been done by some vagrant junkie. Then she'd still be alive if I hadn't leased her that particular house."

"The Chief would like it that way, it would save him some embarrassment. Arthur MacAndie says the fix is as good as in, that this thing won't be solved if it's left to the cops."

I was just making conversation; but after a slight pause she said delicately, "Welcome to Dos Cruces, Mr. Keller."

"You don't trust people either?"

"I trust people a lot, I'm just not a fanatic about it. And there are some people I trust less than others."

It was worth a shot in the dark. "Like some of Helen's old boyfriends?"

"Not particularly. I don't think there were as many as people say."

"Could you name some names?"

"I could, but it might curl the phone line."

Maybe Charles *did* need a lawyer.

I said, "If we met to talk over selling the house, maybe you could tell me directly, over a drink."

There were all kinds of reasons why she might refuse an invitation to gossip with a man she'd never met. I heard a soft but definite intake of breath, as though something had startled her. What I'd just said?

But what she said was, "Why not?"

"I'll call you later this afternoon."

"I'll be showing a house for the next hour or two."

"I've got your card. If I don't get you at the office, I'll call you at home."

"Why not?" she said again, and hung up.

▽

Chapter 10

IT WAS AFTER FOUR when I got back into town. Courthouse Plaza was casually chaotic but unhurried, as though the festival were opening next week instead of tomorrow.

Hank Cronjager, the Laguna potter with the curly beard and the rippling belly, was getting out of a dusty blue pickup parked across from the Barker Building when I got there. He yelled for Carl. The rangy teenager with the sunbleached hair came out from the now completed Canyon Concepts display booth. He climbed over the side into the pickup while his dad lowered the tailgate.

"Hi," I said. "Anyone seen Aunt Kate?"

Two sets of pale bright eyes fixed on me.

"Not lately," the potter said.

The kid said, "You still pricing pottery?"

"Just looking for Aunt Kate, and after her, Fran Rowan. Anyone seen Fran?"

The kid stuck his thumbs in the top of his jeans, flexed his muscles, scowled.

"This morning," Hank Cronjager said. He knuckled his nose and scratched under his beard. "She said you're okay. I told her not to be so damn sure." He wasn't kidding.

"Thanks. Do the same for you one day."

"Don't doubt it one bit."

I assured him he was a rare judge of men, and he and the kid began unloading crates from the pickup.

The county courthouse dated back to a time when all official buildings were built to look self-important. A facelift a few years ago, however, had softened its truculent rectitude, and now it shared a block with the unemphatically contemporary city hall without embarrassment. It was set back from the sidewalk beyond a rising sweep of lawn. Early in the festival's history, well-known artists had been invited to exhibit their work in the ground floor lobby and adjoining rooms opened up for the purpose, but now it was given over to work by school kids; their elders displayed their art on easels set up in the more spacious lobby of the city hall. Charles Cromwell and a few others had grumbled that since the festival was nominally a county affair it had no right to clutter city premises, but for some reason no one had listened.

The festival committee offices were two rooms on the second floor of the courthouse, one donated by the not very busy county public information department and the other a storeroom used the rest of the year by the janitorial staff. A member of that staff, a dignified old cat in white overalls with white hair under a baseball cap, was polishing one of the windowpanes in the courthouse door. The other already shone. He pulled open the door he was working on to let me in. He had the brown sculpted face of a philosophical peasant. The dark brown eyes in the brown face stayed as contained as the desert hills, but appeared to be even more patient. He was Elena Valdez's father and had been polishing these doors longer than she had been answering questions at the city hall information desk. Some Anglos said his grandfather had been a Chiricahua Apache war chief, and found his patience threatening. Others thought he was just dumb. I suspected it was a big joke at our expense. I said, "Buenos tardes, Señor Quijada," to which he responded gravely but without getting chummy.

In the lobby, two guys were setting up the pegboard partitions the kids' artwork would be displayed on. I took the angled staircase to the second floor where, at the rear of the building, a narrow hallway brought me to the festival committee's two rooms.

I found Aunt Kate in the second one. She was sitting at the far end of a long conference table that was decorated with dirty glass ashtrays, mimeographed sheets, and random bits of paper. The air was stale with tobacco smoke, and the burned smell of warmed-over coffee came from a Silex coffeepot on a hotplate in one corner. She was dialing a telephone with a hand that looked as gray and brittle as old paper. The usually neat little bun at the back of her head was coming uncoiled.

She finished dialing.

"Hey, Aunt Kate," I said from the door.

She wrinkled her nose, apparently not getting any answer, and hung up.

"Hello, Jim. Looking for someone?"

"A certain Katherine Cromwell. Couple of questions I want to ask you. Can I buy you that drink you didn't have time for yesterday?"

"What a lovely idea. But I can't now, dear. I have to wait for June Hostetler and the little Kendall girl to get back. Would the offer still be open in, oh, an hour or so?"

"Sure would. We could make it an early dinner, if you like."

"I'd like it a lot. Thank you."

I left her dialing the phone again. Downstairs Señor Quijada's front windows shone like jewelry. Outside the afternoon was still hot, but the sky was again the serene blue of this morning. I headed for the Ramada Inn. Neither Fran nor Mike Garcia had been in their room when I had called from home earlier.

I was nearly there when a small dark blue Nissan drove past me and pulled into the hotel's parking lot. The woman at the wheel had dark hair and wore heavy-framed opaque sunglasses that masked her face. In the seat beside her, her face pale and strained, her eyes enormous and staring right at me, was Fran Rowan.

The car pulled into one of the short-term parking slots near the hotel's entrance. It was still moving when the passenger's door opened and Fran almost fell out, running, pushing her way through the glass door into the lobby. The driver's door swung open and the other woman got out with a flourish of sleek legs, Maggie Radek in the white blouse and tan skirt I'd seen her in this morning. Without bothering to close the car door she ran awkwardly after Fran, hindered by the skirt and heels.

The lobby door swung open behind her.

I went to the car. Both doors were open, the keys were still in the ignition. I plucked them out and dropped them in my shirt pocket. I closed the doors and followed Maggie inside.

The lobby lighting was indirect and dim. A plump, pleasant woman wearing a plum-colored dress and too many bangles was checking receipts behind the reception desk. In the coffee shop, heavy drapes had been drawn over the windows, and waitresses and busboys were flitting discreetly about in the shadows getting ready for dinner.

The woman at the desk murmured behind my back, "Looking for someone?"

I tried to look disarming with the easy unassertive smile.

"Just waiting for Mrs. Radek."

Her eyes flicked toward the carpeted stairway. After a moment she said carefully, "Why don't you take a seat?"

I thanked her and sat down at the end of the upholstered bench running along the wall opposite the coffee shop entrance. Then two feminine voices wafted briefly from upstairs, as though a door had been opened and closed. I didn't get any words, but the lighter voice was raised in what sounded like passionate denunciation.

The woman behind the desk looked sharply up the stairs, then more thoughtfully at me.

Half a minute later Maggie's legs appeared at the top of the staircase.

Casually, as though she had all the time in the world, she floated down into the lobby. She wasn't involved in anything more emotional than a trip to the store for some shampoo, and oh yes, it would still be too bright out there, so she'd better put her sunglasses back on.

At the foot of the stairs she turned toward the lobby door, the shades hiding the lovely eyes and leaving her face as readable as the far side of a brick wall.

I stood up, taking the keys from my pocket.

"You'll need these, Maggie."

Her face jerked around. If she was glad to see me she hid it well enough.

I dropped the keys into her outstretched hand. She kept on walking without even a nod of acknowledgment, pushing her way through the glass door.

I said to her back, "Did your boss just get through beating up on Fran with the birth certificate?"

She stopped and faced me for a second, then turned and ran for her car. I followed. She wrenched the door open, sat down, and swung her legs in under the wheel in one movement, knees together, a woman besieged.

I closed the door for her. The window was open.

"Does your boss always get you to clean up after him?"

Her mouth was pinched and bloodless. So was her voice.

"You bastard. Leave me alone."

"You want to be unpleasant, go right ahead. It doesn't bother me much, it just makes me wonder why." Which didn't prompt any outpourings of girlish candor, so I upped the pressure. "Who's got the guilty conscience? Is it true that some avenues of investigation have been declared off limits?"

"That's contemptible. Who's saying that?"

"People. Tell me about Helen. She was a friend of yours once."

She closed her eyes and her body sagged. For a while she didn't seem to breathe. Then she straightened with something like a sigh and dropped her hands into her lap.

It only meant she was trying a new tack.

"What happened with Fran this afternoon is simply none of your business." Every syllable dripped with indifference. She was forced to endure this discussion because I was bigger and stronger and a heartless brute. "Yes, Helen and I were friends. First in junior high, then at Marshall High School. Helen was a year ahead of me but never graduated. She dropped out after her junior year and went to work and left town about a year later."

"Keep in touch?"

"Not really. I didn't see her again until she appeared out of nowhere last month. I only saw her that one time. She'd been nineteen, now she was thirty-nine. She'd gained a few pounds but still looked good, still warm and friendly, though I thought she was holding a little more in reserve than she wanted anyone to guess. Maybe she'd found that being too friendly can be dangerous. Or just wasn't sure of her welcome. I'm boring you, of course. I hope I am. I'm certainly boring me."

"Why would she be unsure of her welcome?"

"Don't be obtuse."

"Was she as promiscuous as people say?"

"I don't know what people say. She was a nice ordinary girl who made it with a lot of guys."

"How about girls?"

I wasn't sure why I asked that. No special reason. Just covering the territory, I guess. When she answered, the pose of boredom was forgotten. There was venom in her voice.

"How am I supposed to know? Why d'you ask, anyway? To complete the putdown? She slept around so she's a whore, she slept with women so she's a dyke, write her off, she wasn't a woman at all, she was a joke?"

"Was Helen bisexual?"

"No. Are you?"

The Nissan roared to life. She threw it into reverse and slammed it backward without looking. I barely got out of the way of the rearview mirror. Then the car squealed to a stop and lunged forward as she spun the wheel and blasted away between parked cars to the alley exit.

Maggie and her Nissan disappeared. I went back into the lobby.

The woman in the purple dress was still doing things behind the desk. She gave me a politely speculative look.

"Hello again. May I help you?"

I dug a card out of my billfold.

"Please. Would you ring Frances Rowan or Michael Garcia for me? I don't know the room number."

She looked at the card, consulted the register, and picked up a phone. I craned my neck to see her touch two, one, four. She murmured, "I don't think Mr. Garcia's been back this afternoon .. . No answer." She hung up. "Miss Rowan came in a few minutes ago. Either she took the back way to the pool area, or she's in the shower, or she just doesn't want to talk to anyone."

I thanked her and went out the sliding glass door to the sundeck. The only person there was an elderly gent in a Panama hat and a white shirt with the collar open and the sleeves rolled up over his plump pink forearms. He was reading a newspaper. I went past him and found a door back into the building, then another door that led to a loading dock and a utility stairway going up. It took me to the second floor. A door painted institution yellow admitted me to a carpeted hallway with discreet dim lighting and numbered doors.

Before I found 214 I had turned and gone halfway down another hall. I knocked. No answer. I could hear nothing.

I dug out another card and poked it under the door before going downstairs.

Chapter 11

THE COUNTY COURTHOUSE WAS as reverentially gloomy as a museum after hours. A few matted pictures already hung on the temporary partitions.

On the second floor, muffled voices droned from behind one of the courthouse doors. More voices came from the second festival committee office.

I found Aunt Kate sitting on a straight-backed chair just inside the door, her hands in her lap. June Hostetler was dialing the phone, looking trimly executive in some sort of lightweight jumpsuit. A pretty kid with straight fair hair falling to her shoulders was pouring coffee from the Silex pot into a pair of heavy china mugs. Slender and small-breasted and not tall, wearing jeans and a tennis shirt, she had the compact neatness of a dancer or a gymnast.

"Sorry if I'm late," I said.

Aunt Kate had fixed her hair and recharged her batteries.

"There you are, young man! You know June, don't you? June Hostetler?"

June's compact pewter-streaked head turned a few degrees on her slender neck. Her eyes were disdainful behind their tinted lenses.

I gave her my most winning smile.

"We met this morning," I said warmly.

She said, "Yes," in an indifferent voice, hung up the phone, and made a note on a clipboard.

"And this is Megan Kendall," Aunt Kate said. "Jim Keller."

The pretty kid put one of the coffee cups down by June's phone and raised the other toward me.

"Hi. Want some coffee?"

"No thanks. I'm taking Aunt Kate to dinner."

"Have a good time!"

"Thank you, dear, we will." Aunt Kate picked up her own clipboard, which was crammed with papers. "Shall we go?"

"How about La Creperie?"

"That would be nice."

We left the office and started down the hall. She asked in a low voice, "What was that all about?"

"What was what all about?"

"June!"

"She knew Felicia. Who apparently opened her girlish heart."

"'Oh dear."

"She may have picked up more of the same from her husband. I'm not popular with the Chief. He thinks I'm up to something."

"Are you?"

"No."

"I saw that smile you gave June. I thought you were using your manly charm rather like a club."

"Didn't work, did it? Are you still doing space assignments?"

"Oh no. I've been drafted to help June take care of something called Exhibitors' Liaison. Some of the community leaders we depend on insist on thinking in terms of compartmentalized functions and flow charts, so if it keeps them happy, why not? Heaven knows we'd have trouble without them. Imagine those free-form anarchists from the art colony trying to organize anything! So in general, the Exhibitors' Liaison handles gripes and cross-ups and tries to find participants who haven't shown up, stuff like that. What June has little Megan doing I've no idea. Well, not so little, really. She's sixteen, the daughter of Jennifer Kendall, the real estate lady. A lovely child, and I suspect very bright."

"I talked to Jennifer this afternoon—about selling the house." We came to the landing, where the stairs reversed their angle. Aunt Kate started down the final flight without pausing, though she sensibly held on to the handrail. Once we were outside she stopped and looked over the plaza, her eyes warm, her thin face fond.

Chaos had somehow been replaced by an air of community. A classical guitarist, a street musician in town for the festival, played something with an Elizabethan lilt, and a tiny cool breeze drifted almost hesitantly over the scene, as though uncertain of its welcome.

I said, "What I want to talk about is kind of rough. Maybe it's not fair to spring it on you at dinner."

"Are you withdrawing the invitation, young man?"

"Of course not."

"Good. I'll be better prepared with a glass of cold Chablis in my hand."

I had suggested La Creperie because it was only a block and a half from the courthouse and only two blocks from the lot where my car was. We could walk to the car after dinner, and I could drive her wherever she wanted to go. Home, if necessary. Home was a rambling farmhouse from the same era as Clint Farrell's place. It looked so timeless you were surprised it had electricity. There was a sweet water well on the property, two oaks, an apricot orchard, and an incredibly weathered old barn that had been featured in one of the paintings that had first brought Aunt Kate fame. There was an old ranchhand with a rake in the picture, tall and skinny and exhausted-looking but tough as old leather, a survivor. A glow to the picture suggested sunrise. Technically it was a marvel, but Aunt Kate said it was so blatantly commercial it embarrassed her. The sentimentality was laid on with a shovel, she said, but she hadn't been broke since so it would be ungrateful to repudiate it. Her property, out West Eleventh where it became a dusty country road, hadn't yet been engulfed by encroaching suburban sprawl. So far no one had tried to buy her out. Few people would dare. Except Charles. He would rather see her in an efficiency apartment near County General Hospital, preferably one of those run by the geriatrics industry. Then the house could be torn down and the orchard uprooted and a new development planted to replace them—something called Left Bank Estates or New Greenwich Village, as alien and disfiguring as a tattoo on a virgin's breast.

La Creperie was a dark narrow low-ceilinged place dedicated to cheap pseudo-Parisian ambience and good French cooking. Outside it was a painted wooden sign, ostentatious in its reticence, and a heavy door set into a dark brick wall. I was reaching for the door when Aunt Kate put a hand on my arm.

"I've changed my mind. Let's just walk a bit."

We began strolling down the block.

I said, "This afternoon Fran Rowan and Chief Hostetler had some kind of confrontation."

"Oh . . . Yes. Fran told me she had met you last night. What kind of confrontation?"

"Apparently about the murder of Helen Fairland."

She didn't wilt, the planes and hollows of her strong-willed face didn't change, but something happened all the same. Perhaps hope died.

Her voice was quiet but steady. "I don't understand."

"The police were going through Helen's things today. They found a photostat of a birth certificate. Maybe genuine, maybe not. It says Helen Fairland bore a child twenty years ago. The child's name was Frances Mary Rowan Fairland. The father was Charles Everett Cromwell."

"Yes?"

"Those are familiar names, Aunt Kate."

"I suppose they are. But the presence of what sounds like my son's name on a document of doubtful origin doesn't prove he fathered anyone's child."

"True."

We strolled a bit farther.

"I've known Fran since she was in grade school," Aunt Kate said. "She's the daughter of Fred and Cynthia Rowan of Carpinteria. I suppose she may be about the same age as Helen Fairland's child, but the similarity of names has to be a ghastly coincidence." We reached a corner and turned down toward Fourth. "Jim, for Heaven's sake! I would be delighted to find that I had unacknowledged grandchildren all over the state, but you don't think Charlie would ever tell me, do you? His only passion is discretion—protecting his upright image for future use. But even if I did have all these unknown grandchildren, Fran isn't one of them. She's the sweetest child, and I love her dearly, but I knew her parents. Cynthia was a gentle soul who never quite got over the wonder of having a baby at forty-two, after ten years of a childless marriage. One day she went into the hospital for some minor surgery and died on the table. That was when Fran was, oh, ten or eleven. Fred managed a garden supply shop. He died last January in a car crash. The doctors said he had a stroke that caused the crash—the only disorderly event in his entire life. As a family they were wonderfully close and affectionate. You'd never convince me Fran wasn't their child."

"Adoptive parents don't have to be less loving than the other kind, Aunt Kate."

"That's true, I suppose. But even if you ignore my deepest intuitions, what have you to replace them with? Names on a questionable photostat."

"Back when he was young and not so straitlaced," I said, "Charles had a steamy love affair with Helen Fairland that a lot of people still remember."

"Do they? I hope they're remembering accurately. I'd hate to think that the joys of his life have always involved petty bureaucratic victories and hounding less rigid personalities toward his kind of conformity. You see, I failed Charlie somewhere. Otherwise, he wouldn't be what he is. But until I see some reasonable proof of this affair, I'm going to have to consider it just another item of gossip, probably started by his political enemies. Mind you, I've a lot of sympathy for his political enemies, I'm just not in sympathy with using lies and scandal as political weapons."

We came to another intersection. The light was red. Aunt Kate looked up at me, her glasses flashing briefly in the late afternoon sun. Her expression was weary and disparaging, though it wasn't clear what was being disparaged. I felt a touch of panic. I shouldn't be antagonizing Aunt Kate. I wanted her as a witness at my custody hearing.

The light changed. I took her elbow and we crossed the street. The downtown walls of brick and concrete were beginning to glow with the first intimations of approaching sunset.

We walked on slowly.

"Put yourself in Dave Hostetler's shoes," I said. "Suppose he buys the coincidence of Charles Cromwell colliding with the van carrying the girl who just may be his illegitimate daughter—right down the hill from where the girl's mother just got murdered. It's a lot to buy, but suppose. Then he learns that Charlie's mother, quite by accident, got to know the maybe daughter years ago, in another city. I don't think he'll buy that many coincidences. He'll start looking at that birth certificate as some sort of motive for murder, maybe for Charles, maybe for Fran or her boyfriend, and as a sign that he can stop having to consider some of Helen's old lovers, who've since become prominent, as possible suspects."

"Really." Her voice was acid. "And who might they be?"

"Don't know yet. Maybe Dave Hostetler himself."

"Goodness, gossip about Dave? What gutters do you have to crawl around in to pick up that kind of thing?"

"Probably the same gutters you'll be dragged through as long as Dave Hostetler has that birth certificate between his teeth."

Her voice cracked like a whip. "It's good of you to worry about me."

She had stopped in front of an auto display window and stood straight as a pencil, staring defiance at me. How frail she looked hit me like a blow—a small, thin old lady with thick lenses distorting her eyes and pale, withered skin and white hair pulled into a neat little bun at the back of her neck, carrying an incongruous clipboard and looking haunted and vulnerable.

I said as gently as I could, "Listen, Aunt Kate. Charles keeps trying to hire me. I told him to get lost. Maybe I shouldn't have."

She stared at me mutely. I gave her my expectant look, hoping to coax some response from her. She shook her head briefly, giving an exhausted little shrug. I said, "Have I spoiled your appetite completely? We could still have that dinner."

"I'd better go home."

"I'm sorry, Aunt Kate."

"I know, dear."

We picked up the station wagon. I drove her to the St. Francis Hotel's parking garage, where she'd left her car. I parked on a street and walked her into the building. Her car was a maroon Chevy pickup, aging and dusty, with an art festival committee member's sticker on the windshield. She slid under the wheel. I closed her door.

"Anything you want to ask or tell me, you call, okay?"

She gave me an exhausted wispy smile through the open window. "Poor Fran. If it turns out she is Charlie's daughter, it'll be like losing Fred Rowan all over again."

She started the motor. The pickup backed and turned. Aunt Kate wiggled her fingers at me in a way that reminded me of Fran Rowan last night, when she and Mike were leaving the scene of the accident. It didn't mean anything—except in my head, in the secret unexplored passages where feelings are born and daughters and granddaughters get cross-indexed into an impenetrable reflexive lexicon that can play hell with the emotions without illuminating one corner of them.

Chapter 12

THE HALLWAY WAS DIM, muted. I knocked on 214.

Behind the door Mike Garcia said, "Yes?"

"Jim Keller."

The door opened. "Hi, found your card. Glad to see you." He didn't look it. His face was hard with recent anger. "You look older."

"I am."

"Maybe you need that beer."

I went into an unlighted room. Heavy drapes pulled across the windows admitted too little watery light to melt the shadows.

"Hi," Fran said in a small thick voice.

"Need some light, kid," Mike said. Whoever he was mad at, it wasn't her. He turned on the table lamp that was squatting on the chest of drawers.

Fran Rowan ducked her head and hid her eyes behind one hand. The other hand held a drinking glass. She was sitting propped against the headboard of the bed with a couple of pillows behind her, wearing an old white terrycloth bathrobe. Her legs were stretched out and her feet were bare. She had a towel wrapped around her head like a turban.

"I must've been in the shower when you came by," she said.

Mike opened the portable ice chest that sat on the carpet beyond the bed. Ice cubes rattled. He took out a wet brown bottle and held it up inquiringly. I said fine. He got me a glass from the bathroom and twisted off the bottlecap.

I said, "Things have been happening. Maybe we should talk."

He gave me the bottle and the glass.

"Why didn't you tell us about this murder?"

"I didn't know about it until after I talked to you this morning. I didn't know you were involved until this afternoon."

"God damn it, we're not involved!"

"Fran's name came up!"

"So it came up!"

I pulled the chair from under the dressing table and straddled it, put my elbows on the back, and poured my beer. Fran still clutched her glass and hid her eyes.

"Here's what I know," I said. "Some time last night a woman who lived just up the road from me was killed. Her name was Helen Fairland Pavlik and she used to live here around twenty years ago."

Fran's head jerked up off her hand with enough force to loosen the turban. Her eyes were red-rimmed and puffy.

"I know all about Helen fucking Fairland fucking Pavlik! I've been hearing nothing but fucking Helen's name all afternoon!"

"From our police chief, I'll bet."

"That creep."

"Yeah, he's a charmer. Anyway, Helen had only recently moved into that house. She was shot with a small calibre bullet. A neighbor heard the shot but doesn't know what time it was because he was passing-out drunk. He crossed the street and found her and called the cops. Then he took a nap in a flowerbed just outside the house. He had his own .22 rifle with him, but it wasn't the gun that killed Helen. If the cops suspect anyone, they're keeping quiet about it."

"I could give them a good candidate," Fran said darkly. "Know how I got dragged into this mess?"

"I've seen that supposed birth certificate."

" '*Supposed* birth certificate'! What makes you think it's not *real*?"

"Do you have one of your own?"

"Of course. Somewhere . . . At home. There's no Fairland name on it. Or Cromwell."

"Does it look any less real than the one the Chief found?"

"Now it does." Her lower lip quivered. She looked up at the ceiling, her eyes brimming. She palmed her cheeks impatiently, then drained her glass in three swallows. She studied the ice cube severely.

"What's in the drink anyway?"

"Bitter lemon and vodka," Mike said.

"Hooey. Bitter lemon and tap water. No buzz."

Without warning she tossed him the glass. He caught it in both hands without losing the ice cube. Fran smiled sweetly, rolled herself to the edge of the bed, swung her feet onto the floor, and stood up. Her knees buckled instantly and she sat down again with a startled look.

Mike got rid of the glass and took her hand. She looked up at him trustingly.

"You're not getting a buzz on," he told her, "because the vodka went straight to your knees instead of your head. Better lie down again."

"Have to go to the bathroom."

"Oh. Okay, then."

She got up again slowly, let go of his hand with an air of high adventure, and stayed vertical. She turned to me.

"What's that dumb police chief's name?"

"Dave Hostetler."

Her mouth relaxed into a gentle smile.

"Dave Hostetler," she said sweetly, "sucks dead bunnies."

She walked to the bathroom with the exaggerated care of a circus performer on a tightrope. The light came on and the door shut firmly.

"Two vodka and tonics," Mike said ruefully, "are the most booze she ever had in her life." He called loudly enough for her to hear through the bathroom door, "You're just a cheap drunk, kid."

A minute later the bathroom door opened and Fran came out without her turban, carrying a tortoiseshell comb. Her face was washed and her eyes were less swollen. Her hair hung down her back in a tangled mass. She bent forward and swung it over one shoulder and began to comb it out.

I asked, "So what happened with Dave Hostetler?"

She caught the comb in a tangle and worked it through with absorbed concentration.

"Dave Hostetler," she said at last, straightening up, "has all the charm of a plateful of elbows, only not as many brains. And he's mean. I never felt so shit on in my whole life. I took it all out on that secretary of his, Maggie something, when she brought me back. Boy,

I really dumped on her. You see, it was Maggie who'd come to get me. Around the middle of the afternoon, a knock on the door and there she was, that nice smile and those gorgeous eyes, saying who she was and how her boss wanted to talk to me. I thought it would be about last night—that oncoming car, remember? The one that came around the bend? Though I was sure I hadn't anything to add to what I'd told the cops last night. Anyway, she drove me over to the police station and I met the Chief in his office.

"Maggie sat down with a steno pad and I sat down on this hard chair in front of the Chief's desk, and he sat down behind it, sort of fatherly, and said how sorry he was to drag me away and everything, and then asked what my legal name was and when I was born. I said Frances Mary Rowan, March 23, 1970, and he said where was I born. I said San Bernandino, and then he asked if I knew Helen Fairland Pavlik.

"That surprised me. I was still expecting all this to be about last night's accident. I hadn't heard about the murder—I didn't know she was dead. I started to ask him what she had to do with the accident, and he just pressed me to answer. So I said no, I didn't *know* her, but someone who signed herself Helen F. Pavlik had written me a letter about a week ago."

She dropped the comb onto the bed, swung the now gleaming long dark hair back over her shoulder, and pushed it away from her neck. She sat down on the edge of the bed.

"He asked me if I still had the letter. Sure, I said, in the letter file at home. And then he wants to know what the letter was about. I said it was personal—I didn't think he could ask me about that. And he said was the letter the first I'd heard of her? I said yes, and he said why should someone I'd never heard of suddenly write me a *personal* letter? I said well, because of what the letter was about, and that was personal.

"So he got mad. Not hot mad. Cold, mean mad. He said, 'What do you *mean*, personal? She was murdered last night, and that means there's no such thing as personal, this is a homicide investigation.'"

"By this time I was getting pretty rattled, and then he took this little plastic envelope out of a folder. He held it up and said, 'We found your business card among her papers.' " I started to say we give out hundreds of them, and he fished out another plastic envelope and shoved it in my face and said, 'Now don't tell me *this* is just *personal*.' "

The effect of her two vodka and tonics was wearing off. Her voice had taken on a raw edge.

"What it was was that birth certificate. I looked at it and guess what? I started to cry. Like a four-year-old with a broken heart. Only every time I got a broken heart when I was four my mother was there to mend it, only she wasn't here any more, and besides, I'd just found out a few days ago that she wasn't my mother. I didn't know who was, but it wasn't Mom, childless all those years and then suddenly me. It happens, but not every day, and what that letter from Helen Pavlik was all about was whether I might have been adopted, because she had given a child up for adoption twenty years ago and she had reasons to think I might be that child.

"Well, I first thought the idea was crazy. But then I realized that I didn't really *know*. My parents were both dead, and the only family friends I knew were people we'd met since we moved to Carpinteria just after I was born. But there's Aunt Ethel, who was my mom's older sister. She has to be older than Aunt Kate and doesn't get around too well, but she's got these twinkly black eyes and is still as bright as a button. She lives just outside Vacaville, the only family we had apart from some cousins in Illinois we used to get Christmas cards from.

"So anyway, I scraped up my nerve and called Aunt Ethel and asked her. She took the longest time to think about it, but then said yes, she'd always told Fred and Cynthia they should tell me, but they were afraid to—afraid it would make me feel different toward them or something. And yes, she was sure, no question, that I was adopted, although she didn't know who my natural parents were. She hoped she'd done the right thing telling me, but there'd been so much in the papers and on TV about adopted children growing up and trying to find their real parents. And I said phooey, my real parents were the ones who loved and raised me, which was probably true and seemed to make her feel better but it didn't make *me* feel better. I felt awful. Sort of betrayed. As though I'd learned they hadn't trusted me. Childish, huh? If I was adopted I sure lucked out. I just wished they'd trusted me a bit, that's all."

"They trusted you," Mike said. "Except in that one little corner, and it wasn't so much they didn't trust you as they didn't trust their own good fortune."

She sat very still and thought about that a moment. Then her soft unpainted lips melted into a slow smile. Her look got warm and cuddly. She wrinkled her nose at me.

"Pretty good, isn't he?"

"I think he's right," I said.

"God, how'm I gonna keep him from getting smug about it?"

Mike snorted, grinning. She got up and kissed him on the mouth. Then she picked up her comb and ran it through her hair again.

Mike said, "Tell the man the rest of it."

Fran said, "Why wouldn't they?"

"Wouldn't they what?"

"My folks. Why wouldn't they trust their own good fortune?"

"No idea, kid."

She looked at me. I lowered the level of my glass. She was still looking at me.

"Well, people are superstitious," I said uncomfortably. "Sometimes when they've been lucky they think they're on a roll, then they try again and lose everything. Others want to quit while they're an inch ahead and never take another chance in their lives. Maybe your folks simply didn't want to take that one more chance."

She gave that one a hard stare.

"I get the feeling that nothing's that simple."

"Or maybe," I said carefully, "they had a reason to be extra sensitive."

"What kind of reason?"

"Suppose the adoption had been irregular."

"Oh, shit," Fran said.

"Just suppose, Fran."

"Yeah, but . . . They wouldn't've wanted me to find out if they'd been mixed up in something wrong. Can we find out if they were?"

"If the adoption was legal there'd be a record of it. Chief Hostetler's probably checking into that right now."

Mike said, "Go on about this afternoon."

"Okay. Where was I? The letter and Aunt Ethel and everything." She got back onto the bed, leaning back against the pillows. "Well, all that was the stuff I didn't want to tell. Like I said, I started to cry, but I also got stubborn. The Chief, though—his way of getting me to talk was to scare me to death. If that's my name on the birth certificate he's gonna find out whether I tell him or not, so what am I hiding? How does he know it's not a motive for murder? How does he know we really came in on the Pollock Highway and didn't sneak down the hill from Helen's house? What had Helen threatened me with in that letter? He knows I called Helen when we finally got in last night because I left a message on her answering machine. What was I doing, trying to fool people into thinking I didn't know she was dead?

"Anyway, he'd had more practice bullying people than I'd had being stubborn, so I caved in. I told him what was in the letter and about Aunt Ethel and everything. I told him I'd called Helen long distance a couple of days ago and said I was gonna be in town. I *had* been adopted so maybe we should meet. She said yes, please, why didn't we come by her house on our way into Dos Cruces? I said we'd be arriving late, maybe eight-thirty or nine, and she said fine, maybe we'd just say hello and have a cup of coffee and make a date for later. I was scared stiff. And the way things happened, we never got there.

"I explained all this to the Chief. I don't know how much he believed. He couldn't believe I hadn't brought her letter with me, or hadn't planned to look up my father. I said this was all a great big maybe. I didn't know my father was supposed to be Mr. Cromwell—before last night I'd only heard of his name. He said, 'Who from?' I said, 'Aunt Kate, of course.' He went ape shit. 'Oh, right, you knew his mother. Well, well, isn't that convenient,' rubbing his fingertips together to mean money. I got hysterical. I jumped up and yelled, 'Why are you doing this to me?' And Maggie what's-her-name, she jumped up and said, 'He's not going to do it anymore. And when the Chief started in on her she yelled at him, 'You horse's ass, you want to make sure Keller and'—somebody, Mac somebody—'you want to make sure they run you out of town?' " Then she grabbed my hand and led me to the girl's john. She had me wash my face and tried to give me a Valium, and then took me back to the car.

"Which would've been fine. I was so grateful to her and I was just beginning to climb down off the high wire when *she* had to start in.

That letter from Helen, was it handwritten? Well, no, it was typed. Was there anything special about the typing, anything unusual? She was pretty insistent. I got to feeling all boxed in and paranoid, in that little car, with the questions and everything. I came all unglued again. She reached over and put a hand on my shoulder, and I pulled away and yelled at her to keep her dykey hands to herself, which got *her* upset. We drove here and I ran inside and she ran after me. She caught me before I could get the door unlocked. She was sorry, she hadn't known her boss was going to be that shitty, and she had only asked questions because she and Helen used to be friends back in the old days. I yelled every mean thing I could think of and came in here and slammed the door in her face."

She stopped, looking over at Mike.

"Don't get mad, hon."

"Jesus, I wasn't mad at you. I was mad at them. I think they set you up for a good cop, bad cop routine."

"Is she a cop?"

I said, "I think she's a civilian employee. They could have set it up anyway. Didn't work, did it?"

"No, but I feel real crummy about treating her that way."

"Call her and tell her so. Her last name's Radek. Margaret Radek."

She dragged the phone book from its nightstand shelf onto her knees and began riffling pages. I put my glass down on the dressing table and stood up.

Mike was staring at me thoughtfully.

"Are you working for anyone I know?"

"Just me, I guess."

"Why bother?"

Fran looked up quickly, a finger marking her place on a page.

She protested in a scandalized voice, "Mike!"

I said, "I'm being nagged at by an obscure sense of responsibility."

He gave me some more of that stare. Then he nodded.

"Okay."

It obviously wasn't; he was only giving me the benefit of the doubt. It wouldn't have been easy, explaining that my sense of responsibility had been engaged by hints of malfeasance spoken by a soft voice on the telephone, and by my having disregarded a plea for help from a man I didn't like who might be the father of a daughter he didn't want, a daughter my dreams confused with my own who had apparently stepped into the middle of someone else's nightmare. It sounded pretty thin when I explained it to myself.

I said awkwardly, "Something's going on. Maybe a cover-up. Mike's right, Fran. I'd be careful about taking anything on faith right now—or anyone."

"Some people you just naturally take on faith," Fran said. "Mike, for instance."

"Mike's different."

Mike looked at me. "You'd better be too."

$\triangledown$

Chapter 13

QUINTERO DRIVE WAS AN S-curving street heading nowhere special into some low baked hills on the south edge of town. The lawns were smooth and the flowerbeds well-kept. At the end of the street where I went to turn around, a couple of kids threw a softball through the twilight.

I parked in front of number 1521. The Kendall place was the smallest house on the street, low and red-tiled, with wrought iron bars covering the windows and an exuberant bougainvillea crawling over the porch and onto the roof. A driveway led from the street to a closed garage set back from the house. White-painted stucco glowed with an almost spiritual radiance. The evening was as soft as an Angora kitten.

The front door opened before I reached it. The pretty kid I had met in the festival office stood in the doorway. She had changed into a pale yellow blouse.

She said without smiling, "Hi. Remember me?"

"Hi, Megan. I thought you'd still be helping the committee."

"Nothing was happening so June said let's go home. She gave me a ride. The Hostetlers live just around the corner."

Moving with her dancer's balance, she stepped back to let me into the little hall and led me through an archway into the living room.

It was a welcoming room with burnt-rose carpeting and inviting furniture. Light from a tall floor lamp warmed the pale walls and the patterned curtains drawn across the windows. It also gave me my first good look at the pretty kid's face: silky bangs falling over a clear brow, eyebrows fair and level, eyes light brown with golden flecks in them, surrounded by improbably dark dramatic lashes. Her lips were clearly defined and soft and young. But her look was old and knowing, full of weary distaste.

"My mother will be out in a minute," she said politely but still not smiling. "I hear you have a house to sell."

"That's right."

"Is this a date or a business appointment?"

The question was some kind of challenge. I summoned the easy grin.

"A business appointment, I guess. Does it matter?"

"Possibly. Your reputation precedes you."

Aunt Kate had suspected that Megan was very bright. She was certainly self-possessed.

"Don't believe everything you hear," I said. "Do you always try to antagonize your mother's prospective clients? Or do you just check out her visitors?"

"When I have nothing better to do," Megan said. "You'd be surprised how many of them can barely read."

"What's next, the literacy test?"

Light footsteps came from somewhere beyond the hall.

Megan said, "Do you think you could pass a literacy test?"

The footsteps got nearer and a slim woman in a turquoise blouse and black pants came into the room. Her skin was tanned and her hair was cut in a casual shag. Gold winked from her earlobes. She smiled and delicate lines swept back from the corners of her eyes. Not like Maggie's eyes, or even like Megan's. Jennifer's were honey-colored and clear and one tilted up at a slightly steeper angle than the other. She said, "Jim?" in the tentative voice I had heard on the phone and crossed the carpet between us, extending her hand. "Hi. I'm Jennifer. Sorry to have kept you waiting."

There was silver on her wrist. Her hand was small and well cared for, her handshake firm and businesslike.

"Maggie called when you were in the tub," Megan said.

Jennifer took back her hand. "Anything special?"

"She says the murder last night is beginning to look complicated. And she says don't trust Mr. Keller."

Jennifer blinked. Storm clouds gathered.

"Either I misunderstood you," she said grimly, "or a serious apology is in order—at once."

Megan said patiently, "Don't play the knee-jerk parent, Mother, please. I'm only the messenger."

"Not trusting me is going around," I said. "Maggie must have caught it from her boss."

Megan asked, "Where did he catch it from?"

"Megan, you're grounded," Jennifer snapped. "We'll talk about the fine print tomorrow. You're excused."

The girl's face stayed calm, her voice conversational.

"She's not like this," she told me. "She's putting on this act for your benefit."

"*Megan!*"

Megan gave a small sigh, "All right, Mother. So nice meeting you again, Mr. Keller."

She walked unhurriedly through the archway and disappeared toward the back of the house.

Jennifer watched her go, her expression suddenly bereft and lonely. But when she turned to me she showed only conventional embarrassment.

"The nerve of that girl! I apologize for my daughter, Jim."

"No need to. Really. She's worried about something."

"That's no excuse! Simple politeness makes life bearable."

"I think perhaps she was warning *me*."

"What on earth are you talking about?"

"I think she's heard the rumor that I rough up women."

She became very still, looked at me for a long time.

"Is the rumor true?"

"No."

"Where would she have heard it?"

"Anywhere. I heard it from two people just today."

"She's only sixteen, for heaven's sake! Is she likely to be exposed to the same rumors you'd pick up? No, no, she was just overreacting to what my sister told her."

"I don't think she's an ordinary sixteen-year-old."

The honey-colored eyes flashed like knives.

I said mildly, "Am I wrong?"

After a moment I heard the quiet whisper of a sigh.

"She was right, you know—I *was* putting on an act. Sometimes I just slip into the pretense that she *is* an ordinary sixteen-year-old and I'm a fond mother who's no martinet but who draws lines that don't get crossed. It's to reassure people. Of course, it's not that way at all. We're more like two autonomous adults. I always feel awful when I've pulled rank. Sometimes I wish she were ordinary, you know that? Then she'd be a bit dumb and have the usual dumb friends and the usual pimply succession of boyfriends instead of the dangerous young outlaw she goes with—"

She stopped, making a wry face.

"Is it like this when you're in court? You find that one raw nerve and suddenly witnesses bubble over with personal confidences?"

Nothing she'd told me would make the tabloids; if she felt she'd given anything away then maybe she had something to hide. She went on, "It's that you're so easy to talk to. I don't even know what I'm going to say next."

I guess that sounded as weird to her as it did to me. Her lips stretched and her teeth sparkled in a smile that declared it all to have been a joke. Behind the smile she looked exposed, vulnerable. She even crossed her arms in front of her breasts. There was raw nerve somewhere. It might be Megan, but I didn't think so.

I gave her the easy grin. "That'd be terrible—if we were in some kind of adversary situation. We're not, are we?"

"Oh God, I hope not." The stiffness left her eyes. For a moment I thought I saw not one Jennifer, but two: the appealing woman in the turquoise blouse and—as elusive as the afterimage of a bright light, as haunting as memory—a Jennifer with softer, untanned cheeks and eyes that were clear and trusting, the Jennifer of eighteen or twenty years ago.

Today's Jennifer went on, "After all, I want to sell your house for you. Don't we have a date to talk about it over a drink?"

"I'm hungry. Let's make that dinner. How does the Steak House sound?"

"Lovely. Give me a moment to rescind that sentence and make peace with Megan."

Chapter 14

THE STEAK HOUSE WAS about as close as you could come to cloth napkins and crystal chandeliers without bumping into a dress code. The hostess who showed you to your seat was good-looking but not flashy, the waitresses were smiling and deft. Deep enveloping booths lined the walls and took up the center of the room.

Jennifer Kendall's nerves had stopped jangling visibly, but I thought I still saw signs of tension. Maybe I had scared her.

We were shown to a booth and ordered drinks. I asked to see her bracelet.

She turned her hand palm upward. A slender ankh with a turquoise in its loop hung from a slim band around her right wrist. "This?" She gave me her diffident smile. I think she expected me to take her hand and didn't know whether to let me. I didn't, though it was a nice idea. "I bought it at last year's festival."

"From Mike Garcia?"

"Goodness, is it that distinctive?"

"Something about it brought him to mind. Do you know his girlfriend?"

"He was sharing a booth with a potter, a pretty girl with long dark hair. They're from Santa Barbara. D'you mean her?"

"Yes. Fran Rowan. It's beginning to look like Fran Rowan was Helen Fairland's daughter. And guess who's the leading candidate for the role of father."

Jennifer looked startled. Her caution became palpable. She sat back against the dark upholstery and folded her hands in her lap. A small vertical line appeared between her eyebrows.

"You've been doing your homework. How old is this Fran?"

"Born March 1970."

She looked down at her thumbs, and after a while smiled faintly.

"Helen was Maggie's friend, not mine. Twenty years ago I was only fourteen. Why don't you talk to Maggie about this?"

"I doubt if she'd talk to me. I'm not to be trusted, remember? I'm mildly curious about what's going on in her head, in Dave Hostetler's too, but I'm not obsessed about them. I'm more interested in Helen's old boyfriends."

"I know I promised, but now I'm not sure I should tell you."

No bright reply or dazzling strategy came to mind, so I gave her the shrug and the grin of friendly surrender while the cocktail waitress appeared, balancing our drinks on a little tray. She set them down on little napkins while I said, "Well, I guess that's that. Can I ask what she was like back then?"

The cocktail waitress gave us a conspiratorial wink and said softly, "Enjoy!" and went away. Jennifer brought her hands off her lap and laced them around her glass, forming a protective barrier against table-top marauders.

"Why do I get the feeling that I shouldn't tell you anything?"

"Beats me."

"Something tells me that behind the easy-going manner there's a determined man pursuing a private agenda. And being too sincere."

"Which might explain why I haven't been able to convince anyone of anything all day." I was suddenly irritated and didn't care who knew it. "So cancel the question, forget I asked. I'm sorry I asked. Subject closed. Let's forget the whole thing."

I grabbed by glass and almost bit through the rim. My whiskey sour almost choked me. My throat had been expecting beer.

I put the glass down and stared off at the far corner of the room.

"Aw, hell," I said to no one in particular, annoyed at myself for getting irked and wondering why it mattered.

Jennifer said, "I still want to sell your house for you."

"You've got it."

"Just like that?"

"Sure, why not?"

She made a thoughtful sound, nibbled her drink, and stared abstractedly past my shoulder at the dark upholstery behind my head. Then she sighed and turned on a lopsided little smile.

"All right, I'll tell you. If I don't, a lot of other people will. None of this is secret, you know.

"Her dad was a short order cook with a partial disability pension from the VA. I think her mom worked as a waitress and a domestic, but one day she just quit—up and left and never came back—when Helen was eight or nine.

"Helen was very likable but never any good in school. I think that's why she spent so much time doing what she was good at—fucking. But it always bothered me that this neat girl, who always had time for her best friend's kid sister but always seemed so grownup, could be this dope-off non- achiever who couldn't tell 616 from 161. And why did she have so much trouble spelling?"

I said wonderingly, "She was dyslexic?"

"Didn't you know? No, of course, why should you? She was diagnosed, but no one around here knew what to do about it."

In my head, a penny dropped. Jennifer was about to say something else but I flagged her down.

"Would you excuse me for a minute? Suddenly I've got to make a phone call."

There was a pay phone in the men's room foyer. By a miracle Fran answered at once.

"Do you know what dyslexia is?"

"No."

"It's a learning disability that screws up the way your brain perceives things. Turns them around so you see 616 when what you're looking at is 161."

"Okay."

"Helen Fairland had it. Did you talk to Maggie? That's what she was getting at when she asked you about that letter. Were there any reversed letters, misspellings or anything?"

"In the end I didn't call her. The letter was a perfectly ordinary businesslike letter. Is that bad?"

"It makes you wonder if someone wrote that letter for her."

"Then he—or she—must have written what Helen told him. Remember I talked to her before we came here. Listen, I'll try calling

Maggie now. I'll tell her about the letter."

I thanked her and hung up, then looked up MacAndie's number. No answer. I tried the *Chronicle*. The switchboard was closed.

I went back to the booth.

"Helen's dyslexia causing you problems?"

"No." I sat down. "But Fran got a letter from Helen a few days ago suggesting they might be mother and daughter. Typed. No reversals or misspellings. Was there a typewriter at the Osterreicher house?"

"You probably don't want to talk to Dave. . . . Tell you what. In the interest of putting the client in a mellow mood, I'll ask Maggie." She swung her feet out of the booth and stood up, taking her purse. "You can sit and listen to your ice cubes melt."

She left. The ice cubes made dull music. Jennifer took her time. When she finally reappeared, the set of her shoulders was different and she came drifting across the room on automatic pilot, her face catatonic, avoiding people by sheer accident. The emotional zigzags at her house had prepared me for mood swings, but I'd never seen anyone withdraw so far so fast.

I got to my feet, suddenly aware of having dealt recklessly with my drink.

"Oh for God's sake, sit down." She sat down herself. "Maggie doesn't know one way or the other about the typewriter. She's given me an assignment. I'm supposed to learn who you're working for."

"No one."

"What's this half-assed private eye stuff all about?"

"There isn't any. It's all in Hostetler's imagination."

She gave me a remote stare.

"You're quick with glib denials, but you've been poking around getting in the way ever since last night."

"Listen. Last night, near where I live, Charles Cromwell ran his car into the van belonging to Mike Garcia and Fran Rowan. I got involved when Charles started throwing his weight around and two cops named Hardy and Vasquez were too ready to accommodate him. Then first thing this morning Arthur MacAndie tried to involve me in the murder investigation, implying that Dave was too interested in covering up for his buddies, and this afternoon you practically agreed with him and dropped hints about Helen's big time boyfriends. Meantime, Dave Hostetler is snarling at anything that moves, and Charles Cromwell keeps trying to hire me. He insists Mac is out to get him for political reasons, and that Dave will grab at any chance to stab him in the back. Why does he think that?"

"Ask him."

"Maybe because twenty-one years ago he stole Dave's girl and got her pregnant."

She took a sip of her drink, put the glass down, and laced her fingers around it.

"What keyholes have you been listening at?"

"The cops found a birth certificate among Helen's papers. It names Helen and Charles as the parents of Frances Mary Rowan Fairland, born March 1970. Dave got pretty upset. Was Helen pregnant when she left Dos Cruces?"

"I told you—I was only fourteen."

"Is that a responsive answer?"

"I heard gossip about Helen, but I only believed what I heard from Maggie. And I never heard that. Did you invite me to dinner under false pretenses?"

"Of course not. We were going to talk real estate over a drink, then I met you and decided that dinner might be fun." I gave that a moment and then broke open the big bright candid grin. Or anyway, I flashed a lot of teeth. "I still have faith."

The cocktail waitress came by with a nice smile and inquiring eyebrows. I pointed to our glasses and said we'd do the same again. She nodded brightly and headed for the bar.

Jennifer said, "If you're not working for anyone, why dig through all this ancient history?"

"Because Mac may be right. Dave would give his eye teeth to pin the murder on someone from out of town. He's even picking on Fran Rowan."

"Have you known her long?"

"Since last night."

She smiled insinuatingly.

"She must be very appealing."

"Also very unavailable. But the way things were last night I'd have gotten involved if she'd looked like Quasimodo and had the personality of a flat tire."

Her face mimicked the dawn of understanding.

"So that's it. Under the casual exterior lies a comic book hero."

What I almost said was, "No, I'm just emotionally unemployed," but managed to stop myself—at the edge of a cliff. I scrambled back, imagining her response to my unspoken admission: "You mean you're stirring up trouble because you've let your life get into a rut? You're meddling in people's lives to enact a role in some cheap psycho-drama?" Appalling accusations, even if she didn't voice them. Were they true? What *had* I been up to? Just waiting for the custody hearing next week, trying not to get paralyzed with worry. Or with anger. Winding up things in Dos Cruces, turning my work over to Bert Fowler. Living in limbo, tuning out, turning off. I'd been turned off for weeks. Maybe I *had* been looking for a chance to play hero. Which carried the promise of almost certain disaster.

What I said, as unemphatically as I could, was, "No. One thing just led to another."

She made a meaningless gesture. She neither believed nor disbelieved. Irritation clamored in my gut.

"Can I ask one last gumshoe-type question?"

"I don't promise to answer."

I reached for her hand and turned the bracelet to the light. The hand was no more responsive than a banana peel, but at least it was dry and warm, the fingers ringless, the nails naturally rosy and filed to match the curve of the fingertips.

"Were you wearing this the day Helen came to see you?"

She was briefly startled.

"Well . . . yes. Helen saw it and asked about it. Her husband had only liked to see her in traditional jewelry, but her perspective was widening. I had Mike Garcia's card, so I fished it out and gave it to her."

I dug out the card Mike had given me.

"One like that, yes."

"Could you do me a favor? Tell Maggie what you just told me. Have her tell the Chief. It explains how one of these cards was found in Helen's things. It's probably where she first saw what looked like her daughter's three given names, Frances Mary Rowan, and even an address she could write to."

"Oh, God. And it may have had something to do with the murder."

"Dave Hostetler would like it that way."

"Of course, if the murderer *was* some wandering psychotic, I guess I'd feel guilty about leasing her the house he happened to wander by."

The cocktail waitress arrived just then. She put new drinks between us, picked up my empty glass, and left with a murmured reminder to enjoy. I got a firm grip on my new drink but left it where it was. Jennifer hadn't finished her first drink yet.

"I suppose," she said, "it all means I belong on your side. If things go Dave's way, I'm going to wind up with a bigger share of responsibility for what happened to Helen."

"No culpable responsibility."

"Things like guilt are learned a lot earlier than big words like culpability. My God, I had a grandmother who believed that if you had a vindictive thought about someone, and later something terrible happened to them, then your vindictive thought was responsible—you were guilty of causing the damage. Bad things only happened because someone was mean and unthinking about consequences. 'Consequences,' that was her favorite scare word. It was so loaded with moral tyranny that I was thirteen before I could make myself say it."

"How often did Maggie spring it on you when you were on the phone?"

It was the right thing to say. Her eyes crinkled up and her face tilted and she hit the ceiling with a peal of laughter as bright as a happy child's. Amused faces turned to look at us.

"A couple of times, actually. What really got to me was an argument I had with Maggie—about this conviction Dave has that you're working against him. I said maybe he is, what's that got to do with my having dinner with him? She said all right, if you have to go out with a man who's notorious for beating up women, do something useful, set your feminine wiles to the task of learning who he's working for. I said that unless she was talking about basic biology I wasn't sure what feminine wiles were. She told me not to get cute. I don't think she knows what they are either."

"I thought the women's movement had outlawed them," I said. The change of mood had been dizzying. I hoped this one would last. "She should try using her own."

"Mmm. Gorgeous, isn't she? Especially the eyes and tits. But you wouldn't find it much fun, I'm afraid. Anyway, I said I couldn't imagine you beating up women, and she said she'd heard it from a very reliable source."

"Probably Dave. Or Dave's wife. The story was started by my wife. Ex-wife. God knows why."

"Exes are weird. Mine gave up Megan without an argument. What a shallow jerk."

"Mine's doing the opposite. Yesterday she offered me sixty thousand dollars of her father's money to get out of our three-year-old's life. Permanently. The custody hearing's next week."

"Aaah . . ." The syllable was drawn out softly, hardly louder than a sigh. "So that's what it is—your mind's somewhere else. It gives you a flat, schizzy quality . . . and gives other people an excuse not to trust you."

"You've got to be the only person in town who didn't know about my custody thing."

"But I didn't! This puts everything in a different light. If only we could start over, from the beginning."

"Hi. I'm Jim Keller."

"Oh." She laughed again. "Hi. I'm Jennifer." She reached across the table. I shook her hand. Like her face, like her honey-colored eyes, it was alive again. It was a hand it would be profoundly silly to let go of, but I couldn't think of an acceptable reason for hanging on to it. So I just loosened my grip. Her hand lay comfortably in mine for a few seconds then slowly withdrew.

She finished her drink, set the glass down on its damp paper napkin. With a considered, ritual-like movement, she pushed it as far away as her hand would reach.

She started talking without looking at me.

"The reason phoning Maggie took so long was the line was busy. Guess who she was talking to. Fran Rowan. Maggie told me what happened when Dave called Fran in. Maggie had been feeling pretty bad about her part in it. She said it was obvious all along that Fran was telling the truth. Dave was just being dumb. So when Fran called to tell her the letter from Helen showed no signs of dyslexia, and also to apologize for dumping on Maggie after the meeting with Dave, it made her feel worse. Everyone had ganged up on the poor kid, and here she was saying she was sorry for not liking it. So Maggie was clearly sinking into one of her depressions. Which get pretty baroque—guilt feelings, can't eat, can't sleep, name any symptoms you can think of—all to hide the inadmissible fact that she's falling in love again."

"Why inadmissible? Who's the guy?"

"It isn't a guy. That's why it's inadmissible. This time it's your little friend Fran Rowan.

"I think Maggie was first drawn to Helen because even in junior high she was getting a reputation for sexual adventurousness. Maggie was the prettier of the two, and already had that sexy bod by the time she was thirteen. She thought she ought to be attracted to boys but wasn't. They were attracted to her, though, and she tried a few experiments with some of the big good-looking ones, but they all fizzled.

"When Helen quit school and went to work as a waitress, that's when she started getting involved with older guys. Dave must've been around thirty and already married to June. June was pregnant and having a rough time of it. She wound up spending a month in the hospital and still miscarried. I guess Dave and Helen went on seeing each other for a while, but Dave was a pretty straitlaced old family man even then. Helen dropped him when Charlie Cromwell came on the scene.

"Then, when Maggie was a senior, Helen left town. I never heard a word about her being pregnant. With no Helen around, the field was a lot clearer for Carl Radek. Carl was about twenty-two, a time salesman for one of the TV stations. He'd been warm for Maggie's form for some time, but she wouldn't even date him. Then right out of high school she up and married him. The marriage lasted six months. He was the first person to suggest that Maggie was gay. She was really hurt. She said it was all Carl's fault for not being able to make her want to. Carl gave up and moved away. She eventually got around to divorcing him. After all, she was normal, and someday some guy would come along and prove it. Once in a while she'd try one on for size, but no matter how well-suited they were in every other way, the physical thing always wrecked them. And every so often she'd have one of these emotional involvements with another woman. Only emotional, and there was always some straightforward rationale for her interest. It just didn't fool anyone but Maggie."

"Poor Maggie."

"Yes . . . I didn't mean to get sidetracked. I was going to talk about Helen's lovers—at least the ones who might be able to pressure Dave Hostetler. There was Dave himself, of course, and Charlie, but they came later.

"There were two in Marshall High School. First was Tom Schlieffen. His dad was a deputy city attorney then, and now he's mayor of Dos Cruces. Tom is always Thomas L. Schlieffen in the papers now. He's a corporate lawyer in San Francisco and getting to be someone in the Republican party. Tom and Helen were wildly ill-matched but they lasted almost a year. In the end he was too much of a brain, I guess, and someone got bored and that was that.

"Of course, you know the D.A., Lincoln Fox. Well, her next long-term attachment was Linc's kid brother Harlan, the youngest of the Gang of Three—now a state assemblyman and general hack for the real estate interests. Back then, though, he was just a guy who was so good-looking you could hear the girls whimper as he walked down the halls."

I said, "Is the real estate lady suggesting bad things about the real estate lobby?"

"Sure. I've got a nice little business serving the local community. The big timers couldn't care less about anyone's local community. I don't want my hometown turned into a plastic desert tourist trap."

"Why did Harlan and Helen break up?"

"Most high school affairs do. Maybe his brothers pressured him to end it before Helen became a political liability. They were years older than Harlan. Did you know Marcus Fox was Harlan's legal guardian?

"Anyway, those were Helen's 'serious' boyfriends: Tom Schlieffen, Harlan Fox, Dave, and Charlie. Tom, the Fox boys, and Charlie could bring a lot of pressure on Dave. And of course if the old gossip was true—I guess some of it was—there were all the one-night stands, the weekends in San Diego or Frisco, and the odd moments in basement rec rooms and the backseats of cars. I don't know how you check on it, or find out if any of those guys made contact with her in the years she was away. And I don't understand what you need this for, anyway."

"Nothing, I hope. Thank you."

She batted her eyelashes.

"You mean no more questions? We can actually look at a menu, or just sit here and get smashed?"

"Sure." I gave her one of the menus and opened the other. I said without thinking, "Last time I was here . . ." and caught myself. *Last time I was here.* Golden time, contented time, with year-old Katy asleep at home under the calm, practiced eye of Liz Aparicio, a thirty-year-old niece of Elena Valdez. Felicia in a white dress, smelling of jasmine, sharing a booth with me as Jennifer was doing now; taller than Jennifer, younger, with lightly tanned fair skin and an opulent slim-waisted body, her hair a darkening blond and shoulder length—she never left the house without making sure she looked like a casual fashion plate in *Vogue* or *Harper's Bazaar*. The curious irritations that had grown out of her postpartum blues had not yet hinted at the raging dissatisfactions that would reduce my world to bloody dust and rubble within two years.

I finished the sentence automatically, ". . . the lamb shishkabobs were real good."

$\triangledown$

Chapter 15

I HAD LEFT THE windows open, so the house was warm but not stuffy. I gave Jennifer the ten-cent tour and the spare front door key. She suggested an asking price a little higher than the appraisal made for the property settlement.

I got two beers from the refrigerator, popped one, and gave it to her. She disappeared toward the bathroom, and I dialed Andy Feldberg's number from the living room phone.

"Hi, Andy," I said.

"Oh, hi. Listen. I called Ed Hammond a couple of times at his office," he began abruptly, as though no time had passed since our talk this morning. "Out at big meetings. Tried him at home this evening. I was planning a fishing expedition—was the scandalous offer made by this Engle fellow for real, and so on. He answered the phone himself. Didn't say hello, just snapped, 'Felicia?' as though ready to take her head off. I said, uh, no, actually I was calling *for* Felicia, was she home? And he said no and asked who I was. I said the first thing that came into my head. Burt Reynolds."

"And he said you've got to be kidding."

"Nope. Has to be the only guy west of the Rockies who never heard of Burt Reynolds."

"Why didn't you go luxury class and say Richard Burton?"

"Can't do an English accent worth a damn. Besides, he's dead— and who can imitate that voice?"

"Can you imitate Burt Reynolds's voice?"

"Can't even remember what he sounds like. For all I know he

106

sounds like me. Anyway, he said he'd tell her, and no, he *didn't* know when she'd be back. I started to explain that I thought we had a *date*, but he was already hanging up. Point is, old buddy, that something's worrying old Ed. I wonder where she went this evening?"

"She's old enough to go out without a nursemaid. Ed ought to be used to it by now."

"Yeah." Andy sounded skeptical. "I'll call him tomorrow and give my right name up front and be very businesslike."

"Thanks, Andy."

"Don't worry, I'll bill you. Take it easy."

He hung up. Out of the corner of my eye I caught a movement in the arch into the hall and turned to it. Jennifer stood there, naked as the day she was born and a whole lot prettier.

I almost dropped the telephone. I tried to make my hungry stare look halfway intelligent.

"Wow," I said, hanging up the phone.

"Thank you." She gave her soft smile. "What you see is what you get."

"All I have to offer is an over-thirty analogue of a horny teenager."

"Goody. I haven't had one of those in weeks. Megan grabs them all."

I took her beer can and set it down beside mine.

"Suddenly I feel clumsy. It's been too long."

"I'm not usually this blatant, you know. I just thought it would be nice to dispense with the preliminaries."

I stepped closer and folded my arms around her. She eased against me and I kissed her experimentally, rather gently. Her lips were like petals. "You don't feel in the least clumsy to me." Then, half a minute later, "All this would be even nicer if your belt buckle weren't digging into my tummy."

So we got rid of the belt buckle and a few other things, and dispensing with the preliminaries worked out just fine. Quite a bit later, after some pleasantly strenuous passages of pleasure, she was lying sweaty and disheveled in the light from the nightstand lamp, and I was looking down at her, reluctant to separate, euphoric and smug as an Olympic medal winner.

Jennifer said contentedly, "And you aren't even my type."

"Sorry about that. You are exactly my type."

She hooted with laughter. "Sure. Female."

"Dark and slender, with tits like flowers."

"Mmm. Corny, but nice." She ran her hands outward from my shoulder blades. "I didn't know you were a swimmer. You've still got swimmer's lats."

"What do you know about swimmer's lats?"

"My God, I was married to a set of them. . . . Hey, that's right. You don't know a thing about me."

"Sure I do. You have, or had, a weird grandmother. You may be weak on feminine wiles, but your basic biology is totally gorgeous."

"Thank you. There are a few other details. My father was a doctor who died when he was forty-nine and I was three. My mother was twenty-six. That was when her mother came to live with us. To help out, she said. Old bitch. I graduated from Marshall High at just seventeen, went to UCLA, and got pregnant my freshman year. Megan's father was a sophomore swimmer. He was six-four and weighed one ninety-six and looked like a god—"

"My God!" I said. "Jack Kendall."

"Oh, Jesus. You didn't know him! That'd be too much."

"When I was a sophomore he was a senior. Middle-distance and four hundred IM man. I was a sprinter who never quite made the front rank. I never knew he was married."

"By then I'd taken Megan and moved back here. Went to real estate school and got my license and went to work. By then Jack was just a small mistake I'd made, about as important as a parking ticket. He was one of those dutiful, responsible, *dull* guys. I think I divorced him because he was boring me to death.

"When I got my own place my grandmother wanted to move in with me. To help out, of course. I told her I was only moving from my mother's house to that microscopic apartment to get away from her, and that I needed her help like a peptic ulcer. I got hysterical and she got sanctimonious and said she would pray for me and wouldn't speak to me until I apologized. I wouldn't so she didn't, which was fine by me. In 1979 my mother remarried and moved to Tucson. The old bitch died of chagrin when they didn't invite her along." She locked her arms around my neck, her legs around my waist. "We're a nice fit, you know that?"

"Even though I'm not your type. What's your type?"

The sudden hideous clamor was the bedside phone.

I groaned. Jennifer said, "Couldn't we just let it ring?"

"Yes, but I probably shouldn't."

I picked up the phone and tried not to sound too grumpy.

"James Keller."

"Oh, hi, Mr. Keller," a languid female voice said. "This is Deedee. You know, Diane Witherspoon. Your client. Well, ex-client. Can't afford to pay you a retainer."

"Oh, sure, Diane. You got a problem?"

"Well . . . sorta. Fella who tells me he's a friend of yours, anyway, a neighbor. Drunk as a skunk and can't do nothin' and passed out on the bed. I'd need a forklift and a dump truck to move him outa here."

"He got a name?"

"No. I guess I could look in his billfold—"

"Don't touch his billfold. A middle-aged guy, light brown hair, blue eyes, outdoorsy, with a broken nose?"

"Yeah, that's him."

"Where are you?"

"Where else? Lindero Palms Motel, Ninth and Ocotillo, room four."

"I'll come and get him. Thanks, Diane."

"Nada, Mr. Keller. See ya."

I hung up.

Jennifer said, "Party's over?"

"Put on hold. You hear all that?"

"Most of it. Who's the lady?"

"Diane Witherspoon. Deedee to the customers. I've represented her a couple of times. She's got Clint Farrell passed out drunk at the Lindero Palms Motel. I better pick him up before she runs out of patience and turns him over to the pimps who run the place."

"Who's she doing the favor for?"

"Herself. Wants me to owe her one, just in case, and wants to avoid vicarious liability for any offense committed by a co-felon. I drilled that principle into her head the last time around. If she calls the motel management for help in getting rid of Clint, they'll lift his wallet and dump him somewhere. A gung-ho prosecutor could charge robbery, kidnapping, possible reckless endangerment, and conspiracy. I'm sorry about this. I could take you home, or you can stay naked until I get back."

"Or I could come with you and help you handle him. Then we could come back and get naked together."

It sounded like a good program. We disentangled ourselves and spent a few minutes padding in and out of the bathroom and getting dressed. I put on a clean T-shirt and this morning's jeans. She tugged the black pants over white panties and got into the turquoise blouse, and the exuberant wanton with tits like flowers became the neat dark-haired real estate lady with the beautiful eyes. She put on her jewelry and made a couple of passes with my hair brush and we left.

The electric sign said LINDERO PALMS MOTEL and showed a coconut palm with blue fronds and a red trunk. The motel had been the Waikiki Palms until a change of ownership a few years ago, which explained the coconut palm. Smaller letters spelled out VACANCY.

I turned into the motel's parking lot. It was two-thirds empty. A light burned in the office. Under the office window a tiny spotlight glared on a painted sign: $22.95 Per Night, $15.95 Per Siesta.

I parked next to a dusty old pickup. We got out and found room four a couple of doors down. I knocked.

Diane's languid voice said, "Mr. Keller?"

"Yes."

The door opened cautiously. A tallish woman in a snug low-cut white dress stepped out a little, blocking the light. She saw Jennifer and froze.

"She's a friend," I assured her. "Jennifer—Diane."

". . . Okay." Diane stepped back into the light. Her hair was honey-blonde with dark roots. Her nails were bloodred and matched her purse and her spike-heeled shoes and the filmy scarf around her neck. Her face was almost pretty and freshly made-up, but without hope. The breasts restrained by the white dress were the size and shape of a pair of watermelons. "Sure took you long enough. I gotta get back to work—Close the door, honey."

Jennifer closed the door.

The room was cramped. An open door showed a small bathroom. The closet had no door and the chest of drawers had been painted a muddy chocolate brown to hide the cigarette burns. The radio on the bedside table was bolted to it. An almost empty pint of bourbon stood by the radio. The 19-inch color TV set bolted to its stand across the room was tuned to a closed circuit channel playing something pornographic.

The top sheet and blanket had been pulled over the foot of the bed, leaving Clint Farrell sprawled across the bottom sheet like a specimen awaiting the experimental knife. He wore socks and plain white jockey shorts and a singlet and looked limp enough to melt. Breath whistled and scraped through his nose.

"He owe you any money?" I asked Diane.

"Naah. They hafta pay in advance. When we got here he was already too drunk to get it up. He said he needed more vitamins and went out to his pickup and got that pint. It didn't work. Nothin' worked. *I* worked—worked my ass off. He can't say he didn't get his money's worth of honest effort."

Clint's slacks were thrown carelessly on a chair. Jennifer and I began dragging them onto his uncooperative frame. His wallet was a chunky weight in his hip pocket.

"I never touched his billfold," Diane said.

"How did my name come up?"

"It was the radio. The ten o'clock news mentioned you. Something about that murder last night, and an accident you were a witness to or something. This guy perks up and says hey, Jim Keller's a friend of mine, a neighbor. When he passed out I figured I better call you."

"Real thoughtful of you, Diane. Thanks."

"Sure. Nada."

I was getting Clint's pants zipped when, with infinite effort, his eyes opened and struggled to focus on Jennifer. Then his throat made a strangled sound. He said distinctly, "No—!" and sat up in a single heave and grabbed protectively at his crotch. Jennifer jumped away from the bed. Farrell's eyes went vacant, and he toppled slowly sideways.

His head hit the sheet and bounced, but he was already out. His breathing was a tortured rasp.

A sound came through the door. A key turned in the lock.

Diane said, "Oh shit."

$\triangledown$

Chapter 16

THE DOOR OPENED. A man in an open-necked shirt and tan slacks stood there leaning on a sturdy rubber-tipped cane.

"You didn't pay for no party. You owe me another twenty- five."

His voice was full of grating contempt. He had a thin tapering face and an air of authority more menacing than a gun. When he stepped into the room he reeled slightly to maneuver his left leg, leaning on the cane. A sharp piranha smile flashed at Jennifer.

"It ain't no party, Vic," Diane said hurriedly. "This—"

"You know the rules, you know the rates."

"Sure I do, Vic, but this guy passed out. I called his . . . *friends* to come pick him up."

Vic showed me his teeth. "I know you, seen you in court." Probably when I'd represented Diane on charges of soliciting and assaulting a police officer. "Who's your girlfriend?"

The carnivorous smile turned on Jennifer. He stared at her breasts, then lingeringly at her crotch. His tongue came between his teeth, slowly curling up to touch his upper lip.

Blood drained away from under Jennifer's tan until her face looked dead. Two patches of red began to flame over her cheekbones.

"Her name's Jennifer," Diane said.

"Nice name," Vic said, still looking at Jennifer through her clothes.

Diane said in a placating voice, "I just thought calling them would do everyone a favor, Vic, 'specially you."

During all this I had been wrestling Clint into his shirt. Keys rattled in his pocket. I fished them out and offered them to Jennifer. She didn't even see me, just stared at Vic. I shoved the keys into my pocket and Vic suddenly shifted his attention from Jennifer to the man on the bed.

Vic began tapping the heavy cane against his shoe.

He said slowly, not taking his eyes off Clint, "Never try to think, bitch. You thought this guy was just another horny drunk? You didn't even *recognize* him?"

"Huh?" Diane said, and began breathing through her mouth.

"He's a big landowner. Owns Carver Canyon and God knows what."

Diane took a while to get her mouth closed. Then her manner underwent a change. Her face softened. "Well, sweetie," she said to no one in particular, and turned and smiled at me. "I shoulda known you had well-heeled friends. Tell this one not to drink so much next time."

I got Clint's feet off the bed and pushed his shoes on. Then I went around behind him and hauled him into a sitting position.

Quite distinctly Clint said, "Whass goin' on?"

"God damn it, will you stand up?" I almost yelled.

"Of course, for Chrissake." He started to collapse again. I jerked him upright. He made a whimpering sound. "Hey, gimme twenny minutes, okay? Who the hell are you, anyway?"

"Jim Keller. We had lunch today at Bernie's."

"Oh sure," Vic said. "You two are great friends. Anyone can see that." He swung the cane and brought it down on the mattress. It was obviously weighted. "You better leave him right there, mister. You take him, it's kidnapping."

"Call the cops," I said.

Clint slurred, "Where's the broad with the big boobs?"

"Right here, honey," Diane cooed, kneeling in front of him. She began fumbling with her dress. "Look, you wanna see?"

Clint's arms flailed.

He slurred, "Kendall . . ."

Behind me Jennifer snapped suddenly to life.

"Right here," she said clearly, sounding surprised.

Clint heaved himself to his feet, knocking Diane onto her rear and stumbling to the door. He made a hurt sound when he hit it but at least stayed upright. I went across the bed and reached around him for the door handle. He sagged. I think he went back to sleep, standing up, his head on my shoulder. In five seconds I began to feel I was holding up a three story building.

"Come on, Jennifer."

I had lost her again. She looked at me vaguely across the bed. She couldn't go around it because Vic was in the way, and she hadn't the initiative to follow me over it.

Vic limped toward her. "Why's the lush afraid of you?"

Her head shook slowly.

"I'll tell the cops he was afraid of you and you dragged him away against his will. So be nice, stick around, have some fun."

He reached for the front of the turquoise blouse and tweaked her left nipple through the fabric.

For seconds, nothing. Then she reared backward onto the night-stand and knocked the lamp to the floor. The bulb smashed noisily.

Diane struggled to her feet, shrieking, "Jesus, lady, he's gonna make me pay for that!"

Jennifer didn't seem to hear. I tried leaning Clint against the door to free one hand. I held it out to her.

"Over the bed," I said sharply. "Help me with the door."

She turned to me vaguely. Then she said, "All right," just as vaguely, and climbed onto the bed and walked across it.

"Look at those *footprints*!" Diane wailed. "When I find out what this is costing me I'll send you a fucking *bill*!"

I jockeyed Clint around and Jennifer got the door. I almost carried Clint through it. Jennifer closed the door behind us, moving like a sleepwalker. I muscled Clint toward my car.

"I can drive your car," she said unexpectedly. She sounded anesthetized. "You drive him in his. If we leave it here, there's no telling what those awful people will do to it."

I propped Clint against the station wagon. In the dim light Jennifer's face looked slack with shock.

"You sure?"

". . . Oh, yes." The ghost of a smile. "Trust me . . ."

So I did. She made the trip without running any red lights or driving on the sidewalk and turned off Fox Hollow onto Carver

Canyon Road ahead of me. A light burned over the front door of Clint's house. She parked a few yards beyond it so I could stop the pickup opposite the door. Clint was snoring.

I got out and went around to the passenger's side. I opened the door. He almost fell out on top of me.

Jennifer approached from the station wagon. Her step was firm. Her trancelike state seemed to have passed.

"Need some help?"

"You could open the front door."

I gave her Clint's keyring. She opened the door to his house while I got his feet onto the ground so he was almost standing. In the dome light his face looked drawn and ghastly, the hair plastered to his skull.

His eyes came open and stayed open.

"Sorry to be such a fucking nuisance. . . . Gimme a hand."

Hanging on to the pickup door and my hand, he levered himself fully upright and paused, panting. Jennifer came over and tucked his keys into his shirt pocket. He convulsed suddenly and vomited. Jennifer jumped back, but too late.

I let go of him. He sagged against the door and held on with one arm and kept retching. I stayed out of the way. Jennifer retreated to the front door and examined the ruin of the black pants in the porch light. Farrell threw up until there was nothing left, but still kept on heaving.

Finally the heaves subsided. He looked blearily at me, then at Jennifer.

He said obscurely, "I hope you're satisfied."

"Not really," Jennifer said. "You're more than a fucking nuisance, Mr. Farrell. You're disgusting."

He let go of the pickup door and began weaving his way toward the house. He disappeared inside. Lights came on.

Jennifer looked down at her black pants, then at me. She was close to tears.

"I'm sorry, Jennifer. I should've taken you home."

"Do things always happen around you, or is tonight special? First that horrible Vic—now this." She raised both fists and slammed them down on my chest. Her eyes shone wetly. "My God, he walked in and turned my bones to yogurt. I almost wet my pants. I never saw anything so . . . totally hateful."

I made a sympathetic sound. I wasn't her type. Her type was tougher, with an air of menace. Maybe sometimes they roughed up women. Sometimes you were surprised they could even read. Only the tough guys who turned Jennifer on had all been pale imitations of Vic. The real thing scared her silly. Maybe because it turned her on too.

I said, "You're not much of a masochist if you don't like getting thrown up on."

She gave me a stony stare, then laughed weakly. "Oh shit, I don't believe any of this." She reached behind her and unzipped the pants and dragged them down past her hips, then sat down on the front steps and kicked off her shoes. Then she leaned back on her hands and raised her feet toward me. "Help me out of these, will you?"

I took hold of the pants legs and tugged. The snug garment came off without much argument. She stood up and tugged the panties up and took the black pants from me.

"I'll find a garden hose and rinse these off."

"Come into the kitchen, rinse them off in the sink."

"I wish I could rinse me off."

"Take my car. You know where my shower is."

"You're going to stay and tuck him in and sing him a lullaby! Do you mother-hen everyone you know?"

"Only the orphans."

We went inside. The old-fashioned hall had a hatrack and a clothes closet with a mirror in its door and a table with a phone on it. The lighted living room was on the right, an unlighted dining room on the left. Somewhere water ran heavily. Jennifer said, "I bet the kitchen's this way," and found a switch. A milk glass chandelier leapt into bright soft light over a noble old dining table, matching chairs, and an impressive sideboard. All the wood was unpolished, the corners of the room were unswept. Everything was drab and neglected.

At the other end of the dining room a door led past a pantry and a passageway to a spacious kitchen. There was a big, fairly new refrigerator. A table-model color TV set on the counter beside the toaster. There was a cold, half-full glass percolator on a wrought-iron trivet in one corner of the dinette table.

Jennifer threw her pants into the sink and turned on both faucets while I went looking for Clint. I found my way across the house to the master bedroom. Except for one corner, which had a small cot and a low bedside table with a radio and an alarm clock on it, it looked unused since World War II. Blinds were drawn over uncurtained windows.

Water was running in the adjoining bathroom, where I found Clint kneeling beside an old claw-footed metal bathtub with his head under the cold water faucet, his shirt wet and clinging. I spoke to him. No response. I watched him a while. I was ready to give up and leave when he moved his head and saw me.

He fumbled for the tap and turned the water off, then rested his arm on the edge of the tub and laid his face on it. His mouth stayed open.

"Yeah. You."

"Diane says don't drink so much next time."

"Who?"

"The broad with the big boobs. It hurts her professional pride, I guess, when a customer can't get it up."

"Fucked up, did I?" He turned around and leaned his back against the tub, groaning. "Musta mis . . . miscalc'lated somewhere. Window of opportunity gets narrower alla time. Don't drink enough, can't get it up. Drink too much, can't get it up. Jesus . . ." He looked up at me suspiciously. "Whatcha doin' here?"

"I brought you home, remember?"

". . . Naah."

"Blacked out again?"

"Musta."

"You threw up on a friend of mine." He groaned again, closed his eyes. "You seem to know her. Jennifer Kendall."

He became so still I wondered if he had died. Then his eyes opened, blue irises trapped and hurt in their nest of wrinkled skin. Breath wheezed in his broken nose.

"Whatcha tryna do to me, huh?"

"Trying to get you settled for the night."

"Leave me the fuck alone."

I wished him pleasant dreams and left him, dripping and combative. Jennifer was waiting in the kitchen. She lifted a green plastic sack.

"Got the pants in here."

I took her hand and we walked through the house turning off lights. While I made sure the front door was locked, she slipped into her shoes. I closed the pickup's door and we walked to the station wagon.

Her bare legs stuck to the vinyl seat cover.

"I think I should've put my pants back on."

"Get 'em clean?"

"Not really."

"It's not far to my place. I'll fix some scrambled eggs while you do the laundry."

I U-turned the wagon and turned left onto Fox Hollow. Once the street light was behind us there were no lights but our own and the companionable stars.

She asked abruptly, "Do you suppose I'm really a masochist?"

"Do you like being hurt?"

"God, no!—but . . . some people have an air of danger about them that makes being with them an . . . adventure. Of course, sometimes you think it's there but it's just their size, their sheer physicality. Like Jack Kendall—what a washout. I guess there's something exhilarating about taking chances. Maggie says I'm an unconscious Puritan, trying to guarantee that fucking around will have nasty *consequences*."

"No wonder Megan worries about you."

"Oh God. Do you suppose she knows?"

"We know she hears things. She picked up my reputation for sadism, probably from June. Where'd you pick it up?"

"Oh God," Jennifer said again. I swung the car onto the future Fawn Lane and stopped in front of the house. "Am I that obvious? . . . I should have told you, but first I didn't, and then I didn't know how."

"From Felicia."

"Yes. I'm sorry. I met her just that one time, almost a year ago. She dropped a few hints, that's all. I thought you'd be . . . interesting."

"Sorry to disappoint you. Why's Farrell afraid of you?"

We got out of the car. She gave me a small conspiratorial smile.

"I've no idea. And you didn't disappoint me at all, or didn't you notice?"

Inside the house was a little cooler. I took her down into the basement, where she dropped the black pants into the top-loader, added detergent, started the cycle. Going back upstairs, we stopped to neck in the kitchen.

"I'm taking you up on that shower," Jennifer said. "Join me?"

"I'll get the coffee on first."

She disappeared into the bedroom. By the time I had the percolator loaded up and on the stove I could hear the shower going. Then a car drove up outside.

It sounded big and not new. It turned around, the headlights flaring against the kitchen curtains.

I hoped it had learned it had taken a wrong turn and was on its way.

But it stopped. The motor died.

In a few seconds someone knocked quietly on the front door.

I turned down the gas flame under the coffee before going to answer it. I opened the door.

Megan Kendall looked up at me.

Chapter 17

SHE STOOD LIKE A dancer awaiting a cue, or a deer on the knife edge of flight.

"Hi."

"Hello, Megan."

I stepped back from the door. She hesitated, bit her back teeth, then came inside. I closed the door and saw her glance briefly toward the sound of water running through the bathroom pipes.

She was wearing the soft yellow shirt and snug jeans I had last seen her in. She began unbuttoning the shirt.

"Want to fuck?"

"No."

"Given it all to my mom?"

"I don't fuck high school kids. Is this a practiced technique for compromising older men or just for demoralizing them?"

"I'm not a kid, no matter what the law says. So?"

"So why look for trouble?" I steered her into the kitchen. The water was beginning to climb the rod in the percolator. "I'm not so drunk with male vanity that I think you're remotely interested, so I wonder what you're really up to."

Her eyes swiveled to the sound of the shower.

"Your mother's all right," I said. "Those stories are all bullshit. June Hostetler didn't start them, my ex-wife did."

"Why?"

"You'll have to ask her."

"I'd like the opportunity. Not getting rough with my mother

"I'd like the opportunity. Not getting rough with my mother doesn't prove anything."

"No. And so far you've only got my word for it, though the proof should be walking in here any minute. Did you come here just to check on your mother?"

Slowly she rebuttoned her shirt then crossed her arms and leaned back against the draining board, giving me a level stare. I pulled out one of the dinette chairs for her. When she ignored it I took it myself. The coffee began to perk.

I gave her my expectant look. She shook her head.

"Got your own car, Megan?"

"No. Kenny drove me. Ken Allen."

"The fella Jennifer's not too crazy about?"

"Did she also tell you he gives me multiple orgasms?"

"No. Does he?"

She smiled faintly, a rebuke.

I said, "Why didn't you bring him in?"

"I wanted to talk to you. Look, I wanted to check on my mom too, okay? She gets involved with creeps. One yell from me and Kenny'd come busting in that window with a tire iron in his hand. But I came in alone so if everything was okay I wouldn't have to turn around and ask him to wait outside after he was already in. I had to talk to you without him because, well . . . it'd be easier."

"Okay."

She looked up at the ceiling for a long moment, then took a deep breath and sat down in one of the other chairs.

"Kenny wanted to go to the police," she began. "I said, What do you want to do that for? You know they're just waiting to drop something heavy on you. When he was in grade school he got hauled into juvie for stealing hubcaps. In junior high he got tagged as a serious delinquent because some kid said he'd stolen something, which he hadn't, and a teacher went through his pockets and found a little weed in a matchbox. And he wouldn't tell where he got it. Wow. Uncooperative. A gangster in the making. So what does he want to go to the police for? They'll probably say he did something to cause the whole accident."

"What accident?"

"The one down the hill here last night. The one the radio said the police want to talk to witnesses about who maybe saw it. Another car went by when a car driven by Charles Cromwell ran into a van. Well, the car going by was Ken's, and the witnesses were Ken and me."

I said carefully, as if one wrong word might break something fragile, "And Kenny wants to go to the police with the story?"

"Yes."

"And you don't?"

"No."

"You're not exactly a fan of mine. Why tell me?"

"Because you're a lawyer the police don't like, and because you were with Aunt Kate this evening and Aunt Kate is Charles Cromwell's mother, so you'd probably know if anything Ken or I saw might be important. If it isn't, why risk telling the police anything?"

The coffee was percolating happily, dark and pungent. I reached over and turned off the burner.

"Okay," I said, turning back to her. "What did you see, and what time was it?"

"Around 8:45, the radio said. We weren't paying much attention to the time—we figured it out later. You can even check with June Hostetler. When Kenny picked me up last night, June was just getting home from the festival office and the disc jockey was giving the 8:30 station break. This evening we took the same route, through downtown, and made it out on the Pollock to Fox Hollow in fifteen minutes. The radio said one thing wrong. It said Mr. Cromwell was driving in from the Steak House. Ken and I saw his car turning out of Fox Hollow Road."

"How did you know it was Mr. Cromwell's car?"

"Because we heard it smack into the van, and the radio said it was Mr. Cromwell's car did that."

"You heard it smack into the van, but you didn't see it?"

"Kenny almost did. I mean he saw the van parked beside the road, then the car turned out of Fox Hollow without stopping for the stop sign. It went past us and we heard the crash and Kenny looked back and the car had hit the van. The van had tipped off the road and had its emergency flashers going."

"And the car had definitely turned out of Fox Hollow."

"Yes."

"You know about anything else that happened up this way last night?"

Her front teeth dug into her lower lip.

"Yes."

"You could be criticized for not stopping to see if anyone needed help."

"Who wants to get involved?"

"Why don't I believe that?"

"What's not to believe?"

"Kenny wasn't really driving, was he?"

Her face came up. Her eyes were suddenly bereft.

I went on, "You have no driver's license and no learner's permit. Kenny was afraid you might get nailed for somehow causing the accident, but he thinks you should report what you saw, so he wants to tell the cops he was driving."

She could be put at a loss for words after all.

"If he has to lie about driving the car, the cops'll smell something wrong and wind up not believing the important part. So you guys sit tight. I'll try to get an admission out of Charles Cromwell. If I can't, you will have to go to the cops, but I'll come with you."

"Kenny's pretty impatient. Can you talk to him?"

"Okay. Promise me something, Megan."

Her face slipped into neutral. Megan in waiting mode, ready to harpoon any adult absurdity I might come up with.

"Driving with no license and no insurance is dumb. It could cost your mother a fortune. Get your learner's permit and go legal. It shouldn't wreck your nonconformist karma."

A corner of her mouth twitched.

"Okay. About not stopping. We were going to trade places and go back to the accident, but we looked back and saw another car already stopping there. A station wagon. So we just went on."

"That was me. You guys hungry enough for scrambled eggs and bacon?"

"No, thanks, we gotta go. Unless . . ." Now the golden highlights in her eyes sparkled. Suddenly she was just a pretty kid without a worry in the world. It was either a considerate way of assuring me that everything was cool, or a practiced way of turning grown-ups into compliant putty. "Unless you got a paper cup I could take some coffee in."

A cupboard produced paper plates and plastic spoons but no cups. I got out a pair of utility china cups instead.

"How d'you take it?"

"It's just for Kenny. He takes it straight black."

I filled a cup at the table. "One black coffee to go."

Jennifer said from the door, "Did you open a fast-food franchise? Megan, what on earth are you doing here?"

Megan looked at her mother and froze. Her mouth fell open. Suddenly, with her soft uncolored lips and the hair falling over her forehead, she looked about seven years old. Jennifer, fresh from the shower, hair damp and skin glowing, was barefoot and wearing the turquoise blouse and white panties and nothing else.

Megan found her voice. "My, aren't we dressing casually this evening."

"Some of us are," Jennifer said. "Those who got thrown up on by drunks."

"A likely story. I never realized what gorgeous legs you have."

"That ain't all, kid."

"I believe it." Megan stood up. "Hey, gotta be going."

Jennifer said, "You haven't told me what brought you here."

". . . Oh, conference with an attorney. Confidential stuff."

"Yes?"

"Later, okay?"

". . . Okay," Jennifer said uncertainly.

Megan made an uncharacteristically random gesture.

"Oh, Mother, don't be obtuse!" She picked up the coffee cup. "I'll bring your cup back."

"If I'm not home, leave it on the front doorstep."

Jennifer's face was slack, her eyes misty.

"Love you, baby."

On her way out Megan gave her a one-armed hug. Jennifer kissed her temple. I followed Megan out into the hall and opened the front door.

"Is there any reason why Clint Farrell should be afraid of your mother?"

"Not as far as I know."

"You know him?"

"Only sort of vaguely, since I was a little kid."

We stepped outside. The air had definitely cooled off. It carried the smell of cigarette smoke. Beyond my car was a beat-up old Cutlass with someone leaning against it. He straightened up and approached, flipping his cigarette into the darkness. He was about my height and wore a white T-shirt and low-slung jeans. He carried something down by his pants leg—the tire iron he'd been ready to rescue Megan with. He looked capable of doing it. There was a combat-ready urgency about him, a jungle alertness. His face was young and bony and uncompromising.

"It took you long enough."

"There were things to talk about," Megan said. "I brought you some coffee. Jim Keller—Ken Allen."

"Hi, Ken."

"Did Megan tell you what we saw last night?"

"Yes. Now you tell me."

"Around 8:45 we came around that curve in the highway and saw a car swing out of Fox Hollow without stopping for the sign. It swung wide and cut back toward the shoulder and smacked into a van parked there. I didn't see it, but I heard it. When I looked back the van was tipped off the roadway."

"You know whose car it was?"

"The radio said Charles Cromwell's. It also said he was coming from the Steak House."

"Have you talked to anyone about this?"

"Just Megan."

"For now, don't tell anyone else. Megan's right, the cops'll skin you alive and probably won't believe anything you tell them."

"That Cromwell had to have a reason to lie about where he was coming from."

"Sure. Maybe it had something to do with the murder up the hill, maybe it didn't."

"You want to protect him, right?"

"He figured out I was driving," Megan said patiently. "If he can, the cops can."

"Give me a day, Ken," I said. "I don't like Charles much more than you do, but let me see if he has an explanation."

"What makes you think I don't like him?"

"Sticks out a mile. If I can see it the cops can too. Maybe they even know *why* you don't like him. Anyhow, they'll guess you're lying and Megan's lying for you. They might get it right eventually, but who needs the grief? So give me a day, then if you *have* to go to the cops I'll go with you. I'll contact you through Megan."

"What's your angle?"

"No angle."

He had trouble believing that. No surprise there. More tractable types than Ken had been having the same trouble all day. But after a while he gave a short nod.

"Okay. You got a day."

"Thanks."

"Your coffee's getting cold," Megan said, offering him the cup.

He took it, sipped experimentally, then took a couple of healthy gulps.

"You don't have to swallow it whole. We can take the cup," Megan told him.

"Okay, let's go."

Megan thanked me. I told her anytime. Ken gave me a thoughtful stare, maybe already resenting the delay in nailing Charles. But he said grudgingly, "Yeah. Good coffee."

"No sweat." I managed not to say anything too parental, like *drive carefully.* "Have fun, you guys."

They climbed into the Cutlass. The lights came on. The starter sounded resentful but the motor caught. At least they didn't take off like the start of a drag race.

I felt suddenly older than God. I went back inside and locked the front door.

Jennifer had poured herself a cup of coffee and was sitting on the edge of one of the dinette chairs. Her eyes were suspiciously bright; an inexplicable joy lay half-hidden behind unshed tears.

"What do you think of Kenny?"

"He's scary."

"What does she see in him?"

"He's scary. Maybe she takes after you."

She moved her cup half an inch and slopped coffee onto the Formica tabletop. Her lower lip curved into a smile like a flower unfolding.

"I don't need you to rain on my parade, you son of a bitch. I need someone with swimmers' muscles to take me to bed and keep me there till my brain melts. Cheap shots are a dime a dozen."

I said, "My God, that kid came in here full of fight and scared half silly. What she had to talk about could've waited. Mostly what she came for was I'm supposed to be dangerous and you get involved with creeps. Doesn't that mean anything to you?"

Her smile was unchanged, but her eyes flooded. "Of course it does. Don't you realize what happened?"

Tears spilled indifferently onto her cheeks. She palmed them away, streaking her face.

"Hell," I said, "you're the last person on earth I want to yell at." Except for Katy. "What am I yelling at you for?"

Jennifer said, "Because your bitch ex-wife took away your little girl and you have to play daddy to every stray orphan in California. The Rowan girl, that pitiful alcoholic up the hill, probably that dumb hooker Diane, Megan—who else?"

I remembered my dream last night.

I said, "Megan's no orphan."

"Oh? She's always been so smart and capable—and terribly direct. I never thought there'd be anything she couldn't be direct about. Well, I just realized she couldn't be direct about *me*. I always knew she was a loner, I never guessed she was so *alone*. At school she's just too damn smart, she's never really made close friends. Hence Kenny. She says he has charisma. And I guess he's a good lover. She's been on the pill since she was fourteen—she said she was going to be sexually active whether she had it or not, the only question was whether I wanted to worry about her getting pregnant. Well, I didn't. I was only a year older than she is now when I got pregnant with her. God. That poor kid."

She stopped, shook her head. A minute passed. She stood up. Barefoot, she had a dancer's balanced walk, like Megan. She put her hands at the sides of my neck.

"You're pretty new at being a parent. I've been one half my life. You know what a parent is? A teacher, a worrier, a provider. Not so much an individual as an institution."

"No argument."

"Today I got promoted. When I got out of the shower and heard you two in here, I almost went looking for a dressing gown or something. Then I thought, hold it, who do I want to kid, and why? So I didn't. I walked in here, into the presence of my daughter and an attractive man, dressed like this—'casually.' Tonight Megan finally met Jennifer: not the parent, the person; a little older than she is, a little taller, not entirely dissimilar, and at least as sexual."

"With gorgeous legs," I said.

"That ain't all, kid. That's what I mean. She's seen them before and never noticed. Institutions don't have gorgeous legs, sexy women do. Suddenly I'm not only an individual, I'm her equal."

"Is she ready for that?" I had my hands in her clothes.

"I hope so. We'll find out at breakfast. What time is it anyway?"

"Bedtime, as soon as we throw your pants in the dryer."

"God, you're practical. Or is that more compulsive parenting? If it is, does it mean this is incest?"

"I could check the appropriate authorities."

"Oh no, I'll risk it. If you're having fun, don't stop on my account."

$\triangledown$

Chapter 18

THE MOCKINGBIRD TOOK a practice run at an arpeggio in the eucalyptus tree outside the bedroom window.

Making love is a better tranquilizer than five thousand yards freestyle. I don't think I had been quite asleep, just floating in a lagoon of allayed anxieties—an illusion, of course, since what I was anxious about hadn't gone away, but nice. If I wasn't asleep I soon would have been, if not for the mockingbird.

I touched Jennifer's shoulder. She uncurled and stretched out on her back, breathing softly, her body slender and intelligently cared for, soft hills and shadowed hollows accented by clearly defined aureoles and a small dense pubic patch.

I said, "Coffee?"

After a while she sighed, exhaling with a small sound I took for approval. I pulled on shorts and jeans and padded into the kitchen, turning on the overhead light.

The glass percolator stood on the dinette table, three- quarters full. I took out the stem and the basket containing the coffee grounds and set the percolator on the stove to reheat, then went down to the basement and fetched Jennifer's pants from the dryer. I had just returned to the kitchen when a car—not Ken Allen's rattletrap—drove slowly past the front of the house.

There was nowhere for it to go. The future Fawn Lane ended in a ridge of desert a few yards farther on.

For no particular reason I killed the kitchen light before parting the curtains over the sink and peering outside. My station wagon was where I'd left it. I remembered leaving the garage door open.

I heard a car door close gently.

A key made a sound in the lock of the service porch door.

The door opened, closed. Someone was making as little noise as possible. The heavy claw hammer was in the tool drawer on the service porch. No gun in the house. No workout weights, no golf clubs.

The door from the service porch into the kitchen began to open. I flipped the light switch on. The woman in the doorway blinked in surprise.

I hadn't seen her for a while. She had hair that was too dark for a real blonde but too light to be anything else. It was pulled back gently and gathered into a chignon; the effect was the executive look made soft and appealing. Her eyes were cornflower blue, her nose was short, and her mouth was generous and lightly colored. She looked good in a cool blue blouse and designer jeans, five feet eight and 130 pounds any man would be glad to be seen with.

She said crisply, "Does playing tricks like that with the light make you feel powerful?"

"What are you doing here, Felicia?"

I was still carrying the black pants. Felicia looked at them.

"Who's the whore?"

I repeated, "What are you doing here?"

"I came to see you, dear," she said sweetly, pulling the door shut behind her and going on in a voice suddenly as cold as surgical steel. "Have you got some cheap tramp in my bed?"

"No," I said as mildly as I could. "And it's not your bed. I paid you cash for your share of the furniture."

"That settlement charade! You want your money back? Stick to the point. Have you got some whore in my bed?"

I tried to smile. It didn't work.

"The divorce was your idea. The settlement was real. The house is mine for a year, at which time I pay you your half of the fair market value. If I sell it before then, I pay you your half immediately. Meantime it's my home."

"That's just lawyer talk," she said calmly, starting down the length of the kitchen. "I'll see who's in there myself."

The coffee pot began to grumble. I turned off the burner, then stepped into the door to the hall.

She stopped two feet away. She smelled of jasmine.

"Out of my way. I want to know what you're bringing into my house."

"It's not your house, Felicia. Where's Katy?"

Her nostrils got that pinched bloodless look I'd seen too often in the last couple of years.

"Where my daughter is is no concern of yours."

"God damn it, Felicia! You must've had some reason to drive all this way and break in at nearly four A.M."

"To see what sort of squalor you want to introduce my daughter into . . ."

Her voice trailed off. Her eyes focused behind my shoulder.

Jennifer said, "Hello, Felicia."

Felicia snapped, "Do I know you?"

"We met last year, at a fund raiser put on by the Jaycees. I'm Jennifer Kendall." She moved up beside me. "My pants?"

I gave them to her.

"Kendall . . . Of course! You're in real estate." Felicia laughed her cool silvery laugh. I thought of shards of glass falling into a tin bucket. She smiled at Jennifer's bare legs. "This is how you drum up business."

Jennifer smiled back. "Not usually. If you'll excuse me I'll get dressed."

"I won't excuse you of anything."

Jennifer began stepping into the black pants.

I said to Felicia, "Let's go out to the car, the one you drove into the garage."

"Certainly not."

"Yes, Felicia."

"No."

Standing very still, blue eyes stiff and level with denial and rejection, she began very slowly to shake her head.

"*Yes*, Felicia," I repeated.

"You've no right. The car is mine."

"Sure it is. But earlier this evening your dad was worried because he didn't know where you were. It couldn't be because you were out of sight, you're a big girl now. But . . . suppose you'd had some kind of disagreement"—or done something to make him feel you're unreliable, I thought—"and suppose you'd taken Katy with you, then he might worry a lot."

"Where my daughter is is none of your business."

"Just satisfy me she's not in the car and I'll gladly apologize." And immediately call Ed Hammond and make sure she was with him.

"I'm not putting up with any more of your bullying," Felicia said in a voice as smooth as marble. She reached unhurriedly for the percolator on the stove, picked it up, and in a smooth motion swung it at my head.

I was almost too surprised to move. Luckily the coffee pot was heavy enough to be clumsy. I bent at the knees and waist and the whole thing swept over my head and shattered against the wooden door frame. Hot coffee splashed my neck and shoulders and splinters of broken glass rained everywhere.

For a few seconds no one moved or spoke, as though no one quite believed what had happened. In the silence I became aware of a dry mouth, a hammering pulse, my awkward bent-kneed stoop, of my ex-wife not two feet away standing in a coffee-colored puddle with the calm pattern of the linoleum showing through it. Somewhere, I remembered, Jennifer had cried out and jumped away from the exploding glass. I asked her if she was all right. She said yes from somewhere behind me. It seemed unwise to take my eyes off Felicia, whose marble calm had become pale frozen fury. Her white-knuckled fist was still curled around the coffee pot's glass handle, from which a few viciously curved spikes stuck out.

I straightened up slowly. Felicia began backing away toward the door to the service porch. I hoped she wouldn't suddenly decide to run at me with that fistful of glass. I also hoped that when she reached the door she wouldn't just keep going. She was wearing shoes and I wasn't and there was glass everywhere. But when her hips bumped the door she stopped, eyeing me balefully.

"Don't come near me."

"Okay. But how long can you stand there on guard?"

"Until you come to your senses."

I licked my lips, which did no good at all. My mouth was as dry as the noon desert, dry as hopelessness.

"Jennifer?"

"Yes?" she said from behind me.

"The nearest phone's in the den. You'd better call the police."

Chapter 19

THEY MUST HAVE BEEN close. When she put down the phone, Jennifer went into the bedroom to bring me a pair of sandals from the shoe rack. I had barely got them on when strong headlights flared against the kitchen curtain.

Jennifer opened the door for them. An almost familiar male voice asked, "You the lady who called?"

"Yes. Jennifer Kendall." Two pairs of heavy, hard-soled shoes entered the house. "Through there. Watch out, there's glass everywhere."

The front door closed. The footsteps paused behind me.

"Jennifer, see if Katy's in the car."

She went out the front door. Felicia, slightly hunched in front of the door to the service porch with the glass weapon in her fist, didn't take her eyes off me. I risked a quick look at the cops.

Indoors, Hardy looked taller and blonder and bonier, his nose shorter. His eyes were a nondescript blue and a bit bloodshot. Vasquez looked burlier, older. Both men looked tired and sweaty. Hardy made his face carefully neutral.

"What's going on here, Counselor?"

I indicated Felicia. "My ex-wife, Felicia Keller. Officers Hardy and Vasquez."

"How cozy." Felicia's lip curled. "Friends of yours."

Hardy said, "Who's gonna answer my question?"

Felicia said instantly, "I came home and admitted myself with my key. That man challenged my right to be here and was threatening and abusive. I had to defend myself."

"Mr. Keller?"

"Mrs. Keller drove in from L.A. without telling me she was coming. She parked her car in my garage and illegally entered the house through the service porch. When I wanted to see if she had our three-year-old daughter in the car, she tried to brain me with an eight-cup glass percolator."

"That's who the other lady went to check on?"

Felicia said, "The child is mine, the house is mine."

"We've got a custody hearing next week," I said. "As to the house, I can show you the settlement papers."

"Sounds like we got a simple domestic dispute," Hardy said. "Come on, lady. Put down that piece of glass, okay?"

"I need it to defend myself."

"We'll protect you, that's our job. You let him see that the kid's all right, if she's with you, then we can escort you out and we'll all go home and get some sleep, okay?"

Jennifer had come in quietly through the front door.

"Sound asleep in the back seat with a yellow teddy bear," she told us.

Felicia ignored and overrode her.

"You mean you're going to let him get away with those false charges? How could I illegally enter my own house? I had to *defend* myself."

"I saw what happened," Jennifer said. "She tried to hit him with the coffee pot without provocation."

"Going to believe that whore?" Felicia said.

"Come on, lady, that's no way to talk," Hardy protested. "This is what we're gonna do. First, you're gonna put down that chunk of glass, okay?"

"Get lost, officer," Felicia said. "And I'm not 'lady,' or 'Mrs. Keller.' I'm Miss Hammond."

"Ma'am . . . Miss . . . if you don't cooperate we're going to have to arrest you."

She smiled slyly, secretly.

"Don't try it."

"Lady, please. If you don't put that thing down we'll have to take it from you."

"Don't try it!"

"You wouldn't have a chance, ma'am, you're not so tough. Let's just do it the easy way, okay?"

All the time he was getting closer to her. He was almost within grabbing range. Slowly he extended a hand.

"Or if you like, you can just hand it to me."

"Well, if you put it that way," Felicia said, and struck like a snake. Glass stabbed into Hardy's palm. Her fist pulled back, but before she could strike at his face his opposite hand clamped around her wrist, forcing it down to the counter top. She sank the nails of her free hand into Hardy's temple and raked them down his cheek before Vasquez could pin her arms. Cursing, Hardy put pressure on the wrist, shaking the glass weapon from her fingers. He swept it out of reach into the sink with his injured hand, leaving a bright smear of blood across the counter.

Vasquez held Felicia in an iron bearhug. Hardy held up his hand in front of her face, blood running over the heel onto the floor. The skin was pulled tight over her cheekbones and jaw and her face was pale and pure as carved bone. The cornflower-blue eyes were enormous.

"You shouldn'ta done this, lady," Hardy said. "Now you got troubles."

Without changing expression she kneed him in the crotch. He twisted to avoid the worst of it, but his face got mottled and his lips turned gray.

Vasquez moved his forearm up under her chin. "You want the chokehold, lady?"

At the sink Hardy turned on the cold water and stuck his hand under the stream. Then he took off his hat and put his head under it too. I told Jennifer where the first aid kit was and headed for the service porch. Vasquez told Felicia she was under arrest and, in a mechanical drone, recited the Miranda formula.

Felicia said as I opened the door, "I didn't know you employed a uniformed auxiliary."

"Be quiet, Felicia. You're in enough trouble already."

"You hypocrite! What do you care? D'you think the glee cavorting behind that dishonest, manipulative lawyer's face is invisible? You're as transparent as mountain air."

I closed the kitchen door. My mouth had gone dry again. As I hurried to the garage door I felt a mounting tide of anxiety. It couldn't be for Katy—Jennifer had said she was all right. But my head wasn't really working. I only knew that the Felicia I had seen tonight might be capable of anything.

In the garage I hit the light switch. The almost-new Toyota Felicia had taken when she left now occupied its old spot in the near parking space. A rear window was open an inch or two. The back doors were locked but the driver's door wasn't. I opened it and stuck my head in.

The car was full of the warm, close smell of a child sleeping. She was stretched out on her tummy on the back seat, her dark head on a small white pillow, wearing her pajamas and barefoot. There was a shiny quilt comforter under her and a big woolly car rug stuffed between the back seat and the back of the front seats. Reaching up toward her from the rug were the stiff arms and legs of her big yellow Pooh Bear.

Her breathing was quiet, blissfully rhythmic. I unlocked the back door from inside, opened it quietly, and got in and knelt on the rug. I touched her cheek. Her hand came up and brushed my fingers away, and for a while I just looked at her, not thinking, my head swimming in an ocean of relief.

When I heard Hardy and Vasquez take Felicia out to the cop car, I gathered Katy and backed awkwardly out of the Toyota.

"Hello, Kate," I said as Jennifer came quietly into the garage. "Remember me?"

Her head came up. She began to poke at one eye with the fingers of one hand. The other eye opened and regarded me solemnly.

"Hi, Daddy."

"This is a friend of mine. Her name's Jennifer."

Katy's head sank onto my chest again. She said something blurry and sighed and zonked off to sleep again. Vasquez came into the garage carrying a flashlight as big as a war club, saw Katy, and stopped.

"Everything okay here, Mr. Keller?"

"Everything's fine."

"Yeah. Thought I'd better check. Cute kid. Good night, folks."

"Tell Hardy I'm sorry about his hand. Thanks."

"Welcome," Vasquez said. He glanced around the garage, looking for God knows what, then marched without hurry to the prowl car.

I heard him get in, then the car drove off.

"Your mom had to go into town, honey," I told Kate. "You're going to spend the night with me, in your old house."

No response. Jennifer dragged the comforter and the pillow and the Pooh Bear out of the car. We went through the front door into the house and into what had been Katy's room.

The bed was made—my excuse had been readiness for unexpected guests I had never had—but the walls were bare; tape marks and pinholes showed where Katy's posters and pictures had been. Her bookcase stood empty. The whole toy chest was in Beverly Hills, but the Mickey Mouse nightlight was still plugged into the baseboard outlet. In a minute we had her asleep with her head on the pillow she had traveled with, the comforter folded across the foot of the bed, and the Pooh Bear within reach. I kissed her on the temple and murmured goodnight as I always used to, then took Jennifer's hand and led her from the room, leaving the nightlight on and the door in the hall ajar.

"Okay," Jennifer said crisply, "now you get to be Daddy. Have you got anything to feed her?"

"Milk and juice in the refrigerator," I said. "She used to be a bear for Cheerios. I don't have those, but breakfast won't be a problem. Dressing her might be. I hope she's got some clothes in the car."

"You go look. I'll sweep up the broken glass."

I got her the broom and dust pan and went out to the car. Behind the front seat, under the rug, I found a small blue T- shirt with red piping around the neck and sleeves, a pair of jeans, a slightly grubby pair of socks, and a pair of small blue sneakers—presumably what Katy had started out in. Nothing of Felicia's except her purse, which lay on the front seat.

A little lever on the driver's side popped the trunk open. The only things in it were a tire iron and a sturdy cardboard carton containing six highway flares and a quart thermos bottle more than half full of liquid. I unscrewed the cap, took the pressure off the inner stopper, and smelled the contents.

A pint and a half of gasoline.

I closed the thermos, replaced it among the flares, and left the carton where it was. I took the purse and Katy's clothes, closed everything up, and went back inside.

"We'd better mop the floor before the coffee dries," Jennifer said in practical tones. "Especially if we're going to be showing the house. Or is that off, after what's happened?"

"Better postpone it." I dumped the clothes and purse on the kitchen table. "I'm sorry, Jennifer."

"Don't be silly." She returned the broom and dust pan to the closet on the service porch. "The officers took that glass dagger she stabbed Hardy with. Here's the mop. Got a bucket?"

"Somewhere. Do you also do windows? There's no reason you should have to clean up the battlefield after a Keller war."

"No, but . . ." She found the bucket, set it on the floor, and dropped her arms around my neck. Her touch was light and self-deprecating. "All of a sudden you've stiffened up on me. Not to be intrusive, but when you're with Katy your heart's on your sleeve. But now suddenly it's invisible and so are you. Okay, Felicia does that to you. Well, don't let her. And I don't care how much you still love her."

"I didn't have to call the cops," I said. "You saw the kind of shape she's in; she didn't need the cops. I called them to make her look bad. I hoped she'd do something stupid and score me some points at the custody hearing. When she did I almost crowed with delight. I've got this terrible feeling I must have failed her miserably somewhere along the line."

"Maybe you did. People fail people. You're not God, for God's sake! How much are you supposed to do for her? She just knows how to make you feel guilty. You *had* to call the police. Felicia's not your baby, Katy is. What matters is you and Katy."

Suddenly, as though aware that all this was getting pretty heavy, she gave me a bright look. Her arms tightened. I got a firm squeeze from collarbone to knees. "And things like swimmer's lats and tits like flowers, not necessarily mine. I'd better call a cab."

"Take the station wagon, with my spare key. I'll pick it up in the morning."

"Okay. Thanks—but after we mop the kitchen floor. You can give me a hand, if you like."

So we did it her way, and all the while a knowing sneer inside me whispered that Felicia might once have been my tormentor, but she was now definitely my victim.

Chapter 20

THE SNEERING WHISPER WAS with me from the moment I woke up.

I had set the alarm for 8:30. Her face clouded, Katy padded into the room before I got it turned off.

"This is my old house," she said accusingly.

"That's right, Kate. Your mommie brought you here last night, while you were asleep. Then she had to go into town. Ready from some breakfast?"

"Cheerios," Katy said.

"Sorry, love, we don't have any. How about one of our old Sunday grown-up breakfasts, pancakes and scrambled eggs and stuff?"

She nodded doubtfully, then brightened.

"Can I watch cartoons on TV?"

"Sure, if there are any. I'll help you look."

We found a program aimed at preschoolers. I left her cross-legged on the floor in front of the set and went into the kitchen. The empty months had rusted my coordination, but everything was ready more or less at the same time: three modest pancakes, two strips of bacon, and a scoop of scrambled eggs for each of us; orange juice for Katy; and a mug of clearly evil coffee for me made in a small metal drip-type pot that dated back to law school.

I poured boysenberry syrup on Katy's pancakes, she picked up her fork, and the phone rang. It was Andy Feldberg, calling from his office in Westwood.

"Can I call you back, Andy? Right now I'm having breakfast with my daughter."

Pause.

"Run that by me again?"

"I'm having breakfast with Katy."

"Ed Hammond's frantic."

"Call and tell him she's okay."

"Is her mother there?"

"No. In custody for assaulting a cop. Can't talk now, Andy."

"Understood. Call soonest."

I hung up, cut a wedge of pancake, and the phone rang again.

"Keller," I said into it.

"Hi, Jim. This is Walt Gilfillian, Public Defender's office. I've been talking to a prisoner down here at the calabozo. Gives her name as Felicia Elizabeth Hammond, Beverly Hills address."

"Yes. What are the charges?"

"Just about everything short of armed insurrection. Assault with a deadly weapon, assault on a police officer, resisting arrest, you name it. The arresting officers identify two witnesses, you and Jennifer Kendall. She was given the opportunity to make a phone call but refused. She was advised that she needed a lawyer and insisted she didn't. Which is nonsense. Even Dave Hostetler seemed shook up about it. Is he a friend?"

"Not of mine. I didn't think he knew her."

"He told me to see if she'd accept me. She didn't even recognize me. Okay, I never knew her well, but Jesus! She gave me that icy blue stare and assured me that if she needed a lawyer she hadn't been reduced to requiring the services of a public defender. Anyway, she had a lawyer. Guess who."

"Clue me."

"James Keller, the Barker Building, Courthouse Plaza, Dos Cruces."

I almost said, "That's crazy," but my tongue stuck on the first syllable. Instead I said, "Oh. God."

"Uh, look," he said, suddenly awkward. "Should I get the shrink to see her?"

"Jesus, Walt, don't ask me. We're on opposite sides of a custody case. If she's crazy, it's to my advantage. If she's not crazy, it's to my advantage too because it'll mean last night may have been impulsive, but it was done in full knowledge and understanding. Either way I can impugn her fitness. Any suggestion I make is going to be tainted with self-interest. I'll call her father as soon as I finish breakfast. He'll send one of his lawyers down. When's the arraignment?"

"Scheduled for ten A.M. I can get it postponed till this afternoon, since she's without counsel acceptable to her."

"Good. Can you tell her I'll be in to see her as soon as I can?"

"Okay. See you."

"Thanks, Walt."

When we had finished breakfast I stacked the dishes in the sink and helped Katy dress. Then, feeling guilty about it, I parked her in front of the TV again and called Andy Feldberg from the bedroom phone.

"Biggest break you've had in years," he said briskly.

"I don't know how planned this trip was; she brought Katy's pajamas and a stuffed toy but nothing for herself. There was a cardboard carton in the trunk containing six highway flares and a thermos bottle, quart size, more than half full of gasoline."

Just telling him was a betrayal, involving a vicious hope.

He said intelligently, "Huh?"

"Highway flares and gasoline. I'd said I might sell the house and use my share of the proceeds to finance the custody fight. I think in some dim corner of her mind she was ready to burn the place down."

"You'd never prove it. Anyway, she knows you're insured, for God's sake. "

"In some *dim* corner of her mind."

"Oh, God. If you're right, that could be the whole ball game. Of course, they're going to yell illegal search."

"I thought she might have brought along at least a change of socks for Katy, so I went looking. Nothing. Just the stuff I told you about. And her purse, of course. I went through it."

"Blatantly illegal search."

"Sure. It contained three hundred and fifty-two dollars in folding money, Auto Club card, bank and gas cards, bank deposit book. One of those calculator-checkbook-desk calendar things in real leather. Appointment reminders in the calendar: attorneys, her hairdresser, court appearances for the divorce, the hearing. One appointment for next week with a Dr. Bergstrom, address on North Camden. The fact that the address is on the calendar suggests it's her first appointment."

"I'll look him up. Anything else?"

"This morning Felicia refused to call a lawyer. She said she already had a lawyer. Guess who."

"Richard Nixon. Melvin Belli. Clarence Darrow."

"Me."

"She's trying to give it to us on a platter, Jim."

"Jesus, Andy, I don't want to screw her."

"You're not afraid of winning, are you? You can't afford to be. We're going for broke, remember? Will you call Ed Hammond?"

I said I would. He told me not to step on any land mines and we hung up. With the sounds of an old Rocky and Bullwinkle cartoon coming from the living room, I picked up the phone again and dialed the Hammond home number.

"Hammond residence," said a cool male voice that didn't want to be mistaken for the butler's.

"Mr. Hammond, please."

"I'm sorry, Mr. Hammond can't accept calls right now."

"This is Jim Keller, his ex-son-in-law. I've got news for him."

"Oh. Sorry. Engle here. News about his granddaughter, I take it. Your attorney already called to tell him."

"That was the good part."

I heard muffled sounds. Then someone breathed heavily into the phone.

"Okay, Jim," Ed Hammond said. "Let's hear the bad part."

"I'll give you the bare facts—*you* make sense of them. Last night Felicia drove to Dos Cruces. Sometime between three and four she drove into the garage and invaded the house. I was up. I asked if Katy was with her and could I see her. She snatched up a partly full glass coffeepot and tried to brain me with it, then stood guard at the door to the service porch with the remains of the coffeepot in her fist. She kept calling the house her house, my guest a whore that I'd had the temerity to introduce into her bed. I called the cops."

Ed Hammond exploded, "You *what*? You underhanded self-serving little shit. You *what*?"

"Blow it out your ass, Ed," I said wearily. "She's spread some pretty wild slanders about me, and I wasn't going to risk laying a glove on her. And she had that chunk of glass in her hand—"

"Oh, bullshit!" Ed snapped. "She wouldn't have used that and you know it."

"She used it on a cop named Hardy. He bled like a stuck pig. Hardy's partner pinned her from behind and she kicked Hardy in the gonads. So they booked her. Assaulting an officer, resisting arrest, et cetera. She wouldn't call you or anybody, and she said she already had a lawyer—namely me. That's pretty far out, Ed."

After a long moment I heard him draw a deep breath. I imagined him pursing his lips thoughtfully, nodding his big cropped graying head, his thick, once-muscular body slumping into his chair. He exhaled noisily.

"Okay, Jim, we'll do what needs doing, though I don't doubt your account of events was highly colored and prejudicial—"

I interrupted, "What d'you mean by doing what needs doing? Covering things up? Listen. I didn't have to call you. I could've left her in the hands of court appointed counsel, which at least would have meant honest representation."

"Who's the D.A. down there?"

"Lincoln Fox. Someone in your shop will know about the Fox brothers."

He grunted. "Where's Katy?"

"In my living room, watching TV."

"Well, take care of her. I'll be out as soon as I can to take her off your hands."

"You'll do nothing of the sort," I assured him, and cradled the phone.

A couple of days ago I had lectured myself on the need to maintain a dispassionate, analytical attitude. It wasn't working. That was why I had Andy Feldberg working for me, wasn't it? Wouldn't he have insisted I call the cops? And I knew just what he would say if I told him about the snide, condemnatory inner voice I kept hearing. *Was* I afraid of winning?

I called for a cab. While we waited for it the phone rang again.

"Hi," Jennifer said. "How are you fixed for babysitters?"

$\triangledown$

Chapter 21

THE KENDALL HOUSE GLOWED less magically than it had by twilight. My station wagon was parked at the curb.

I paid the cabbie and took Katy's hand as we walked to the front door. Katy poked the button. A chime sounded. The door opened and Megan stood there barefoot, fair hair drawn back into a pony tail, the pretty kid of every California ad and poster, with small high breasts under a yellow T-shirt and a pair of white running shorts setting off the tan of her smoothly muscled young legs.

She gave me an opaque stare, as though I meant as much as a mud fence, then smiled at Katy.

"Hi, you must be Katy. I'm Megan."

Katy said "Hi" in a small shy voice.

"Thank you for volunteering," I said.

"Oh sure. Mother hardly had to twist my arm at all."

We went inside, following Megan into the kitchen where Jennifer stood finishing a cup of coffee. Her late night hadn't taken any visible toll. She wore fawn slacks and a white blouse—business formal in Dos Cruces from May to November—and her earrings were gold-mounted with cat's eyes.

I introduced her to Katy, who didn't remember her from last night.

Katy asked, "Are you the babysitter?"

"No, that's me," Megan said. "Want to come outside and see the swimming pool?"

Katy hugged my leg.

"Sure," I said. "Why don't you?"

Megan extended a hand. Katy didn't quite take it.

"Does she know how to swim?"

"Not quite," I said.

Katy said, "I can swim almost all the way across," eyeing Megan's hand all the time, "in my pool at my new house."

"I expect your pool's bigger than ours," Megan said.

"I used to go to the day care place."

"Hey, so did I, but they don't have a pool," Megan said. "Here we can have a swim, then I can fix us some lunch, then if your dad doesn't get back for you real quick, we can go down to Baskin-Robbins for an ice cream."

Megan was still holding out her hand. Katy finally took it, but only after more thought did she let go of my leg. Megan led her to a back door. Katy paused to look back doubtfully. I waved and she waved, then they disappeared outside.

"In case you're worried," Jennifer said, "she has her senior livesaving certificate."

"Another swimmer?"

"A diver. She was in county age-group competition when she was eight. Now she dives for Marshall High—so did I, way back when. She's better."

"Thanks, Jennifer."

"Don't be silly." She put her hand on my arm and kissed me briefly, but not so briefly as to seem merely pro forma. She was wearing a fragrance so light its effect was almost subliminal, evoking a fleeting nostalgia for a time and place that never were, eager pure emotions that could never be. "This is a lot less public than any of the day care places. Gotta go. I know rank has its privileges, but I already took an extra hour's sleep and time for a good breakfast."

I headed downtown with the air conditioner going full blast. To avoid the blocked-off streets, I approached Courthouse Plaza from Eleventh and parked in a lot on the corner of Padre Sierra Place, which gave me a three block hike to the copshop.

Officer Hamill was at the desk again, jaws grinding and suspicious stare in place. Ray Gallardo, the skinny detective with the clipped mustache angling past the corners of his mouth, looked up from a desk and saw me come in.

"Morning, Counselor. Can I talk to you a minute? Buzz him through, Ron."

Officer Hamill gave me a visitor's tag and leaned on the hidden buzzer. He obviously thought I was getting away with something. I told Gallardo I had come to see Felicia Hammond and he took me into the interior of the building and down a flight of stairs to a small interrogation room near the lockup.

It smelled of old tobacco smoke and contained a small wooden table bolted to the floor and two straight-backed chairs.

"I heard you're wondering was there a typewriter at the Osterreicher house."

"Yes."

"No typewriter."

"The letter Helen Pavlik sent Fran Rowan was typed and postmarked Dos Cruces. It could've been written anywhere."

"You reported the letter contained no signs of dyslexia. Have you seen it?"

"No. That's what Fran Rowan told me. Maybe Helen was one of those people who learn to overcome dyslexia."

"Not according to the handwritten stuff in that lockbox. So maybe someone helped her. Any ideas?"

"No. Did the search team ever find the weapon?"

"Naah. Have a seat. I'll have them bring in Miss Hammond."

He went away. I sat in one of the chairs. It was anything but comfortable.

In seconds, the silence of that squalid little room had made it an emotional deprivation chamber. Three years of regrets and disappointments and mindless antagonism came flooding to the surface, clamoring for attention in voices that nagged and whined, raged and goaded, called for compassion, demanded revenge. I wanted desperately to be out, away, having a picnic with Katy on the banks of the Rogue River in Oregon. I wanted to be in bed with Jennifer, the phone off the hook and nothing on the calendar till next month. I wanted to be anyone but me, sitting on this punitive chair like a ten year old waiting to see the principal and not knowing why, or what I'd done, only that it must've been something real bad.

The door opened.

She stood in the opening with a tall, young-looking policewoman behind her. Felicia looked drab, without her affluent confidence that the world was built to accommodate her. The policewoman had short gleaming back hair and smooth brown cheeks and eyes big and lustrous but without humor. Her name tag read L. Gutierrez.

"Mr. Keller?"

"Yes. Thank you, Officer."

"Thank you, Luisa," Felicia said in the absent manner of a lady talking to her maid.

The policewoman closed the door behind Felicia, who didn't move.

She said finally, "The only thing to be said about this place is that the toilets work. Are you going to get me out?"

"Sit down, Felicia."

I pulled out a chair for her. She brushed the seat with her fingertips, examined them; her nostrils flared fastidiously. She was still in the cool blue blouse and designer jeans. Behind a lingering trace of the familiar jasmine was the smell of sweat.

She gave a shrug of resignation and sat down. I sat down opposite her. Grave cornflower-blue eyes looked at me steadily.

I said carefully, "I can't represent you, Felicia. It would be a conflict of interest." Faint puzzlement came into her eyes. "So this morning I called your dad. He'll be flying in with a lawyer, who'll probably bring an army of assistants—"

At the mention of her father an extraordinary expression settled on her face. It was the look of someone incomprehensibly betrayed. Her lips came apart; I heard a short intake then an expulsion of breath, almost a voiceless sob. The she looked away and seemed to take counsel somewhere over her right shoulder.

After a few moments she took a deep breath, sat up straighter, folded her hands in her lap.

"So," she said calmly, "you won't represent me, you won't get me out of here, and you've shifted the burden of responsibility onto my father and his legal staff. What I fail to understand is—why?"

"The responsibility was never mine," I began.

"Are you my husband or aren't you?"

"I was, till you divorced me.'

. . . A tiny pulling of brows together, an infinitesimal frown, as though trying to remember something . . .

Unless I imagined it.

Her face cleared. She said in voice of quiet scorn, "And you, of course, bear a grudge."

"It's simply this: we're on opposite sides in a custody battle, and the police listed me as a witness to your resisting arrest and assaulting a police officer. They might not insist I testify against you, but they could, because I'm your *ex*-husband."

"I'm not a criminal and you know it."

"Felicia, last night I saw you commit several criminal acts. You stabbed a cop with a chunk of broken glass, then you scratched his face and kicked him in the crotch. That's why you're in here."

She absorbed this as though it were news to her. A trace of concern came into her eyes. Her brows crimped fractionally, as though she were trying to recall something without letting me know. Why bother?—unless she wanted to hide how little of last night she even remembered . . .

The silence in the small room stretched like molten glass to membrane thinness; cooling and solidifying, it might shatter at the least unsympathetic sound. I found myself illogically in deep dread of that happening. Felicia sat motionless, her hands in her lap, only the lightly incised lines at the corners of her eyes and the slight rhythmic movement of the front of the blue blouse identifying her as a living woman and not a pretty plastic doll.

And then she shrugged one shoulder. Her lips quirked into a half-smile.

"Kid stuff. Aren't I accused of anything serious?"

"Those charges are good for a year in county jail. You mean you can't remember, and want to know if you set fire to the house."

She gave it a moment's thought, then produced her tinkling laugh.

"Did I?"

"No."

"Of course not. Why would I do a thing like that?"

"Why would you spread lies about me, and pretend I'm not interested in being Katy's father?"

"Don't be ridiculous. I never spread lies about you."

"You told them to June Hostetler and Jennifer Kendall."

"June . . . Oh yes, the woman who's had all those miscarriages. She said I had a very pretty little girl and confessed to being envious because she had no children of her own and apparently never could have. Kendall . . . Oh, that titless wonder you took to bed last night. She told me at some function or other that she had a teenaged daughter and was divorced."

"And you said you wished you were, because your husband was a sadist? And what did you tell June? That you were glad you had Katy, but your husband was a brute and you were both in danger?"

"You're delusional. You should be under psychiatric care."

"Just guessing about how the conversations went, but I know they took place. Now d'you see why I can't represent you?"

She shook her head. "I see only that you are being petty and spiteful."

"Felicia—"

"Don't crawl to me, you spineless son of a bitch. If you want forgiveness, go to church."

"All I want is for you to understand you're in a jam—"

"You just want to deny all responsibility!"

"I *have* no responsibility. I won't deny I *feel* responsible for you, but then I get to feeling that way about almost anyone who gets in a jam around here. You didn't approve, remember? But I'm not responsible for you, legally or morally. You left me and ran back to daddy."

Anger flared. "Who the hell do you think you are? Limping Jesus carrying the sins of the world up Calvary?"

My hands began shaking. I knotted the fingers together under the table.

No, I thought, I'm just a poor slob fighting his emotions in his daughter's best interests. And his own—don't forget his own. Felicia, Felicia, how do I get your attention? How do I cradle and comfort you? And if you had any inkling I felt this way, how could I survive your triumphant derision?

To get close to Felicia was to enter a minefield.

I pushed the button that would summon the guard.

"This isn't getting us anywhere. Felicia, I'm sorry. All I can do is make sure your dad gets here real soon."

I couldn't sit still any longer. I got up and crossed to the door.

Behind me she said in a strained voice, "No! No, you son of a bitch, you can't desert me—"

She was half-turned in her chair, her face haggard and appalled and totally defenseless.

"Please. Please don't desert me!"

That must have cost her a lot. What could she fear and dislike more than me?

I heard footsteps coming down the hall.

I said awkwardly, "We're on opposite sides of a court fight."

"Just don't desert me."

"I never deserted you, honey."

"Just don't."

Officer Gutierrez opened the door.

"You all through here?"

I nodded. She walked past me into the room, brisk and no-nonsense and a bit bored.

"Okay, let's go."

Felicia didn't respond. The cornflower-blue eyes were bereft and frightened.

I said, "Why don't you go back with the officer, okay?"

"Don't want to."

"Come on, Felicia, it's what we gotta do," the officer said calmly. Felicia blinked. Her body stiffened.

"I'm Miss Hammond to you."

"Sweetie, this ain't the Beverly Wilshire and I ain't the maid come to make the bed. We don't bother with mister or miss. Inmates are just inmates."

"I am not an inmate. Inmates are thieves and prostitutes."

"Sure you're an inmate—temporary. Let's just go by the rules and no hard feelings, huh?"

Felicia curled her lip at me.

"I hope you're satisfied."

I said, "The charges are bailable. Your dad's lawyer will have you out real soon. And he'll see about getting the charges reduced."

"He'd better." She sighed. Her stiff posture relaxed and she stood up. No trace of panic now. The ice princess was in control again. She said to the officer, "Since there seems to be no help for it, I suppose I can put up with this criminal regimentation a while longer. For which, I assure you, someone is going to be very sorry."

She went out the door with that opulent unhurried grace I was so familiar with, the young matron of aristocratic measurements and coloring who'd kept her figure into motherhood and her style and stature in adversity. Just a role, I thought. Not even that. Just a pose assumed by a store-window dummy with no more volition than a double-headed nickel. Perhaps it was magic, a long-practiced ritual to assure the continued blessings of privilege. Once I'd thought of that it came to me that Felicia had relied on this kind of magic as long as I'd known her, it had just taken me a dismal length of time to realize it. What irreplaceable loss, what unspeakable fear, had brought her to this sterile reliance? Not that it mattered. What was done was done. The woman I had loved had been a broken child all the time, and I had at first not known it and then lacked the skill to mend her. How I must have blundered about, compounding the damage, creating more havoc. But that was done too. All that was left was the sadness of it, and the waste, and the incomprehensibility of how it could have happened to Felicia, of all people, and how it could have happened to me.

By the time I had fumbled my way through this subjective morass, Felicia and Officer Gutierrez had disappeared.

Felicia had not once asked about Katy.

I was going to have to fight her tooth and nail for sole custody, and the saddest thing of all was that she might not even be able to fight back.

Chapter 22

I LEFT THE COPSHOP, found a pay phone, and made a credit card call to Ed Hammond. He was on his way to Dos Cruces. Then I called Charles Cromwell. His secretary told me he was out and wouldn't be back until after lunch.

Courthouse Plaza was hot, bright, and getting crowded. On a small stage opposite city hall two lightly amplified fretted dulcimers accompanied a clear, firm mezzo-soprano in a southern ballad. I wandered through the craft booths and pavilions to Fourth Street and looked into Bernie's. It was packed to the walls. The interview with Felicia had left me in a numb, gutted daze that had not begun to wear off when I walked into the Broadway and bought T-shirts, socks, panties, and a new set of pajamas for Katy. When I got back outside I could barely feel the sidewalk under my feet. The thickening crowd of pedestrians, taking advantage of storefront awnings' gift of shade to ogle the artwork displayed in shop and restaurant windows, was a half-seen, half-heard mob from a disquieting dream.

The first restaurant I found without a waiting line was the Montmartre, a small place across the street from the *Chronicle* building. The menu was limited to exotic soups, salads, pastries, imported beers, and coffee you could float a brick in without divine intervention. It had all the personality of the inside of a refrigerator. Everything was white except the floor, which alternated black and white squares. The proprietor, who was also the chef, looked almost as French as the Pittsburgh Steelers. Prices were absurd, but I needed somewhere to sit and try to think.

The man at the first table put an end to that idea. He put down what looked like an official manila folder and gave me his tight V-shaped grin.

"Hi, Mac."

"Keep me company." He waved at the chair across his table. "You a regular here?"

"Too rich for my blood, but everywhere else is packed." I sat down, parking my Broadway package at my feet. "Are you on the expense account?"

"Doesn't cover the money I feed parking meters." He tapped the manila folder. "I've been reading a xerox of the autopsy report on Helen Fairland."

He pushed it over to me as the waitress brought his order. Bringing your food the length of the room on a tray was supposed to distinguish the Montmartre from Joe's Diner. The waitress, who wore a burgundy blouse and pale rose slacks and only a silly apron to distinguish her from the female patrons, set a bowl of onion soup and a French roll, and a cup of severe-looking coffee in front of Mac and promised to be right back for my order.

Mac dipped into his soup. I scanned the report.

"Nothing much there," Mac said, "except the technical details of the brain injuries, and how they killed her. Otherwise"—he tore the roll in half—"a well-fed, well-taken-care-of dead body, the appendix surgically absent. So was some other plumbing: she'd had a hysterectomy. Some nice bridgework. She was five feet six inches tall and weighed one hundred thirty-six pounds. *Sic transit.*"

He buttered the French roll, his face pale and remorseless.

"Were you one of her exes, Mac?"

"Nope. She was just someone I knew and liked."

"When did you learn she was back in town?"

He took his time biting into the roll, chewing it, and swallowing.

"About two weeks ago. She saw me on the street and recognized me. About a block from here."

"Who else knew she was back?"

"Dave, certainly. When I told him he said he already knew. She said early on she was going to contact Charlie Cromwell."

"How about the Gang of Three?"

"She didn't say. I got the feeling she wasn't interested."

"What was she interested in?"

He shrugged. The waitress came over and I ordered the mulliga-tawny soup and a small green salad and the cheapest beer they had, Anchor Steam at $3.50 a bottle. Mac tested his coffee and looked startled.

When the waitress had left I said, "Did you write that letter for her, Mac?"

"What letter?"

"The one to Fran Rowan, asking if she was adopted."

He took a mouthful of soup, swallowed, then grinned.

"You've been doing your homework. Sure, I wrote it."

"Why?"

"For Christ's sake, because she asked me to."

"And maybe to embarrass Charles?"

"No. I knew there was a kid, but I didn't know who daddy was until that birth certificate showed up."

"But you knew there was a birth certificate."

"Yes. Frankly, I thought the father would be Dave Hostetler. I thought embarrassing Dave might be politically useful, since he was going to support Charles for mayor. Any dirt's valuable if it's used right."

"Did you tell Dave there was a birth certificate somewhere?"

"Hell, no! He might have looked for it himself and suppressed it if it named him. The way it worked out, Ray Gallardo started going through that lockbox and found it right away."

"If he hadn't, I bet you'd have nudged him till he did."

"Damn right. I told you this one wasn't going to come out right if someone didn't work on it."

"If Dave ever learns how much you knew and didn't tell him—"

"Listen, Jim. You've been here what, five, six years? I've lived here all my life. I like it. Especially the way it was: a little oasis, surrounding farms, the art colony, and people doing their thing. Now the creeps are getting control—guys like Charlie and the Fox boys, bringing in outside money to make more money out of our clean air and art colony image. When they're through we'll have resort hotels with wall-to-wall hookers, miles of tract housing, and three times the population—most of them transients, too many of them crooks and grifters. No one'll be safe anywhere at high noon, and the only thing the air'll be good for is cutting into bricks and building high-priced condos with. My God, Charlie's going to run for mayor on a platform to catch up with California! With money behind him you think he can't win?—and take enough assholes into the city council on his coattails? Of course he can! Only he won't. Because I'm going to stop him." He caught himself, jabbed a forefinger at me. "*We*'re going to stop him."

"By nailing him for murder, whether he killed Helen or not?"

"He didn't just happen by your intersection by chance. Of course he killed her."

"Why'd he leave the birth certificate behind?"

"Didn't know about it. Or couldn't find it. Or lost his nerve and ran."

"Why'd he kill her?"

"Maybe she was blackmailing him."

"Was she that kind of woman, mean-spirited and vengeful?" I gave him the sunny grin. "Let's see some evidence, Mac."

"It'll turn up. You're asking me to buy too many coincidences." He dropped money on the table. "Just breathe deeply." He picked up the autopsy report, keeping his voice so low it was almost inaudible. "Charlie Cromwell stinks of guilt. Dave Hostetler doesn't know how to deal with it because, though they're not real friends, they are part of the same power structure."

Yesterday, of course, Charles hadn't thought his membership in the power structure gave him much protection. I didn't feel like arguing about it. "They found the ejected shell case," he said, standing up and tucking the folder under his arm. "It was in the cuff of the robe Helen was wearing. She wasn't wearing anything else. Expecting him, maybe?"

"Maybe."

"Enjoy your lunch," Mac grunted, and stalked out.

I thought about his sensitive nostrils, and about what Megan and Ken had told me, until the waitress brought my food.

Chapter 23

I DIDN'T CALL AHEAD for an appointment.

In the city hall, easels set against the lobby walls now displayed canvasses by artists with established reputations. A crowd of visitors gawked at them and at the distinctive murals. A couple of security men tried to limit use of the building's elevators to people with legitimate business on the upper floors.

Ray Gallardo stood waiting for an elevator, smoking a slim, dark cigarillo. I joined him.

"The Chief Deputy D.A. wants to see you," he said. An elevator door opened and we got in. I punched the fourth floor button and asked him what number.

"The same."

"Don't I rate a summons from Lincoln Fox himself?"

"Linc's out of town. He went to Sacramento to hold Harlan's hand and pick what brains he's got."

"He'll have to wait a few minutes. What's it about?"

"The Felicia Hammond thing, I guess. Her father arrived with four lawyers in tow."

"He'll probably try to fix it like a traffic ticket."

Ray shrugged and stared at the ceiling. The elevator stopped and we got out. I waved at the mayoral suite across the hall.

"What are you doing in this rarefied atmosphere, Ray?"

"Liaison with His Honor on the Fairland killing. Which means assuring him that nothing points to his son Tom, who used to be Helen's boyfriend. As though we'd tell him if anything did. I won't ask what brings you up here."

"Good idea."

"Charlie won't see you. You're not wearing a tie."

He opened one of the imposing doors and I followed him inside. A counter with a gate in it was commanded by a bright-eyed gray-haired woman who recognized Ray and picked up a phone. She announced him in a soft voice, then buzzed him through the barricade. Looking resigned, he went through the gate, then crossed the office and disappeared through another imposing door.

The bright eyes flicked over my T-shirt and jeans and resolutely showed no disapproval. I gave her the easy smile, the respectful tone.

"James Keller to see Mr. Cromwell. You might tell him I've found the witnesses."

She picked up the phone again, dialed, and spoke to a secretary. There were a few moments of silence as the secretary relayed the message. Then the phone began to make angry noises. The gray-haired woman handed it to me.

"Hi," I said.

"What witnesses?" Charles barked.

"To the accident. I found the oncoming car. It had people in it."

"I'll be right out."

I handed the phone back to the gray-haired woman.

"He'll be right out," I told her politely, and a nonimposing door across from the mayor's sanctum burst open. Charles barged out, impatient as ever in another of those three-piece suits.

He came through the gate and opened the door into the hall. Pushing me outside ahead of him, he closed it with a force that echoed.

The hall was deserted. Charles became very still and watchful. His jowls were the color of wet plaster.

"Well?"

"Let's go somewhere and talk."

"Have we anything to talk about? You said you found witnesses." The tip of his tongue crawled over gray lips. "They have names?"

"Sure, but right now nobody needs to know them."

"I do." He glanced furtively both ways down the hall. "For God's sake, Keller! MacAndie's hounding me like he had some vicious personal grudge—"

"Have you seen him today?"

"Jesus, man, he was out at my place before I'd finished breakfast! Did I have a statement to make. Did I want to change the story I'd told the police. What about that . . . that birth certificate the police found in Helen Fairland's papers, naming me the father of someone's bastard, for God's sake—"

"What about that, Charles?"

"It's a lie, a forgery! That's what I told Dave Hostetler. He pretended he didn't believe me. Come on, gimme those names."

"No names."

He sucked in a shaky breath, then turned back to the double doors.

"I could've thrown you to the wolves," I said to his back. "One of the witnesses was all for going to the police."

He stopped with his hand on the doorknob, turned around, and smiled. I guess it was supposed to be disdainful. All it managed to be was ghastly.

"Are you crazy? I *want* witnesses to go the police—to corroborate my story. Your *witnesses* aren't going to do that, are they? What's their angle? And how convenient you found them! All the people driving through on their way from Oregon to Arizona or God knows where, all the people who drive cars in Dos Cruces every day, I mean one particular car out of God knows how many—no make, no model, no license number—and you just happen to find it in no time at all. Isn't that great. Isn't that convenient. Isn't that suspicious. You think MacAndie's not capable of hiring someone to come in off the street and lie?"

"If Mac were going to hire someone to nail you, he'd have them go straight to Dave Hostetler."

"You think Dave's not above doing this *himself*?"

"Knock it off, Charles. The witnesses are real."

"Go screw yourself, Counselor."

"Same to you, Charles."

He charged back into the mayoral suite, slamming the door behind him.

What I had offered Charles was a bluff. Ken Allen's and Megan's testimony wasn't worth much unsupported, and the fact that I had failed to get him to open up might simply mean that he had nothing to open up about. But he had convinced me that Arthur MacAndie was right. Charles *was* guilty—of something.

I went to the elevators and summoned one. It sighed to a stop, the door opening. I got in and was turning to punch the first floor button when Charles barreled back into view. I put my hand against the edge of the elevator door and waited.

"All right," Charles said in a dead voice. "Let's talk."

I followed him to a conference room down the hall from the mayoral suite. It was bare and clean and had metal blinds covering the one long window. Eight wooden chairs surrounded a long table. I sat in the nearest chair, dropping the Broadway sack with Katy's new clothes onto the table. Charles prowled the space beyond the table, slack-gutted and round-shouldered.

"Can't you even dress like a lawyer? . . . I need legal advice. That makes anything I say confidential."

"I can't keep those witnesses quiet for long, Charles."

"What do they say?"

"That you weren't coming from the Steak House when you ran into that van. They saw you turn right coming out of Fox Hollow. The way it looks, you lied about it because you knew about Helen's murder. Some people will assume that knowledge has to be guilty knowledge."

"Do you?"

"Not necessarily. Convince me."

"She was dead when I got there. Or she looked dead."

"Had she been expecting you?"

". . . Yes."

"You told me yesterday you hadn't even known she was back in town."

"What did you expect me to tell you? Sure I knew she was back. She called me a few days after she moved into the Osterreicher house. I told her I didn't want to see her, what had happened was a long time ago and might as well have happened to two other people. She said yes but don't hang up, I've got a couple of things to talk about, then I won't call again."

"And?"

"She wanted to talk about the . . . the kid she'd put up for adoption."

"Your kid."

"All right, *my* kid. She wanted to know if I had any idea where she was. I said no, I didn't even know it was a 'she.' I'd arranged the adoption and paid the bills and given Helen enough to get on her feet again. That was it— the limit of my responsibility and more. She had no complaints. Which she admitted. But she said didn't I ever wonder, my own flesh and blood and all? I said hell, no. She said she did, especially now she couldn't have another kid. I said what was she talking about, she wasn't even forty, lots of women in their forties had kids. She said yeah, but a few years back they'd found what she called a precancerous condition and took out the whole works, so she was sterile."

He grinned unpleasantly.

"I said there were advantages to that. She said disadvantages too, when you didn't have any blood kin, and after her husband died last year she got to feeling left out and began thinking about trying to find the kid. Not too seriously then, but by some stupid fucking chance she learned that a girl named Frances Mary Rowan lived up in Santa Barbara, and did the name Rowan mean anything to me?

"I said hell no, why should it? She said Rowan's the name of the people who adopted our kid, and Frances Mary are the names they gave her. I said how the hell could she know that, and she'd better not try to set me up or I'd fix her ass good. She said don't be an asshole, Charlie, you can't touch me, I've got the *real* birth certificate."

I said, "As opposed to the one your lawyer arranged for the Rowan family to get?"

"Yeah. Adopting parents always get a birth certificate that shows them as the biological parents of the kid they adopt."

"In legal adoptions, yes. This one wasn't legal, was it?"

Charles gave me a fishy stare. When he didn't respond I kept going.

"I'm sure Dave Hostetler knows by now whether it was legal or not. When a kid is adopted through the county adoption service, the adopting parents get a birth certificate naming them as the natural parents. In a private adoption, the adopters get the same, plus a certificate naming the natural mother. What we're talking about was a private adoption—but one that got around a string of legal requirements, didn't it? Maybe the Rowans were a little old, or not too financially secure. The rules aren't so stiff when it's a minority kid, black or Asian or something. I guess the Rowans wanted a kid in their own image."

"Next thing you'll be bitching about how they weren't good parents."

"Apparently they were great parents. Finding them was the one thing you did right for that kid."

"Yeah? Well, I didn't find them. What I found was an upstanding member of your profession. Creep named Cameron Rexford, worked out of a shabby little office in Long Beach. Couple of years later he died of a heart attack under indictment involving an adoption racket. He was selling kids to a Tijuana whorehouse.

"But the deal with these Rowan people was almost legit. They'd hired him to see them through the adoption process, and when they couldn't qualify he promised to help them out some other way. I'd been sniffing around. I'd heard he might be useful, so I called him and said hey, there's this lady who's gonna have a kid and wants to get it adopted the quickest, quietest way possible. In twenty-four hours the Rowans had agreed to take the baby.

"He'd told them that the parents were members of the successful white middle class, which was a laugh. Helen was a high school dropout. Her father was a short-order cook who didn't work too regularly. Her mother was a waitress and sometime domestic who ditched them both for the bright lights of Hollywood when Helen was in grade school. Who knows what happened to her. This shyster had the Rowans eating out of his hand, but he was only half-smart. He thought Helen was just a girl who'd gotten pregnant instead of a dangerous self-seeking little tramp.

"He had her move to San Bernardino, to a cheap hotel a couple of blocks from the county hospital. He had an accomplice on the nursing staff, in the maternity ward. All she had to do was juggle a couple of bits of paper to make sure the birth was registered with the Rowans named as the biological parents. Then they could get a photostat for school, or if she ever wanted a passport or anything, just by paying the Hall of Records the two bucks, or whatever it was. So everything's all set. All that's left is for Helen to have the baby and for the nurse to slip the phony registration into the system. The

Rowans would pay the lawyer his completion fee and Helen would pay the hospital bill with the money I'd given her. So what happens? Helen begins to have second thoughts. Or so she tells me now, twenty years later. Will the baby be okay? What are the adopting parents like? Is she doing, for Christ's sake, the right thing? If the adoption doesn't go through, the shyster doesn't collect, so he wants to slip her a tranquilizer. And of course the Rowans want the baby so badly they'll do anything. So the shyster breaks the rules. And of course I don't know any of this until the phone call from Helen.

"Standard practice is that adopting parents may know who the natural mother is but never the other way around, to save trouble in case the natural mother changes her mind later. But the shyster has Cynthia Rowan visit Helen at the hotel to reassure her. And here's where the real trouble starts, because the Rowan woman tells Helen her real name and what names they've picked out for the kid. Frances Mary if it's a girl, Paul something if it's a boy. Anyhow, Helen gets all reassured and everything's okay again.

"Except that now the nurse, the one who's working with the shyster, gets broadsided in her VW bug by a drunken farmhand in a pickup, and winds up in hospital in Pacoima or somewhere, where she's gone for a birthday dinner with her folks. And four hours later Helen goes into labor and checks into the hospital and has the kid.

"Okay." His color was still awful but now he seemed more mad than scared. "You know how a birth certificate gets into the Hall of Records, you've been through it. When the kid's born they give the mother a form to fill out. She writes in the kid's name and everything, and they take this and type it up and get a few hospital signatures and this is the document that goes on file to be photographed every time a copy has to be made. The shyster's plan, and it had worked often enough before, was that Helen would submit one form, and he would prepare his version with the Rowan names, and his accomplice would switch them. But she can't, she's in a hospital miles away. By the time she's back at work it's two weeks later and way too late.

"The nurse can still slip the fake into the system, but there's no intercepting the one based on the form Helen filled out. And what that bitch had done was send through a document giving the baby the Rowan names with her own surname tacked on—and naming the real parents.

"She tried to tell me she was still a bit dizzy when she made it out. She couldn't think of another guy's name to use, and so what, it was going to get switched, wasn't it? She didn't learn about the nurse's accident until the shyster picked her and the brat up. Bullshit. Why put my name on anything except to use it against me later?"

I said, "So there are two records of Fran's birth, one under the name Rowan and one under Fairland."

"Yeah. I don't know how good the signatures on the fake certificate were, or even if the shyster seriously tried to duplicate the real ones. If a serious comparison were made, the signatures would tell which document was phony, but who'd think to compare them? And why? Well, one guess.

"Anyway, as soon as she'd explained about the two birth certificates she hung up in my ear. For days I waited for the other shoe to drop. It came in a letter. She still couldn't spell worth a damn. The note said she'd written to this girl in Santa Barbara, and that if it turned out there might even be a chance she was the one, she'd decided she had to meet her—but I needn't worry.

"Fat fucking chance! With her holding that birth certificate? And the left-wing environmentalists and the art crowd and the *Chronicle* all wetting their pants to get something to nail me with? So I decided to try a different approach. Last Tuesday I called her. I said hey, let's not fight, it's twenty years later. If you want to call the kid, that's fine. Maybe it'll be for the best.

"She gave me this long pause and then asked, why this sudden turnaround, Charlie? And I said hey, well, I got to thinking, you know? And she said what's in it for you? And I said Jesus, give me a break, can't you, why can't we be nice about this? Cost me half my stomach lining but I got it said, and there was a real long pause and she said, well, it would make things easier if you really mean it. Let's talk about it over a drink tomorrow evening between 8:30 and 9:00. And I said sure, why not? Hell, it might give me a line on what she was up to.

"So Wednesday I went to see her and she was dead."

"Details, Charles," I said. "When did you get there?"

"Around 8:30, maybe 8:35. Everything was quiet. Lights were on inside the house. I parked in the driveway and rang the front doorbell. Nothing. The front door was ajar so I pushed it open and called. No answer. I stuck my head inside—and that's when I smelled the gunpowder.

"I should've gotten scared, but I didn't. I did a lot of competition pistol shooting when I was a kid, so that smell's always been friendly, not threatening. So I stepped into the hall and called Helen's name and looked into the living room and there was someone lying on the floor. *Then* I got scared. *Real* scared. Whoever'd fired the gun could still be in the house, might even be Helen gone on some kind of rampage. And maybe whoever was on the floor could use some help—I could call the cops or paramedics. So I went in to look. It was Helen and she'd been shot in the head.

"I felt for a pulse but couldn't find one. I was too busy being scared and keeping down below the level of the windows so I couldn't be seen from the street, and listening for the guy with the gun. It took me about half a second to figure out that with Helen dead on the floor I couldn't call the cops or anyone, couldn't let anyone know I'd been there. So I got the fuck out and raced down to the highway and . . . had the accident."

He stopped, his face slack and vulnerable and glistening with a sweaty film. Okay, Ken and Megan had told the truth. Okay, it was no coincidence that had brought Charles and Fran to the same neighborhood "between eight-thirty and nine": they'd both been invited.

Charles dropped heavily into one of the other chairs. He knotted his hands together and stared at them.

"I should have suggested that Helen say Fran Rowan was Dave Hostetler's kid. Dave would've liked that."

"How about June?"

"Maybe June too. At least Dave would've had the kid she couldn't give him." He closed his eyes, breathing noisily. "Okay, God damn it, are you going to sit there all day or do I get some legal advice?"

"Go tell Dave what you just told me. You don't want him hearing it first from the witnesses."

"That's not the kind of advice I need. Just give me their names."

"So you can intimidate them, or try to buy them off? You've got several .22 calibre guns, haven't you?"

"What if I have?"

"Have Dave run a ballistics check on them."

He sat up straighter. Something like intelligence glittered wearily in his eyes. He looked quickly down at his hands again.

"What would that prove? He'd only say I used another gun and got rid of it."

"How many guns do you have?"

"Four!" he said too emphatically.

"In your possession?"

"Yes."

"What about not in your possession?"

He shook his head, pulled his hands apart, put them flat on the table, and pushed himself upright.

"I don't need this crap."

He kicked his chair aside and blundered to the door. It shut behind him and latched itself.

If I'd guessed right he owned a fifth pistol—which he'd given or loaned to someone. Not something he'd do lightly. Guns get misused. Even cheap Saturday Night Specials aren't cheap anymore. He must've loaned or given it to someone he trusted.

Someone like Aunt Kate?

Chapter 24

THE CHIEF DEPUTY D.A.'S office was down a few steps from the rear of the County Courthouse lobby and along a low fluorescent-lit hallway. The outer office was presided over by a lean, ironic secretary named Marge Klein, who picked up her phone to announce me as two men I knew came through the door from the inner office.

Ed Hammond looked like a battlefield commander in casual civies. He wasn't tall but had the physique of an aging weight lifter, and he wore gray slacks and a white shirt open at the neck. Behind him was John Engle, taller and slimmer, in a brown summer suit and carrying an unostentatiously expensive briefcase.

Ed's face congealed when he saw me.

"Great little system you got here," he growled. "Justice by cronyism and conspiracy."

"Careful, Ed," Engle said, the smile in his voice not masking the urgency. His clean-shaven face was narrow and his hair was fair and thin; unremarkable blue eyes picked the world apart from behind wire-rimmed glasses. He smiled at me. At least his mouth stretched, with tilted lips. "Hello again, Mr. Keller."

I said hello civilly enough.

"My boss will see you," Marge Klein murmured, replacing her phone.

I went past her desk to the door and Ed Hammond growled at my back, "You just *think* you're getting away with this."

I threw him an unfriendly grin but Engle was in the way, trying

166

to get him out of there before he said something damaging. He wouldn't, though. Ed's bluster sounded eruptively ill-tempered, but what I had seen of it had always been part of a coldly planned strategy. He liked to play the battering ram. It put subtle minds off guard.

I went through the door and said hello to the Chief Deputy D.A.

He sat at a small cramped desk in his small cramped room, his face weary and ironic. He was a narrow hard whip of a man named Paul Franken. His dark hair was short and lay close to his head and his eyes were so deepset they peered out from permanent shadow. His mouth looked like a guillotine blade.

"Hi, James," he said when the door closed on its pneumatic arm. "What did you do to get that old bastard mad at you?"

"Married his daughter. Where's the rest of the team? I heard he arrived with four lawyers."

"That's what I'm told. He's spending big bucks. I guess he's got 'em, huh?"

"Compared to General Motors he may be small potatoes, but compared to you and me he's the whole potato patch."

"He's convinced we're ganging up on his little girl. What's this all about?"

I said slowly, "My ex-wife wants complete custody of our three-year-old daughter. The hearing's next week." I sat down on a hard wooden chair in front of his desk. Paul Franken leaned back and lifted his feet to the corner of the desk and crossed his ankles. His shoes had almost new heels, but the gleaming neatly laced tops looked old and comfortable. "Last night she drove here from L.A. with the kid, and you've got the rest in the police report."

He folded his bony hands across his shirtfront.

"So?"

"She said she wanted to talk but never said about what. Then she said she'd come to see what kind of squalor I hoped to bring her daughter into."

"A comment on your housekeeping?"

"No, on the fact that I wasn't alone. Jennifer Kendall was with me."

"You determined to push this illegal entry charge?"

"No."

"And the assault on you?"

"No."

He stared at me thoughtfully, then reached for a folder and glanced at some papers in it.

"Jennifer saw it?"

"Yes."

"My, my," he said dryly. "It must be true love. This morning she insisted you were her legal counsel."

"Yes."

"Wasn't that pretty baroque?" When I didn't answer he dropped the folder back onto the desk. "The police report describes some pretty wild behavior."

"Yes."

"Is that all it was—loss of control due to emotional stress? Or is your ex not competent to stand trial?"

"Come on, Paul. I'm not a disinterested witness. Anything I might say would have to be suspect, even to me."

"Say it anyway."

"No way. Look, last night she got violent and didn't make much sense. Didn't this morning either. I'm not sure how much of last night she even remembers."

"Oh, fine," Paul sneered. "She's confused, violent, and amnesiac. She's everyone's ideal of mental health. Tell me she's competent to have custody of your daughter."

"No."

"Joint custody? Equal time?"

"No. Though I may have to settle for that."

"Hell," he said, smiling like a knife, "you just don't want to be seen playing the heavy. You think she belongs in a rubber room, but you just don't want to say it in case she proves she's sane as a summer day. Just the way you'll look spiteful if you press those charges, but such a concerned Mr. Nice Guy if you don't. Okay, you want all charges dropped? No, because you think the defense will have to introduce psychiatric evidence to mitigate and give you the ammunition you need for the custody hearing. Don't want much, do you?"

"Enough." His smile died and left his face bleak and bitter. His sunken eyes, stared at me across the desk. "Look, Paul. Two days ago I only wanted joint custody. Then I began to wonder, and last night it became obvious that Felicia isn't just a neurotic bitch, but is actually dangerous. Now all I can think of is how sad it'll be if she turns out to be a clinical basket case."

"So what are you going to do?"

"Go for full custody."

He swung his feet off the desk and opened a belly drawer, from which he took a fresh cigarette pack and a book of matches. He gave me a noncommittal sort of nod, then tore open the pack with savage precision.

I said, "You need me for anything else, Paul?"

"No." He worked a cigarette loose, plucked it free with his lips. "Incidentally. When Engle presented himself at the copshop as Felicia Hammond's attorney, she refused to see him. Or her father." He lit the cigarette with a paper match. "Neither of them saw fit to mention it—I got it from Ray Gallardo. Of course, Engle can represent her without consulting her, but it might make things interesting at the arraignment. You going to be there?"

". . . I've got things to do," I said awkwardly.

"Can't say I blame you. See you around, Counselor."

In the lobby, I called Andy Feldberg from a pay phone. He said he had checked on the Dr. Bergstrom who was listed in Felicia's appointment book.

"Dr. Henry L. Bergstrom, psychiatrist, highly thought of. Felicia's appointment for next week was made the day before yesterday, the day they offered you money to concede the custody fight. Were the two events related?" He didn't wait for an answer. "She's obviously disturbed. Either she or her father knows it; maybe both do. You've got to take advantage of it. You've got to be willing to win—"

"Yeah, yeah."

"Think of Katy. Do anything dumb and I'll double my fee."

"Okay. Lighten up, will you?"

"No. That's how serious I am. Stay in touch."

I said I would and hung up, then went straight to the bigger festival office.

Aunt Kate, holding her rectangular reading glass, was passing a sheet of paper across the table to June Hostetler, who looked cool and efficient. The hair brushed forward over her ears was pewter-colored in the backlight from the window behind her. I said hello.

June's face froze into a mask of boredom as soon as she recognized me.

Aunt Kate's expression was welcoming.

"Hello, dear. What can I do for you?"

"Can I have a word with you outside, Aunt Kate?"

"Of course." She stood up briskly enough. "Excuse me a moment, June; I won't be too long."

She followed me into the corridor. I drew her down toward the central hall, where there were built-in benches along the walls.

"What's on your mind, young man?"

I stopped short of the central hall. A few voices echoed meaninglessly, as if in a slowed-down dream of nameless fears. At least there was no one to hear us.

"Do you have a gun, Aunt Kate?"

She looked up at me, her eyes behind their distorting lenses intelligent and watchful. After a long moment she fixed her gaze on my chin.

"Yes. Charlie gave it to me years ago. He was worried about rattlesnakes where I live. I thought I'd be telling Dave Hostetler about this one day, but I'd rather tell you. I think you'll understand . . . why I had to."

"Had to what?"

"Don't pretend to be dull, it won't make it easier. Had to kill Helen Fairland."

"I don't believe you did, Aunt Kate."

"Oh, but I did. I'll show you."

"Show me the gun too?"

"Of course. I'll get my purse."

$\triangledown$

Chapter 25

THIS TIME ON THE stairs she took my arm as well as the bannister. In the lobby a uniformed guard held the door open for us, smiling. Withdrawn and inaccessible, she caught herself in time to respond with a smile and a nod, but they had nothing in them. She had retreated so far she almost disappeared.

Outside, a guitarist, probably the street musician we'd heard yesterday, was playing Castelnuovo Tedescu. Aunt Kate didn't seem to notice. By the time we got to my car the lines were cut deeper into her face and she looked bloodless.

I took West Eleventh. Neither of us said a word until we were almost at Fox Hollow.

"I told you some awful nonsense yesterday," she said suddenly.

"You weren't too convincing, Aunt Kate."

"Oh, you didn't believe a word, I could see that. But I was still trying to do things Charlie's way, because he believed his whole future might be at stake. He's so concerned about appearances! I know children are often the direct opposite of their parents, but I was never enough of a rebel to account for Charlie's desperate conventionality. I hate to dispel old myths, but Tom Cromwell and I were married quite prosaically on a gloomy afternoon in Burbank in 1943. Charlie was born early in 1945. The marriage was already in trouble. I was beginning to get some recognition. Tom had tried to enlist right after Pearl Harbor but was rejected because they found a heart murmur, so he'd never been in uniform, and now he was frittering his time away writing obscure poetry and painting and drawing cartoons and trying to start a little press to print beautiful little books full of shallow thoughts. I think he was working hard not to realize that he had some skill but no real talent. Tall and good looking with the body of a Greek god, and quite marvelous in the sack, if that recollection doesn't shock you—if he could only have been content to be a garage mechanic or mailman! Turn right here, dear, onto Fox Hollow."

I made the turn. She was quiet for a block or two.

"We broke up in 1946," she went on then, "and a few weeks later, in a heavy rainstorm, his old Ford convertible skidded out of control on Santa Monica Boulevard in L.A. and hit a light pole; he was killed. I mourned for a little while, then got on with my career and with bringing up Charlie.

"I was an indifferent mother, I'm afraid. I loved Charlie, but I've seen how so many women have done so much better. The war was on, most of the young men were away, and I was busy and quite successful. Charlie got . . . misplaced in the shuffle. By the time he was a teenager he was, oh, a little cool, a little stiff emotionally, and I was beginning to realize all the things I'd done wrong and how little I could do to make them up to him. And I think he was left feeling that I owed him . . . something. When there was anything special he wanted, which was rarely, he'd come right out and ask. Very stiffly and formally, but at least he'd ask. A few months after he graduated from college he asked to borrow two thousand dollars.

"He told me just how much he was making at his new job with the city, and how much he could afford to pay back each month, so I said okay, I hope it's important. He said I stupidly got a girl pregnant, it's too late for an abortion, and the least I can do is pay the bills. I said, you could marry her. He said no. So I wrote him a check and asked him who it was. I was holding the check out to him. He stood there a long time without taking it, as though wondering if his getting it were conditional upon his answering the question. Then he took it and put it in his billfold. Perhaps he decided now *he* owed *me* something. He said, her name's Helen Fairland, she's a nineteen-year-old waitress. Next right turn, Jim."

I thought the next right turn was onto a dirt track leading nowhere. I said so.

"Nowhere much," Aunt Kate said. I made the turn. The tires

crunched and the station wagon bucked mildly. "Now turn left."

I turned onto a broad track that wandered into the hills that ran alongside Fox Hollow. It looked as though someone had started a development but changed his mind. I drove up to where the graded surface petered out.

I stopped and set the emergency but left the motor and the air conditioning on. Aunt Kate didn't seem to notice.

"He told me that a private adoption was being arranged, no names, and assured me that the situation was under control. He made it sound like an outbreak of plague. I guess to him it was. He was beginning to see his future in political terms and wanted the whole incident over, this waitress out of his life permanently, and no smudges on his reputation. But right from the start I was looking for ways to betray him.

"You see, I had been guilty, apparently, of the stupid, crippling rejection of my own child. I wasn't about to consent to the rejection of my only grandchild.

"I thought, it'll be simple. I'll just find this girl and—But I realized that she would see me as an interfering old fool trying to complicate a situation she and Charlie were trying to keep simple. Besides, if an adoption was being arranged, there would be no way to learn who the adopting parents were from her because she wouldn't know. So I was going to need help. The long and short of it is that a Los Angeles art gallery manager put me in touch with a detective agency that charged me an arm and a leg, but came up with Fred and Cynthia Rowan's names, the address they moved to in Carpinteria, and even a photograph of them with the baby and the old car they all drove away in.

"A few years later, when her grade school put on a little art festival, I was able to meet Fran and her new parents in natural, unforced surroundings. They were a close family and for a long time I was almost a member of it. Now Fran has Mike, but our closeness is still there. Isn't that miraculous?

"Now we come to two days ago. You and I had just talked to Charlie, then you went off and I went back to work. Afterward, I walked back toward the festival offices. As I was crossing Fifth, I saw a couple going to a car parked across the street, in the last place before the no-parking zone in front of the courthouse. The woman was rather handsome, about forty, and the man was Arthur MacAndie. They seemed friendly together and I thought, it's about time! Mac's got himself a nice-looking lady friend. She got into the car and drove off, and he saw me and waved. I said something or other and he said oh, that was Helen Pavlik, the widow who leased the Osterreicher house. She grew up here in town. Her name used to be Helen Fairland.

"You know, for quite a few seconds the name didn't mean anything to me. I said goodbye to Mac and went up the walk to the courthouse, and had time to wonder at this little tickle of apprehension that was turning into some kind of panic. I thought, my God, I'm going to have a heart attack, and then the significance of the name hit me and I thought, my God, *the* Helen Fairland, after all these years—Fran's mother! and I had the horrid conviction that she could spoil everything.

"Mind you I didn't stop to analyze *how* she could spoil everything, I just ran to the nearest phone and called Charlie's office. He'd already left. I didn't get him until I got home and called from there. I said, get set for a shock, Helen Fairland's back in town. He said he already knew, and yes, she had been in touch with him. In a cold, driven voice he said she was trying to track down the kid she'd put up for adoption. There was someone in Santa Barbara who might be the one. He didn't know what she was up to but count on its being vicious, she probably had a campaign on to bleed half the prominent men in Dos Cruces. And suddenly I got to feeling very calm and dispassionate. I said why Charlie, you mean you were silly enough to get the town slut pregnant? And he said that's right, now you know why I wouldn't marry her.

"Well, he said he appreciated my concern, but he wasn't a kid any longer. Whatever Helen was up to, he'd handle it. He wouldn't know what he would do until after he found out what she was planning, but I wasn't to worry. Then he hung up.

"I sat there by the phone for half an hour with my brain in neutral. I simply couldn't *think*. But I suppose I must have been thinking under the surface because suddenly I just knew what I had to do. Charlie and his holier-than-thou ambition weren't what mattered. What mattered was Fran. Soon Fran was going to discover that Fred and Cynthia hadn't been her parents after all, that her *real* parents were a self-important stuffed shirt and a promiscuous bitch who carried grudges. And no doubt she'd consider me a part of the original deception and never trust me again.

"So I dug into a closet for the gun Charlie had given me years ago. I took it out of its little box and loaded it, took along a few extra bullets and a flashlight and put them all in a Save-a-Tree tote bag with an old work shirt on top of them. I'd never used the gun, but Charlie had taught me how. So I got into the pickup and drove up here. This is about where I parked."

She opened her door. I turned everything off and went around to help her, but she already had both feet on the dusty ground and was pushing herself off the upholstery. A long wisp of white hair was kept moving over her forehead by the furnace-dry desert breeze. The afternoon was hot enough to bake bread.

"Know where you are, young man?" Aunt Kate asked.

"I'd guess," I said, closing her car door, "that the gap between those hillocks comes out in the Osterreichers' back yard."

"Good for you!"

"How did you know about it?"

"This whole country's my back yard." Walking carefully, Aunt Kate headed for the gap. I followed. "I've known Mel and Julia Osterreicher for years. I found my way through here by flashlight two nights ago with no trouble at all."

The gap ran uphill for a few yards then turned downward. Rock and dirt walls on either side cooked us like an oven. Sweat squirted energetically out of all my pores.

Then the gap widened and we were looking at the rear of the stone barbecue. The grass beyond it was already scorched and untended, the house beyond that secretive, withdrawn, ashamed of itself.

Clint Farrell was sitting in one of the weathered wooden patio chairs I had seen yesterday. His legs were stretched out in front of him, the ankles crossed. One hand hung down almost to the grass. The other cradled a flat half-pint bottle in his lap.

Aunt Kate murmured, "What's he doing here?"

"Drinking, apparently. We'd better get you into the shade."

"Shade would be nice."

I walked her across the ragged lawn and onto the verandah, then turned to Clint. He saluted me with the bottle and took a healthy sip.

I said pleasantly, "Drinking out here in the sun, you're going to get so dehydrated they'll never get your motor restarted."

"This ain't recreational drinking, son," Clint Farrell said. A small philosophical sip this time. "I got to thinking if I did just enough careful drinking, not a sip more but sure as tomorrow not a sip less, I just might achieve that dead-center moment of clarity in which I could remember those parts of Wednesday night I *don't* remember—the times I blacked out. Who knows what I mighta seen, Jim? Or *who*? Maybe with his pants open. Maybe with a gun in his hand—"

"Maybe nothing."

"Sure. But I gotta find out. And the key . . . is here."

He lifted the bottle.

"Like the key to that window of opportunity you told me about last night."

He nodded peacefully. The sweat poured out of him and his face looked like crinkled wet suede. His eyes were tired blue marbles in puddles of vinegar but looked calmly intelligent. He hadn't achieved his revelatory state, but seemed to have made it to a plateau of quiet lucidity. Seemed to. I didn't know if it was even possible; I didn't know enough about drunks.

He took another drink and looked to see how much whiskey was left—about a third of the bottle. Breath whistled in his nose.

"Well, frankly, I wasn't being too strictly truthful last night," he said matter-of-factly. "It ain't so much a window as a hairline crack. A service connected disability, happened on my first weekend pass after boot camp. I was twenty, been dipping my wick in the honeypot since I was twelve. No one ever had so much fun in high school, all that pussy and most of it mine. Guys like MacAndie and Dave Hostetler used to hang around me trying to figure out how I operated. I didn't even know, it just came naturally. So that weekend after boot camp I got cheerfully boozed up and got caught in the back of an old DeSoto doing it with another guy's girl. He wasn't any bigger'n me but he sure was meaner. Name was Winslow Parker, from Salinas. Beat me up good. Concussion, three broken ribs, punctured lung, bunch of other stuff. Gave me this with the heel of his boot when I was lying on my back not expecting to live." He rubbed the bridge of his nose with a flat forefinger. "Beat the girl up some, broke her jaw, then went AWOL. They never found him. Coulda reenlisted somewhere under a false name with a fake ID, or maybe just ran into someone with an even shorter fuse than he had and wound up dead in a ditch.

"Well, son, they patched me up okay, though the nose never worked too good again and the fungun hardly at all. Except sometimes, just sometimes, when I was exactly drunk enough, at the moment when I hit that dead center calm and all things got clear and not to be worried about. Been drinking in search of that righteous calm ever since. Except today. Today I'm turning that old bromide upside down. I'm drinking to remember."

"Think it'll work?"

A shrug. Another drink.

"Suppose it does," I said. "Suppose you remember everything back to the day you were born, including everything that happened that other time you blacked out—"

"Yeah, yeah. Might find out why I don't want to remember that."

"Get out of the sun or it won't matter either way."

"Don't crowd me, son, you're not my keeper . . . though I guess I gotta thank you for last night. Don't remember that any too well either. Kept drifting off and having nightmares about an avenging angel with a scalpel . . ."

I remembered him on the bed at the motel, protecting his crotch.

"I was with Jennifer Kendall," I said.

He became very still. Even his shirtfront didn't move. Eventually the tip of a gray tongue came out and tried to moisten his upper lip.

"She say anything?"

"Nothing to explain why you're afraid of her."

The tired blue eyes looked at me for a moment. Then he put his hands on the arms of the chair and pushed himself slowly upright, holding the neck of the bottle between two fingers.

"Man, you're muddying the waters."

"Or is it the kid you're afraid of?"

His knees sagged. I took an arm and kept him standing.

"Into the shade, Clint."

He gave me a cagey drunk look and I tugged him toward the verandah. We went up the two wooden steps. At the far end Aunt Kate sat with her feet over the edge on the steps down. I heard water running. Her light summer sandals were on the verandah beside her.

She heard us coming and stood up, holding the end of the garden hose, from which water gushed brightly. She went down to garden level, bent to turn off the water at the standpipe, then came back up the steps.

"I've been cooling off."

Clint Farrell stopped moving.

"There was a woman," he said suddenly. "Wednesday night. Here."

"Of course," Aunt Kate said. "I was here."

"You remember seeing a woman?" I asked him.

He gave a slow nod.

"What did she look like?"

"Can't quite see . . ."

He took a sip from his bottle.

"When was this?"

"I dunno. After I heard the shot."

"Was she inside or outside the house? What was she doing?"

"Dunno."

"Maybe you saw Helen Fairland."

". . . Naah."

"How can you be sure? You didn't know her."

"Not then. But I'm the guy who found her, so I know what she looked like. This wasn't Helen. Leave me alone. It'll come."

$\triangledown$

Chapter 26

I AGREED TO LEAVE him alone if he would go home and stay indoors. He smiled benignly and said okay, home was where the booze was. I asked Aunt Kate to wait for me and left her turning on the hose again while I escorted Clint toward his house.

It sprawled like some graying relic of pioneer days, its windows blind secretive eyes under the blazing white sky. I looked back. If I hadn't know who was sitting on the edge of the Osterreicher veranda I might not have recognized her. The only way anyone could have recognized her after dark, I thought, was if she had been standing at the front of the property under the streetlight.

He opened the front door. I followed him into cold like the air off a glacier and heard the muted roaring of an old- fashioned air conditioner. After the glare outside, the shaded windows made the interior as dark as a midnight cave. He maneuvered carefully into the kitchen and sat down at the dinette table.

"Eat something," I told him. "And drink something besides that embalming fluid."

"The Kendall kid." He sounded unresentful, almost wondering. "How old d'you suppose she was when she lost her cherry, huh? So many kids now, they hit twelve, thirteen, all they got left's the box it came in. Pretty as a picture on a Christmas card, polite as you please. What would her mother say? Broken homes, I guess. Broken homes'll do it. Little bitch sure had me worried.

" 'Course, the only reason she could do that was I was sauced. Winter of last year, been raining. I went outside mid-afternoon to see if it was dry enough I could set me up some targets in the canyon. Puddles everywhere but the sun was out and the day was purely pretty. Thing was, there was this car parked on the private road runs from Carver Canyon Road to where some of the old buildings used to be, back when my granddaddy was mining gold there. Only an old shed there now. Big hoot of laughter coming from the shed. I thought maybe some sleazy biker types mighta come over to get outa the rain and smoke dope. Didn't want strangers messing up my property, so I went over to tell 'em to git.

"Door was latched inside with a hook-an'-eye latch, so I gave it the old shoulder, tore the hook clean off the door. They had a sleeping bag on the floor, a six-pack, clothes scattered all over. The guy was sitting up in the sack pulling a sweater on. He got real spooked and yelled and grabbed his pants, but she said, cool as iced tea, it's Mr. Farrell, and came over and eased me back out the door. She was wearing a man's shirt came down to her knees. All the time I'm talking about trespassing and does your mother know and you oughta be ashamed, and she's unbuttoning this shirt and opens it and she's stark fucking naked under it. Cute as a bug's ear and not a stitch on and there's this cute little blond pussy in the afternoon sun, and she says, Want some? like she's offering cream for my coffee. It's sad, cute little thing like that, beat up old wreck like me, fifty years old. Last time I had a fourteen year old with a shape like that I was sixteen. Her name was Marcie Kaufman—great body but a sad little face with a crooked front tooth. When you're sixteen it's young love, when you're fifty it's child molesting. They throw you in jail, you're lucky if the other cons don't carve your liver out. But do I stop to think that far? Not on your life, neighbor. All I can think of is how long it's been and how good that little pussy looks. Next thing I know, I'm coming through that door."

"You blacked out?"

"Like a light. You said yesterday, go with the evidence. Well, there's other kinds of molesting besides fucking."

"You'd caught her and she was counterattacking, trying to throw you for a loop or compromise you. She tried it on me last night. No one's holding anything against you. I think you blacked out so you'd be sure not to mess with the wrong girl again."

"If I could black out and still find my way back here, I could black out and still do something disgusting."

"I can't argue maybes. Go with the evidence."

"You figure I blacked out Wednesday . . . to keep from seein' something I shouldn'ta?"

"No idea, Clint."

"But I'd have to've seen something . . . to know I shouldn't've seen in. I'll work on it. Lot's more memory juice in the cupboard."

I reminded him to eat something, and headed back to Aunt Kate.

She was still sitting at the edge of the verandah, the garden hose still running. She pointed the nozzle my way.

"Need cooling off, young man? No? You don't know what you're missing. Did he remember it was me Wednesday night?"

"No."

She turned off the faucet.

"I could have jogged his memory, but I knew it would be better if he remembered all by himself. Anyway, where were we?"

"You were telling me how you drove here Wednesday night."

"Yes." She slipped on her sandals and buckled them, then took my hand to help her stand up. "I parked and picked up my tote bag, walked here the way we came, and knocked on the door. A woman in a bathrobe answered. I asked if she was Helen Fairland, and when she said yes I took my gun out of the tote bag. I pointed it at her and said I was Charles Cromwell's mother, and that I was going to protect my granddaughter if I had to kill her to do it. She got scared and backed into the living room. I followed. I didn't waste time talking to her. I picked a cushion off the sofa and held it in front of the . . . the muzzle of the gun, got it as close as I could to her head and pulled the trigger. She fell in front of the sofa. I thought she was dead, of course.

"I was quite calm, and took time to think about anything I might have left fingerprints on. Nothing. Except the cushion. I wasn't sure I hadn't read somewhere that they can get fingerprints off cloth now, so I decided to take the cushion with me. I didn't know about the birth certificate, and that I should find that and take it too. So I just left everything except the cushion and went out and back to my car, using the flashlight. Then I remembered half a can of paint thinner in an old tool box behind the front seat, with some old brushes and palette knives and stuff. I doused the cushion with the paint thinner and set a match to it in the gap, out of sight of the house. Then I put the empty can back in the tool box and drove home."

"What time did you get here, Aunt Kate?"

"Well, I wasn't checking my watch and making notes," she said tartly, "but I suppose it had to be, oh, just after eight."

"Didn't see anyone?"

"No."

"Or hear anything?"

"Nothing unusual, no."

"You promised to show me the gun."

"All right."

"Wait here, I'll go get the car."

"Oh, nonsense, dear, I can still walk. I'll show you where I burned the cushion."

We walked back through the gap in the hills. The place she showed me seemed to match Officer Vurpillat's description. I tucked her into the station wagon.

A quarter mile past the last gas station on West Eleventh a dirt track turned off to Aunt Kate's place. It was a welcoming oasis. The old barn, its loft converted into a busy studio during her most productive years, was a sleepy ruin dreaming ancient dreams under the unfeeling sun. The track curved around to the twin oaks shading the front door of the ranch-style house. Behind the house spread the orchard.

I parked close to the front door and we went inside. The living room was elegant in its lack of clutter, the furniture low and comfortable, not new, never expensive. Three striking canvasses hung on the walls, only one by Aunt Kate.

"Sit down, dear," Aunt Kate said almost absently. "I won't be a minute."

"Can I use your phone?"

"Of course. Right over there."

She went away. I sat down by the phone on a cane sofa with firm flower-patterned cushions. I dialed Jennifer's home number.

A clear young voice answered, "Kendall."

"Hello, Megan. Jim Keller. How's Katy doing?"

"Oh, hi." The voice was instantly cool. I still hadn't proved myself. "She's taking a nap. Want me to wake her?"

"No, she had a rough night. I'll pick her up as soon as I can, but I don't know just when that'll be."

"No problem."

"Thanks, Megan. Here's what I really called about. Looks like you guys won't have to talk to the cops. Details later. Tell Kenny, okay?"

Sudden excitement flashed over the phone line, but she had caught my guarded tone.

". . . Uh, okay. See you."

I hung up and Aunt Kate came back. She handed me what looked like a hefty old cigar box.

I raised the lid. Inside was a cardboard box containing, the label said, .22 calibre short ammunition, and something wrapped in a faintly oily yellow cloth. I unwrapped it.

It looked like a Luger automatic. It was neither. Instead of containing a clip the butt was solid. Fiddling with the milled knobs lifted the breech block and exposed a spent shell in the chamber. I extracted it and set it down by the phone and sniffed the muzzle of the gun. The barrel had not been cleaned since the gun was last fired.

I put the gun back down on its yellow cloth and looked over at Aunt Kate. She was in a chair across the room, feet together, hands folded in her lap, patient as death.

"It won't work, you know, Aunt Kate."

"What won't?"

"This is a single-shot gun. One bang and you have to reload. The murder gun was an automatic. An automatic ejects the empty shell after each shot and puts another into firing position. We know that an automatic was used because they found the empty shell in the cuff of Helen's bathrobe."

"I'll go and tell the police. Of course I won't tell them all the reasons for it that I told you, that would defeat my purpose and make everything public, but Dave Hostetler will believe me."

"No, he won't, Aunt Kate. The first thing he'd do is order a ballistics check on your gun. Every gun leaves marks on a bullet that's fired from it, marks as distinctive as fingerprints. It wouldn't take long to prove this gun didn't kill Helen, and then he'd start to wonder who you're trying to protect. He'd like it to be Fran. No political embarrassment if it were an out-of-towner like Fran. But it isn't Fran, is it? It's Charles. And not long ago Charles was trying to protect *you* by denying he had a gun not in his immediate possession.

"I think it happened this way. On Wednesday evening, you decided to go and talk to Helen, maybe convince her not to contact Fran. You didn't take the gun along; it would never have occurred to you. And if you'd got there a little after eight you'd almost certainly have heard Clint Farrell's target practice. You actually got there around 8:35 or just after. Before you turned into the driveway you saw Charles's brown Cougar parked in front of the house. So you stopped at the curb and turned off your headlights, and right away, before you had time to start wondering what to do, he came tearing out of the house and jumped into his car and took off like a rocket, going out the other end of the driveway. He wouldn't notice a darkened vehicle that far behind him.

"You got scared. What had he told you? That he'd take care of the problem. You had to make sure he hadn't done something real stupid. So you turned around and went back to the road we took and drove up behind the Osterreicher house and came in that way. Charles had found the front door open but he'd closed it behind him. You rang the doorbell but got no answer. You went around the front of the house where you could see Helen lying on the floor through the French door—which was unlatched, so you went in. You saw that Helen had been shot and thought that Charles had done it. You saw that cushion the shot had been fired through. You took that with you, left the way you had come, and burned the cushion just like you told me—to make people think the murderer had escaped out back instead of out onto Fox Hollow."

I paused. Aunt Kate said, "Why on earth should I have done all that?"

"Because you're still trying to pay Charles what he feels you owe him. Trying to pay him what *you* feel you owe him. And on Wednesday night after you got home you dug out the gun he had loaned you, or given you—it's not a competition gun, I'll bet he's had it since he was a kid—and you fired a shot into the ground, so you'd have a recently used gun to show if you needed one."

She shook her head regretfully.

"I'm afraid you're dreaming, dear. It's sweet of you not to want to believe me, but I'm afraid you must. And where did you get the idea that Charlie was there that night?"

"He told me, Aunt Kate. Witnesses saw him turning out of Fox Hollow before the accident. Charles says he denied being on Fox Hollow because he had to deny being anywhere near the Osterreicher house. He'd found Helen dead there. If anyone knew he'd been near the place, he'd be accused of killing her."

She shook her head again, very faintly this time. She looked fragile, as though the skull beneath the parchment skin was as thin as eggshell. Then she sighed. The sound had the autumnal finality of the touch of dry leaves.

"Did he?"

"I don't know, Aunt Kate."

"No, nor do I . . . I wonder what sort of person she was. Helen, I mean. I said some terribly mean things about her to Charlie."

"Some nice people liked her, in the old days," I told her. "When she came back here she was a financially secure widow who had never had any other kids and wanted to find the one she'd given up for adoption. Charlie was convinced she was planning something mean. She invited him over for a drink and a talk, without telling him that Fran was going to be there too. Of course, Fran never got there. It would have been rough on Charlie, but I didn't think it was meant cruelly. I don't think Helen had it in her to be vindictive."

". . . No, nor do I," Aunt Kate said. "That was all in Charlie's mind. Oh, poor Charlie. Poor Charlie."

Chapter 27

AUNT KATE GOT OUT at the rear entrance to the County Courthouse. Against all odds I found a parking space in the metered lot a couple of blocks along Sixth and hiked back to the courthouse myself.

A woman, Clint Farrell had said; he had seen a woman. Who it might have been concerned me less and less the closer I got to the courthouse, because the little knot of apprehension in my gut was growing into a fist of ice. I had told Paul Franken I wouldn't be at Felicia's arraignment. As though I had a choice; I'd promised I wouldn't desert her.

By the time I got to Franken's office my stomach was a clamoring pit of helplessness.

Marge Klein looked up from her word processor.

"My boss isn't here, Jim. Judge Goetzmann's court. Your ex's arraignment."

I thanked her and went to the lobby and up the angled stairs. June Hostetler was coming down them.

Concern was all over her face. When she saw me her feet hesitated on the stairs.

I gave her a nod. "Mrs. Hostetler."

She said abruptly, when we were almost level, "Have you been giving Kate Cromwell a bad time?"

"No."

"She left with you and came back in a very bad state indeed."

"If she wants to tell you about it, I'm sure she will."

I climbed past her. She made an impatient sound behind me.

"Do we have to feud, Mr. Keller?"

"I'm not feuding, Mrs. Hostetler. You are."

"Oh, for heaven's sake call me June, everyone does. Whoever's feuding, let's stop it, shall we? Kate said you'd seen Clint Farrell and he was drinking."

"Yes."

"Don't you think it's too soon after last time?"

"Of course it is. Last time was last night, and the time before that was the night before. No one can keep that up indefinitely."

"No, of course not. I hadn't heard about last night . . . How did he seem to you?"

"Someone should be looking after him. It's not very neighborly, but I can't. He's a friend of your husband's, maybe the Chief can arrange something."

"Yes. There are too many people in the committee rooms right now, I was going to call Dave from a public phone. Maybe he can send someone out to check on him."

"I hope he can. You'll have to excuse me, I'm late already—"

"Yes, of course, sorry to've kept you."

She gave me a jittery smile and a tentative wave, sort of a we're-friends-now-but-I'm-still-not-sure-of-you gesture, and turned back downstairs.

An arraignment is the first step in the judicial process. Arraignments are usually cattle calls in crowded courtrooms where charges are read, plea bargains set, pleas entered, trials scheduled, and bail set or refused. But when I slipped in through the double swing doors, Judge Goetzmann's courtroom held fewer than a dozen people, including court functionaries. The judge himself was a small thin man whose rimless glasses and black robe made you think of a small town preacher.

Felicia stood facing him, tall and erect. It was weird. She was without counsel. The only others beyond the fence separating the public section from the court proper were the bailiff, the court reporter, the prosecutor Paul Franken, and the tall policewoman Luisa Gutierrez.

In the front row of the public section, Ed Hammond slouched

characteristically next to John Engle, who was on his feet. A blond young man in a gray suit sat with them. Walt Gilfillan, the deputy public defender who had phoned me at breakfast, sat alone on the left. At the back of the room, across the aisle from where I sat, Arthur MacAndie took notes in a spiral notebook.

Judge Goetzmann was talking to Felicia.

". . . I know this isn't a trial, Miss Hammond, but these are serious charges." His tone was dry, patient, unshakably friendly. "You ought to have competent counsel even at this stage of the proceedings."

Felicia said, "Counsel of my choice refused to represent me."

"But then you should make another choice, shouldn't you? Or the court can appoint counsel, or you can reconsider your objections to Mr. Engle and accept his offer for the duration of these proceedings."

"Mr. Engle is not acceptable. He represents my father, not me."

"Your Honor," Engle said smoothly, "Miss Hammond's wishes are of course paramount, but I would remind her that I represented her in her recent divorce and am doing so again in her child custody case next week."

"That can be changed," Felicia said icily. Her voice rose in pitch but not volume. "Get off my back, John."

"Please address your remarks to the bench," Judge Goetzmann said mildly. "That way we can avoid getting into personalities and wasting time."

"This entire business is a waste of time." Under the well-bred tones I heard a passionate wail of protest. "These absurd charges are a waste of time. They are also a serious reflection on the competence and good faith of the policemen who filed them, and on the probity of the—"

"Be quiet, Felicia!" The judge had begun tapping his gavel, but it was Engle's sharp order that cut off her accusations. As far as I could tell she hadn't moved an inch since I came in. She didn't move now. Just stood there, as still as frozen marble.

Engle went on, "My apologies, Your Honor. When Miss Hammond has had a moment to reflect, she's going to be very chagrined and sorry for that outburst. I can only ask the court to consider the effect on any young woman—especially one who has been fortunate enough to lead a comfortable and sheltered existence—of being thrown in jail like any street tough on charges involving gutter violence. Especially at a time of such mental and emotional strain."

Paul Franken asked, "Is the defense planning to introduce psychiatric evidence to mitigate?"

"No!" Engle snapped.

"Or perhaps to claim that Miss Hammond is unable to comprehend the charges, or help in her own defense?"

"Mr. Franken," Judge Goetzmann sighed, "that was really unnecessary. No, Mr. Engle was merely letting his rhetorical skills get the better of him, in spite of which the court is inclined to accept his apology while at the same time reminding him that Miss Hammond has again indicated his unacceptability. Mr. Gilfillan, since you're here may I assume you're free to assume this task?"

Walt Gilfillan stood up. He was about my age, with a round face that made him look like the kind lawyer you hope the other guy has, which he wasn't. He said yes, he was free to be Felicia's counsel pro tem. Judge Goetzmann passed him a thin sheaf of papers, and said he would no doubt want to consult with his client in private.

And from then on things went normally. The judge retired to his chambers. I practiced being unobtrusive, and Walt led Felicia out by a side door. A few minutes later they came back.

Walt looked awed. Felicia looked tense enough to make her joints creak. The bailiff went to notify the judge, who resumed the bench. Whatever Walt had told her, Felicia was now the ideal client, unargumentative, letting her lawyer do the talking. It was a triumph of brains over raw feeling, the kind of performance I was afraid she would put on for the custody hearing. Walt entered a plea of not guilty to all charges, requested a jury trial, orally noticed a 1538.5 motion, and served stipulated discovery on the People. The judge set a trial date three weeks away with a compliance date one week later. He released Felicia on her own recognizance, and the court's business was over. The bailiff told us all to rise, the judge left the room, and Ed Hammond launched into a violent whispered argument with John Engle. Engle whispered back, vigorously shaking his head.

Clipping his pen into a shirt pocket, Arthur MacAndie unfolded his frame and ambled to the center aisle, pretending not to see me as he turned toward the front of the room.

Ed Hammond was throwing off Engle's hand and lumbering to his feet. Mac caught him by surprise.

"Mr. Hammond," Mac said. "Arthur MacAndie, *Lindero County Chronicle.* What can you tell me about the pressures brought by several outside sources today to have the charges against your daughter reduced or dismissed?"

"Pressures?" Ed rumbled. "What d'you mean, pressures?"

"Calls to the mayor's office, the office of Harlan Fox in Sacramento, the office of his brother, local businessman Marcus Fox—"

"Just like you guys," Ed interrupted. "The story's under your noses, but you gotta go after someone from out of town so you don't step on any home toes. You want the real story, just ask Mr. Prosecutor Fucking Franken there. Ask him about his flagrant bias. Ask him if his ex-wife didn't win a disputed child custody case in which he lost three kids. He's not only helping a buddy in this malicious prosecution, he's expressing a malignant prejudice against any woman involved in a child custody dispute. Don't tell me this farce this afternoon wasn't planned to prejudice my daughter's custody case. All of which will be proved when I bring suit in Superior Court."

"For Christ's sake, Ed," Engle began.

"You getting soft?" Ed snarled at him. "You think every dispute can be settled over lunch?"

"You won't settle anything this way!"

Mac said cheerfully, "What about those accusations of bias, Paul?"

"They're false," Franken said shortly.

He snapped shut the latches on his briefcase. I hadn't even known he'd been married, much less about his divorce and his children. He was the Chief Deputy D.A., not someone with a home life.

"He knew about your kids," Mac said.

"Public record. As to the rest, Mr. Hammond is simply mistaken."

He picked up the briefcase and came up the aisle, hesitated when he saw me but kept going. He wouldn't want to be seen talking to me. I didn't doubt he'd made the decision to prosecute in good conscience, but may have begun to wonder what made his conscience so pure. He pushed savagely through to the hall.

I stood up and walked to the aisle. Felicia turned away from Walt

Gilfillan and approached her father. She moved like an imperfectly articulated robot. Her face was empty, the blue eyes shadowed, dark, enormous. She and Engle saw me at almost the same time, Ed a beat later.

"Hello, Felicia," I said.

"Of course. You came to witness my humiliation."

"I came because I said I wouldn't desert you."

She studied me remotely.

"What happens now?"

"A few formalities, then you're free. You have to be back in three weeks for the trial. If the prosecution isn't ready to go to trial by the compliance date, the case is dismissed. The other stuff Walt talked about means the prosecution will have to give you a checklist of everything the cops saw and who their witnesses are, and they won't be able to introduce any surprise evidence—some stuff like that. Purely technical."

"What about right now?"

"You're still officially in custody. The officer will take you back to the copshop and they'll do the paperwork and give you back your stuff, whatever you had in your pockets. I've got your purse at home. Your car, too."

"You won't need those," Ed Hammond said. "Let's get you sprung and pick up Katy and fly you both home." He grinned at me. "Oh yeah, we know where she is. George here"—he jerked a thumb at the blond young man in the gray suit— "figured you probably left Katy at the broad's place you were with last night. Her name's on the police report. We got a couple of guys out there right now, seeing Katy comes to no harm."

I looked at George. His face was classic Sigma Chi marred by ruthless confidence.

"Who's George?"

"George Ferguson," Engle said. "Admitted to the California bar last year, an associate of our firm since January. James Keller, Dos Cruces attorney."

"Hi," I said.

"How do you do, sir?" George stuck out a hand. I shook it. His grip wasn't quite strong enough to crush granite.

Felicia said, "This courtroom charade—am I supposed to sit and play with myself until the trial?"

Her father's face went gray.

"First get yourself a good lawyer," I told her. "Someone who doesn't work for your dad, someone who won't be bullied."

"We don't need advice from you," Ed rumbled. "Just call your girlfriend and tell her to give us Katy. If you don't we'll just have to go and take her." He said to Felicia, "Okay, kid. You go with the officer."

"If you take Katy," I told him, "it's kidnapping."

"Oh, come on!" Engle scoffed. Sweat had broken out under his eyes.

"If Felicia takes her," I plowed on, "I'll immediately sue for temporary custody pending the outcome of this case, arguing her disturbed and violent behavior."

Felicia made an impatient gesture.

"Why do I have to go through all this shit?"

"Why?" Ed snarled, his face ashen. "Because this guy wants to take your kid away from you, that's why."

Felicia looked at him, her expression chilled, fastidious.

"You mean he's trying to take my kid away from *you*. I have to go through all this shit for *you*. Just so you can have another kid to raise. Why? Didn't you like the way the first one turned out?"

MacAndie was still there. He gave me a startled look. Engle had suddenly aged ten years. I was dimly aware of his trying to tell Felicia that she hadn't meant what she had said, but no one paid any attention.

Ed cleared his throat.

"Aw, c'mon, kid," he said.

She mimicked savagely, " 'Aw, c'mon, kid!' I'm not a kid. I'm twenty-sev—no, almost . . . I'm *thirty* years old. You still think I'm a kid and you don't even *trust* me! You—and Dr. Phil's no better— you both want to send me to that other doctor . . . What's-his-name . . . Bergstrom!" She stared at her father in bitter accusation. The performance for the judge was over. Controls were visibly unraveling. "A head doctor! A *shrink*!"

"Yeah, well, Dr. Phil thought—"

"Dr. Phil, Dr. Phil! As though I were a six-year-old with chicken pox! He's Dr. Philip Markham, M.D. Can you handle all that? Call him anything, I don't care. Call him a cab, call him a doddering old fake past due for retirement. 'Well, little Felicia Hammond! Where've you been all this time? Goodness, how are you?' I tell him I'm shitty and he says go see a fucking *shrink*!"

"God damn it, Felicia," Ed ground out, "I won't have you using that kind of talk—"

"Oh, go fuck yourself. Everyone wants to get me to a shrink. Even this pie-faced twerp." She pointed to Walt, whose mouth hung open. "Do I even know you? Even you! First you want to plea bargain. What am I supposed to plead guilty to, pissing on the sidewalk? I say no, not guilty or forget it! So he *threatens* me. 'Listen,' he says, 'one more wingding and that judge is going to order you held for psychiatric evaluation. Behave yourself and you'll be out of here in five minutes.' "

"It worked," Walt said placatingly.

"Shut up, I'm tired of you. My turn to talk."

"Sweetheart," Ed began.

" 'Sweetheart,' " she mimicked, making a face.

His shoulders fought an invisible enemy. He took a heavy breath.

"You want to get out of here? Okay. Easiest way is to go with the officer and get checked out. We'll meet you over at the police station and take you to the hotel. I got you a room already—brought a coupla suitcases of your clothes and stuff. You can take a nice long bath—"

Felicia pounced. "And not have to listen to anyone."

"Not to anyone."

"No more shit, no more threats—no more doctors?"

"No more."

The frozen fury began to melt out of her face. I almost heard the ice in her eyes crack and flake away. The corners of her mouth began to tilt upward. The smile was slightly malicious and very, very crafty.

"For how long?"

"Long as you like."

"Promise?"

"Promise. Yeah."

"Your promise isn't worth much on the Big Board, you know."

"Maybe. But it's all I have to offer."

"Just this once maybe I'll take it. Remember you made this promise in front of witnesses, in a court of law!"

"Yeah."

"I'm going to soak in the tub, then I'm going to order a delicious room-service dinner, and eat it with the phone off the hook, and no one's going to bother me."

"You got a deal."

Felicia stood straighter. "Luisa?"

"Right here," Gutierrez said, "I gotta put the cuffs on you to take you back next door."

"That's silly," Felicia said, "but all right."

MacAndie followed me out of the courtroom. He didn't speak until we were clattering down the stairs.

"What happened to her mother?"

"Lit out years ago. Felicia was only a kid."

"Rejected child syndrome."

"That a guess?"

"Of course it is. I'm a newspaperman, not a child psych expert. I'm more interested in local developments."

We crossed the main lobby between panels of children's art and went down the steps to the low hallway leading to the rear exit.

"Old Ed's got some folks around town scared silly, others couldn't be happier," Mac said. "The development scheme the Fox boys and Charlie are involved in? Turns out a lot of the money is Ed's. He's threatening to withdraw his participation."

The V-shaped grin showed teeth.

"Got to hand it to the old bastard. He really goes all out for his kid. Let's hope he keeps it up."

$\triangledown$

Chapter 28

I MADE IT TO Quintero Drive without hitting any cop cars or pedestrians.

It looked torpid. It was a suburbia Norman Rockwell never painted: a couple of parked cars, sleek empty lawns, low houses huddling vainly in search of shade, unseeing windows, no signs of occupancy, no voices.

One of the cars, parked way up the block, was a roadster of some kind protected from the sun by an all-over dust cover. The other was a blue Nova two-door parked across the street from Jennifer's house. I parked behind it. I could see two men in the Nova, one pretending to study a newspaper, the other catching a nap. I got out and crossed the street and turned to give them a friendly wave, then approached 1521's front door. The drapes behind the iron bars and the big glass pane moved slightly. Seconds later the front door opened.

"You look like a man who could use a beer," Jennifer said.

"I could, but I better not." I went inside. Glare and heat gave way to dimness and deliciously cool air. Jennifer had changed her work clothes for worn jeans and a dark T-shirt, and once she shut the door I could hardly see her. Then I felt her hand on my arm and her mouth on mine, not erotic but friendly, reassuring. I inhaled contentment with the fragrance of Jennifer. Who, I reminded myself, was turned on by menace. My ex-wife had other demons to contend with. I wondered if she were soaking in the tub yet, but couldn't bring that opulent image to mind. I could only see her in the cool blue blouse and designer jeans, standing alone and head-on, feet together, in a featureless expanse as lonely as a desert, as imprisoning as any cell, a frightened little girl.

I said, "I thought you were at work."

"Megan tried to call you after those two outside showed up. She couldn't get you, so she called me."

"I'm very glad you came. Where's Katy?"

"She and Megan went over the back fence and three houses down the block to the Millers'. Joyce Miller is a swim team mate of Megan's. Her brother has a car. Megan called and offered to treat them to ice cream if Norm would drive them, so they're all at the Baskin-Robbins on Verde Oak!"

"And those guys didn't even spot them?"

"They went in disguise, in case they'd been seen. Katy with her hair tied back in a ribbon, Megan in an old gray sweatshirt and her hair in a blue bandana with a cowboy hat on top. One of several kids piling into an old clunker down the block. Who'd make the connection? Can you stay to dinner?"

"Love to, but I have to buy Kate a toothbrush and lay in some groceries."

"Like some company?"

"Please."

She picked up her purse and clamped a pair of big-framed sunglasses on her nose. I installed Jennifer in the station wagon then went to the Nova and tapped on a front window.

It came down a few inches. A young face with a truculent jaw looked up and said, "Yeah?"

"In case you weren't sure, I'm James Keller. If anyone so much as looks cross-eyed at anyone in 1521 . . ."

"We figured it was you from your car. And yeah, we understand the rules."

"Didn't know the law could be this dull, did you?"

"Hell, I'm just a law clerk—with a Juris Doctor." He pointed to the guy at the wheel. "He's another. We get to do this gumshoe shit to keep us humble till we get the results of the bar exam."

"Well," I said, "keep up the good work."

The Baskin-Robbins shared a tiny parking lot with a Minimart and a dry cleaner's. I parked next to an old Dodge Dart held together by new white paint and baling wire. Jennifer said it was Norm's clunker.

The ice cream parlor was a small one. I followed Jennifer into cool air fragrant with a fresh dairy smell and the scent of several of the 31 flavors. Along the shaded front windows were three unitized table-and-four-chairs modules with three teenagers and a little kid sitting at the farthest one. It took me a second to recognize Katy because the top part of her face was hidden by dark glasses with pink frames and the lower part was daubed with chocolate ice cream. Megan sat next to her. She had gotten rid of the gray sweatshirt, but the fair hair was still gathered up in a blue bandana and held there by a black cowboy hat.

Katy saw me and touched her sunglasses.

"Megan gave these to me!" she crowed.

"That's nice," I said. "Did you remember to say thank you?"

She poked a last spoonful of ice cream into her mouth and nodded solemnly.

"She thanked me very formally," Megan said. "She has beautiful manners." Up close Megan looked like a calm, polite high school freshman with a pretty unmade-up face, the idealized babysitter. Until she impaled me with those gold-flecked eyes. "Let me introduce Joyce and Norm Miller from down the street. Joyce is going to be a junior at Marshall starting next week and Norm and I'll be seniors. Joyce swims two and four hundred free and IM. This is Jim Keller, Katy's dad."

Norm was slim and pleasant-looking, with a lot of disorganized hair. His sister was taller and outweighed him. She had an exuberant grin and wore a pink-and-white tank top that exposed well-muscled shoulders and sleek, powerful arms.

We traded hellos.

Megan said, "I didn't tell them what all this was about."

"All this what?" Joyce asked blankly. She squirmed in her seat, suddenly avid. "What all *what* was about?"

"I apologize for my sister," Norm said. "It's not that she doesn't mean to pry, it's that she does."

"I gave Kenny your message," Megan said. "He's getting impatient."

"He promised me a day."

"He said it's been almost a whole working day. He's almost decided you've got some angle you never told us about."

"Where can I find him?"

"He works part-time at Las Palmas Auto Supply. He gets off at four."

"Better give me his home phone."

She wrote it on the back of a business card from my billfold.

"Thank you for taking care of Katy."

From under the level brows came the disquieting stare.

"Do you? Have some angle you haven't told us about?"

"No. Come on, Kate. Time to go."

Katy stopped licking her plastic spoon and grinned brightly.

Megan dipped the corner of a paper napkin in her water glass.

"Goodness, we can't have you going out looking like that!" She mopped Katy's face. "There, that's better." Megan crumpled up the paper napkin and Katy got down off her chair. "You're a good kid, you know?"

"Yes," Katy said matter-of-factly, extending a small moist hand. "Thank you very much, Megan."

For a fleeting moment I saw her mother in her: ritual politeness and social formality used as magic. But Katy didn't need magic. Megan shook her hand and said, just as formally, "You're most welcome, Katy."

I took Kate's hand and said goodbye. Joyce had obviously picked up on Megan's doubts about me and didn't know whether to be friendly or stand-offish, so she just looked bewildered. Her brother had become still and watchful. I thanked them for helping in Katy's getaway and asked Megan to explain—but not about Wednesday night until we got it cleared up.

"Okay," Megan said. "Have fun."

Joyce giggled nervously.

"Count on it," Jennifer said over her shoulder.

Outside the sun still glared off chrome and glass. I opened up the station wagon and got Katy to take off her sunglasses while I tugged off her T-shirt. A yellow and white one from the Broadway sack replaced it.

"Well," Jennifer said, "at least my kid likes your kid."

Katy put the sunglasses back on. With the new shirt they were enough of a disguise to work. Or else we got lucky. We crowded into the front of the station wagon with Jennifer driving, visited the Alpha Beta at Fourth and Palmetto, then went home by way of the Pollock Highway, driving up to the front door and carrying in the groceries just like an ordinary family on an ordinary day. Which of course we weren't, and the day wasn't ordinary, or even over.

Jennifer and I put away groceries while Katy wandered through the house, opening and closing closet doors. Finally she came into the kitchen clutching the yellow Pooh Bear.

"There are no toys in my old house," she said in a bereaved voice.

"Sorry, Kate. We'll get some tomorrow."

"I want some paints."

"Okay. And a coloring book and some crayons."

"Crayolas."

"Okay."

"Can I watch cartoons on TV?"

"If there are any."

"Sailor Sam's on from three to six Saturday afternoons," Jennifer said.

"Sailor Sam!" Katy brightened, remembering. "He has a little dog called Sea Dog. It walks a tight-rope!"

"Channel Four," Jennifer said.

Katy scampered into the living room.

"So the real estate lady is a cartoon rerun freak."

"As long as they've got Augie Doggie," Jennifer said.

"I was a mad fan of Crusader Rabbit."

"Top Cat! Of course, that was later. We must have been teenagers . . ."

A triumphant shriek came from the living room. I went in to see if the picture needed adjusting, which it did. Then I picked Katy up off the floor and moved her six feet farther from the screen. A wave of nostalgia bowled me over, but Katy never took her eyes off Sailor Sam and Sea Dog.

When I went back into the kitchen Jennifer was popping a can of beer. She gave it to me and moved in close, silently locking her arms around my waist. I slid my free hand down inside her jeans, and the phone rang.

"Spoilsport," Jennifer murmured.

I led her into the den and picked up the phone.

"James Keller."

"Yes," an aggressive voice said. "George Ferguson. I'm the—"

"I know who you are, George."

"I understood you to say earlier that you are in possession of the former Mrs. Keller's car and purse."

"Yes."

"When would it be convenient to pick them up?"

"Any time's fine. Just call ahead. And I'll need some kind of authorization from Felicia—"

"Oh, come on, Mr. Keller. Is it really that complicated?"

"Yes. Of course, if she's keeping the phone off the hook and the door locked, getting anything from her will be a problem. It's your problem. My problem is she's already accused me of some pretty wild stuff, so I don't want her adding a charge of turning over her property to persons not authorized to receive it. Your firm isn't high on her popularity list right now. Neither is her father."

"If you could see your way to being a touch more cooperative . . . "

"I am being cooperative. You aren't. May I speak to Mr. Engle, please?"

I listened to his teeth grinding. Then he said disgustedly, "He went down to dinner with Mr. Hammond."

"Would you have him give me a call?"

"Yes."

"Good for you," I said encouragingly, and hung up. "I'd better call Kenny."

"I'll start the hamburgers." Jennifer took a healthy swallow from the beer can and went into the kitchen. I got Ken Allen's number from my billfold and dialed it. No answer. I called Andy Feldberg at home.

He swore luridly at me for not pressing the illegal entry and assault charges.

"This is no time for sentimental gestures, you dumb shit."

"She's got enough troubles," I said.

"She's got troubles, you take advantage of 'em. She'd take advantage of *your* troubles. Look, she's pleading not guilty to all charges in an attempt to avoid weakening her custody case."

"I don't even know how interested she is in that anymore. I don't know why she's denying everything. Maybe because she believes she isn't guilty. Or doesn't remember. Maybe she just can't admit to being less than daddy's perfect little girl. Maybe all the above, or none of the above. Maybe looking for motives that half-way make sense is expecting too much."

"Bottom line, old buddy: who cares? You want a nut case to have custody of Katy?"

"Of course not."

"She must've known there was something wrong, if she made the appointment with Dr. Bergstrom."

"Her father knew. She still won't admit it."

"Sounds to me like she's in some kind of heavy rebellion against him, but what do I know? Of course, Engle's going to ask for a continuance. You realize you could win this by default?"

"Yes."

"But don't count on it."

"Yes."

"Talk to you tomorrow."

I hung up and sat looking at the phone as though waiting for moss to grow on it.

He had actually said it.

You may win this by default.

Perhaps it was only a remote chance. I should have cheered it on like a runner to the tape, but even the thought brought a wave of guilt that left me cringing. There could be no default, even a temporary one, unless Felicia was unable to press her case, or couldn't be trusted not to ruin her case if she even tried. In which case she would be . . . too disturbed? Unstable? A nut case? How could I hope for any of those? "People fail people," Jennifer had said. "You're not God." How had I failed Felicia? I hadn't a clue. Perhaps because I wasn't God, perhaps because gorgeous Felicia was only a little kid in disguise, deeply injured by her mother's desertion, under enormous pressure to keep her father's love by being anything except herself, whoever she was. . . .

The sizzle was a ground beef patty hitting the frying pan. I decided the phone wasn't going to grow moss and went into the kitchen.

While I was setting the table Sailor Sam's program ended and Katy, looking zonked, dragged the yellow Pooh Bear into the kitchen. I sat her down with Pooh on the next chair and poured her a glass of milk. Jennifer slid the first hamburger onto Katy's plate and the phone rang again.

I returned to the den.

"Is there some problem about Felicia's car and purse?" John Engle asked.

"I can't deliver the car because I don't have the keys. Get her keys, plus some kind of indemnification so I don't get accused of turning over her stuff to persons not authorized to receive it."

"You're being overly cautious, but all right."

"When you get in the car, look in the cardboard carton in the trunk. You'll find six highway flares and a thermos bottle more than half full of gasoline. She came ready to torch the house."

"Nonsense," he said automatically; then, after a pause, with less conviction, ". . . nonsense."

"I don't know if she could actually have done it, but it's the kind of thing that's going through her head. Didn't know about Dr. Bergstrom, did you?"

"I'm sure your curiosity is natural, but you realize it would be most improper for me to discuss the subject."

"Why wouldn't she accept you as counsel?"

"Same answer. Please, Mr. Keller."

"Bear with me, Mr. Engle. She wouldn't accept you because she sees you as representing her father's interests, not hers. Which means she finally turned against Ed. I have an idea why."

"Mr. Keller, I'm going to hang up."

He wasn't, or he'd simply have done it. Maybe he was curious to hear me out. Maybe he had another reason.

I said, "Felicia wasn't feeling well. Ed got her to see old Dr. Phil, who's a pretty smart old coot. He knows there's no physical reason for her symptoms, whatever they are, and that the trouble goes deeper than temporary situational tension. So instead of patting her hand and prescribing Valium, he tells her to go see Dr. Bergstrom. Felicia complains to Ed, who calls Phil—and Phil convinces him. Maybe Ed's been noticing things, and the custody hearing's getting close. He can't afford to have her mess that up, so he offers to buy me out of the fight—providing Felicia agrees to see Bergstrom. I turn down the money. Felicia says that cancels her obligation to keep the appointment with Bergstrom. Ed says it doesn't. Felicia feels betrayed."

Engle said without interest, "Why would she resist seeing Bergstrom?"

"Why do people resist seeing a dentist? They don't want their fears confirmed. Same with a shrink. How can Felicia be daddy's perfect little girl if she's found to have a screw loose? He would be justified in replacing her with his granddaughter. Which she thinks he's trying to do anyway."

"You mean she's in some kind of sibling rivalry situation with her own daughter? Felicia's not a little girl, after all."

"Why, because she has tits and a driver's license? For God's sake, John, this didn't start last week. It probably goes back to when Ed's wife left him. Felicia's mother. Twenty-seven years ago. Now . . . aren't you at least going to hint that what you've learned today confirms some of my guesswork?"

"Of course not."

"Then why don't you hang up, Mr. Engle?"

". . . Uh, there was something I wanted to ask . . ."

"Ask away."

"Yes. Well . . . we recognize that we're going to have a problem talking to Felicia about getting help for her. No one's thinking of involuntary hospitalization, anything like that. Her father is convinced that less . . . drastic measures will be beneficial."

"But he's talked himself into a corner."

"Well, hell, you know Ed: say what works now, then find a way out later." It was the first unlawyerlike thing I had ever heard him say—it clearly made him uncomfortable. He went on awkwardly, "Look. He knows Felicia doesn't trust him, which for Ed is something. He knows he can't simply break that promise you heard him make, it would only reinforce her conviction that he's the enemy."

"Yes?"

"So . . . he wants to enlist your help."

I had seen that one coming. Now it was here I couldn't believe it. I was still standing, so I sat down. The ordinary sounds of what was again, however temporarily, a household—the TV on in the living room, Jennifer and Katy in the kitchen—all faded out, until my world had shrunk to a soundproof bubble enclosing me and the telephone, through which a vague sense of presence eventually got through to me.

I murmured intelligently, "My help."

"Yes," Engle's distant voice said.

"You've got a hell of a nerve."

"I'm sure it must seem that way, but . . . She has no friends."

"Ed doesn't want to be the enemy. He wants *me* to be the enemy."

He said in a suddenly exhausted voice, "Think about it, will you?" and hung up.

Household sounds reasserted themselves. I cradled the phone and rejoined Katy and Jennifer like a zombie. Jennifer gave me a concerned look but didn't say anything. Katy, her eyes at half-mast, could only eat half her burger. I ate the rest. She wanted a bowl of Cheerios for desert, so I poured her a small one.

And the phone rang again.

This time it was Ray Gallardo at the copshop. He said Dave Hostetler wanted to see me soonest. I told him I hadn't finished dinner. He said I still had a few minutes before the car they'd sent arrived but there wouldn't be time for brandy and cigars.

"I've got my own car."

"The Chief doesn't want you stopping off to visit sick friends."

"I've got my three-year-old daughter with me."

"We thought so. We're sending a police matron to babysit."

Jennifer said Katy already had a babysitter. I gave her my car keys without being too sure why.

The cop car drove up two minutes later.

∇

Chapter 29

I HAD BEEN EXPECTING a weight lifter type with baleful eyes, but the police matron had a motherly face and was no tougher than the average grade school teacher. When I told her that a friend was going to babysit she just smiled and said too bad, she'd been looking forward to a couple of hours of easy time. She rode back into town with us, as discreetly silent as the two uniforms in the front seat.

We went down the Courthouse Avenue ramp and in the back way. I was logged in and Ray Gallardo appeared from somewhere.

"Thanks for the call, Ray."

"Yeah. Don't tell Hostetler. He wanted the prowl car to come as a surprise."

"Nice of him."

He shrugged distantly, and I followed him down the hall, past the Chief's outer office, which was closed, past the intersecting hallway, and through the double doors labeled DETECTIVE DIVISION.

Ray said, "Clint Farrell's dead."

I blinked.

"Booze?"

"I guess so."

"Is that what this is all about?"

He shook his head. The door to one of the interrogation rooms was ajar, emitting light and a monotonous male voice. Ray opened it wide and ushered me in.

The room was a photocopy of the one I had seen Felicia in that morning, with a couple of extra chairs. Tobacco smoke fogged the air.

Dave Hostetler sat in one of the chairs, filling a pipe in his open tobacco pouch. His face got a look of grim satisfaction when he saw me. Detective Scanlon leaned against a wall, a worn suede boot propped on one of the empty chairs. He was middle-aged, jowly and gutsprung, but there had to be a lot of muscle under the flab because I'd seen him pumping iron down at the health club with the devotion of an Olympic hopeful.

On the table was an open pack of Winstons and someone's police file. Ken Allen sat on the other side of the table, dark hair curling damply over his forehead. His eyes were flinty but he looked physically relaxed, though he might have been working at that.

"Evening, Counselor," the Chief said. "Look who we got here. Know this guy?"

"Sure," I said. "Hi, Kenny."

"Hi," Ken said shortly.

"Ken's been telling us quite a story," the Chief said. "He says Charlie Cromwell lied about driving in from the Steak House before he hit that van Wednesday night. He says no, Charlie was driving downhill on Fox Hollow, and he knows because he saw him. That what you're telling us, Ken?"

"Yeah."

"Why'd you wait this long to come in and tell us?"

"Simple," I said before Kenny could answer. "Because there hasn't been any big media campaign asking witnesses to come forward, and because I asked him to wait."

The Chief's look of satisfaction deepened. He tilted his chair back and reached into his pants pocket for his lighter.

"That's what the kid said!" He smiled suddenly, spun the lighter into flame, and lit his pipe. "Talk fast."

"Nothing to it. I wanted to find a corroborating witness."

"You mean you didn't believe the kid's story," Scanlon said in his monotonous voice.

"I did, but I thought you guys might not."

"Here's a kid doing his duty like a good citizen. Why shouldn't we believe him?"

"No reason—but you didn't. You pulled his file so you could hassle him about his past."

"You're the one with the explaining to do," the Chief growled. "You're not putting us on trial, no one's listening."

"Why not just check out his story?"

"We will—when we think it's worth checking out."

"I already did."

Scanlon said, "Yeah? So what did you do, talk to his girlfriend? And she told it just like he told her to, right? Hell, she's no better than he is."

"So why don't you pull her file too?"

"She goes with this scumbag," Scanlon said. "She fucks around—"

"Who says so?"

"Everyone knows it. She fucks around. Mo Vurpillat says so, he used to date her mother." Scanlon grinned. "You should hear what he says about mama!" He leered at Ken. "Ever make it with mama, scumbag?"

Ken said thoughtfully, "You're a real asshole, y'know?"

"Ever make it with both of them together? Nice little family threesome?"

Ken looked at me.

"Do I have to sit here and take this shit?"

"Why not? You ran in here asking for it."

"You were taking too long, man."

"How would you know?" I said to the Chief, "Scanlon's out of line."

The Chief gave me his disparaging I've-got-your-number look, then turned it on Ken. Ken's lip curled. Hostetler worried his pipestem with his teeth, took the pipe out of his mouth, scratched the side of his nose.

"Go home, kid."

For an instant Ken Allen was just that, a kid, his street smarts and cynicism vanishing in the brightness of sheer surprise. For an instant only. Shutters clanged down over that brief vulnerability.

"That's all? All that hot air, then just 'go home kid'?"

Hostetler growled, "Move your ass before I change my mind."

Ken got up, slowly enough not to seem eager. "Oh, you won't change your mind." Which didn't mean anything, it was just a vehicle for the contempt in his voice.

Gallardo stepped out into the hall. "Let's go."

Scanlon turned on a sweaty grin.

"Hell, you're not so tough, kid."

"Neither are you," Ken said. "You just got a dirty mouth."

Scanlon made a threatening move but I was in the way. Ken gave him the finger as he went through the door.

His and Ray's footsteps echoed down the hall.

"Shit," Scanlon said.

I took the chair Ken had vacated. The Chief eyed me from behind his pipe. Scanlon dropped into one of the free chairs.

"There's something he ain't telling." He started trying to bite a hangnail off his left thumb.

"If his story's verified," I said, "what else is there to worry about?"

"I got a nose for when a witness is holding back," Scanlon said. "Especially when the witness is a chickenshit delinquent we been having trouble with for years. In case you've forgotten, we haven't heard anything to verify his story yet."

Perhaps he had an instinct for sensing an evasion. Like about who else was in Ken's car Wednesday, and who was driving.

"Just name your corroborating witness," the Chief said.

"The most important one is Charles himself. He confirmed Ken's story to me this afternoon."

Scanlon grinned in comfortable disbelief.

"Charlie told you *himself*?"

"Yes."

"Admitted to being in the vicinity of the Osterreicher house about the time Helen Pavlik was shot?"

"Do you know *when* she was shot?"

"Had to be around that time. Clint Farrell heard the shot."

"Clint Farrell heard *a* shot, and didn't know what time it was. Charles told me he got to the Osterreicher house around 8:30 or 8:35. Helen was already dead, or he thought she was."

The Chief said wonderingly, "He admitted to being *inside* the Osterreicher house?"

"Yes. He'd been invited."

"Why'd he admit anything?"

"After I heard Ken Allen's story, I went to warn Charlie he could be in trouble. One thing just led to another. I advised him to come in and tell his story to you."

"He might've," Scanlon said, "if he was innocent."

"He may be. He told me he was in the Osterreicher house and Helen had already been shot when he arrived. You have no real grounds to believe otherwise."

"Aunt Kate told my wife that Clint remembered seeing a woman that night," the Chief said. "He was trying to remember who."

"That's what Clint told us," I said.

"You said Charlie was your most important corroborating witness," Dave said. "Name the others."

"Sorry, Chief. Not yet."

"Aw, shit," Scanlon said in his bored voice. "He's gotta be kidding, Chief, right?"

"Naah, it's about par for this guy." The Chief didn't even look disappointed, just sat there on his wooden chair as lively as a tree stump. He sighed and sucked on his pipe. It squeaked wetly. "Okay, let's see what we got here. Clint said he saw a woman that night. Clint's dead, I don't know if you heard."

"Ray told me. I'm sorry."

"Maybe this woman didn't have anything to do with the murder, maybe she did. Maybe she's one of your witnesses." When I let that one drift by he went on irritably, "You're not counsel representing someone, you're just a witness."

"What did I witness?"

"Don't smartmouth me. You're withholding evidence."

"I'm withholding the name of a witness—not a witness to a crime, only to where someone was at a certain time."

"When a crime was committed. Why withhold the name?"

Scanlon said, "He won't tell us *why* . . . because *why* would also tell us *who*. Right?"

The Chief shifted position. His pipe had gone out; the once fragrant billows it had produced had settled into a rank fog. His gaze went past my left shoulder, and after a while his face suddenly went slack.

"Oh, for God's sake."

Scanlon said, "Huh?"

"What women can we connect up with Helen after she came back? Frances Mary Rowan. My secretary Maggie. Her sister Jennifer

Kendall. Nothing places any of them anywhere near the Osterreicher house that night."

"So?"

"Where was Kate Cromwell?"

"Aunt Kate?" Scanlon said. "Why Aunt Kate?"

"Because she connects up with Helen too. She's Charlie's mother, the Rowan girl's grandma. So what took Aunt Kate to the Osterreicher house, which is where she'd have to be if she saw Charlie there?"

"Slow down, Chief," I said. "I didn't say the witness saw Charlie at the Osterreicher place, and I didn't say it was Aunt Kate."

"No, we figured it out all by ourselves. And if Aunt Kate was there, we gotta talk to her."

Scanlon said, "Ever stop to think maybe she took one of Charlie's .22 pistols in her apron pocket?"

"You want to talk to Aunt Kate, okay," I said. "But maybe you won't have to if you talk to Charlie first."

"What are you worried about?" Scanlon demanded. "What d'you think we do to witnesses, anyway?"

"I think you feed them ice cream and cake, like I saw you feeding Ken Allen."

"Listen, he came in with a story that made Charlie Cromwell look like a murder suspect. He's got a grudge against Charlie that goes back years. Of course we leaned on him. Maybe this time he was going for some serious grown-up revenge."

"What did he do last time?"

"Slashed Charlie's tires. Got caught at it. He was thirteen years old, for Chrissake."

"Why'd he do it?"

"Because he's a hard case delinquent. First it was stealing hubcaps. Then they caught the little shit in possession of a controlled substance in school. He wouldn't tell me where he got it. So he was suspended from school. The welfare people got onto the case about the same time that Charlie made a bid for popularity with 'respectable' voters—the regular church-goers and people who think TV preachers are the greatest thing since sliced bread."

"Did Charles think the drug culture still meant bearded hippies and rock musicians?"

"Who cares? He went on the warpath. Wanted the schools investigated. Wanted the welfare department investigated when it didn't declare the kid's parents unfit and stick him and his brothers and sisters into foster homes. The *Chronicle* printed every word of every speech so they could chop Charlie up like dog meat on the editorial page. The noise got to the kid's mother. She got a bit weird, lost her job clerking at a shoe store, then got born again and began running the house like a prison camp commandant with a Bible in one hand and whip in the other. The husband split. Ken decided Charlie was to blame for everything, so he slashed Charlie's tires and wound up in juvenile court again.

"Big deal. One of those bleeding heart woman judges. The kid's dad paid for the tires and the kid got so many hours community service. Any wonder he's got no respect for authority? Nothing but trouble from that day to this. Truancy, liquor violations, disorderly conduct—"

"Nothing big?" I asked.

"Give him another year," Scanlon said. "Another month."

Ray Gallardo stepped into the doorway.

"Your wife's here, Chief."

"Thanks, Ray. I'll see her in a minute."

"Anything else, or can I go get some dinner?"

"One thing I want you to do first. Both of you. Go pick up Charlie Cromwell."

"Arrest him?" Scanlon said.

"Just say I want to talk to him. If he gives you a bad time, tell him as much as you have to to shake him up a bit. Ray, you do the talking. Remember who he is."

"He's a goddam suspect," Scanlon said.

"He's suspected of not having been where he said he was on Wednesday night." Dave glanced at me sourly. "That do it for you, Counselor?"

I said it did.

Scanlon said, "You gonna represent him, Counselor?"

"Who says he's going to need representation?"

"He looks good for this one," Scanlon said cheerfully, and followed Ray out into the hall.

Voices and footsteps faded out.

Dave Hostetler did nothing for long moments. Then he sniffed, sighed, and tapped his pipe against the heel of his hand. A spray of ash and a few shreds of unburned tobacco fell onto the floor. He tucked the pipe into his shirt pocket and stared at nothing.

I said, "What happened with Clint?"

For a while I thought he hadn't heard me, then he grunted, shrugged.

"Nothing unexpected. Kate Cromwell told my wife he was boozing again, and June called me. Luckily I had Mo Vurpillat just going off duty, so I had him look in on Clint."

"Don't I know him? Young guy, about the size of a two-story house?"

"Yeah, that's Mo. Mo for Maurice, in case you wondered. Mo got to Clint's place around 3:30. He said Clint was okay, ripped to the eyeballs but navigating okay as long as he stayed out of traffic. Mo left the front door unlocked, just on the latch, in case of emergencies."

Hands on knees, he pushed himself up off his chair. He looked spent and slack-muscled. I left the room ahead of him. He turned off the light, leaving the door open.

"A coupla hours later," he went on as we started down the hall, "I tried phoning Clint's place. No answer. No one around to send out this time, so I asked my wife if she'd go."

We left the Detective Division and started down the main hall. There was a light on behind the frosted glass of Hostetler's outer office door.

"She found him sitting at his kitchen table, his head on an outstretched arm. Not breathing. No pulse. I sent an ambulance, but the paramedics couldn't do anything."

He unlatched his outer office door.

"Come on in. I gotta find you a ride."

$\triangledown$

Chapter 30

THE OVERHEAD LIGHT GLARED down on oppressive order. The janitors hadn't emptied the wastebasket yet, so it all had to be Maggie's doing. Her desktop was bare except for the phone and a standing pen set sharply aligned with the edge of the blotter. No book or steno pad lay casually across some empty surface. The typewriter was covered and rolled neatly into a corner. Her life might be unbalanced, but in her office Maggie was in control.

In Dave's inner office June Hostetler was sitting on the old sofa. She looked up; her face was soft.

"Dave, I'm so sorry."

He went into the room and stood behind the desk. His shoulders sagged and his belly hung over his belt buckle.

"I'm sorry you had to find him, hon."

"Better me than no one."

"Yeah, I guess you're right. You know James Keller, don't you? My wife, June."

I summoned the agreeable smile, suitably subdued.

"Hello again," I said.

"Anyway, we're not going to learn whatever it was Clint had to tell us." The Chief sat down heavily in the swivel chair. "If he ever remembered it. I can't even take you to dinner, not yet. Ray and Tim are bringing a guy in, maybe a witness, maybe a suspect. Hell of a thing, when a case involves all the people you know." He studied a typed list, then reached for the telephone. "I gotta find someone to ride this guy home."

She said unexpectedly, "I could do that, Dave."

I started to protest. She plowed right through me.

"Nonsense, Mr. Keller. You don't want to ride in a squad car or wait for a cab. My car's in the basement garage." She offered me a wispy smile, which she turned on her husband. "Besides, it would offer me a chance to coax this young man into telling me what he's been up to the past few days."

"He dug up this witness," Dave admitted.

"Well, then!" June's smile widened. "He may have all sorts of gossipy tidbits I can fish for."

"You can always get those from Detective Scanlon," I said.

She waved a thin hand airily.

"Oh, Tim Scanlon's an old woman. He may be good at his job but all he's really interested in is who's sleeping with whom in what position at what address; and very proud of his daughter, who's a senior at Marshall this year and doesn't go out with boys. Wait till he finds out she prefers girls. No, really, I insist. You come with me."

She stood up, slipping the strap of a flat leather purse onto her shoulder. She looked at me brightly. It was either give in or seem unappreciative. So I thanked her.

"Well, that's settled, then," the Chief said. He gave me a flat look that said he hadn't forgotten the unfinished business between us. "I can always send for you again if I have to." The weary smile said he was kidding. I grinned back to maintain the pretense for June's benefit. He nodded. "I guess that's all for now, Counselor."

June asked, "Should I come back here or go straight home?"

"I don't know how long I'll be, so you might as well go home. D'you mind?"

"Of course not." She turned to me. "It's disgraceful, how often he has to eat TV dinners."

"Drive carefully," Dave said.

We were checked out through the exit leading to the garage with everything still as friendly as could be. Her car was a beautifully cared-for old Mustang, which she hadn't bothered to lock. I got in on the passenger's side while she dug her keys out of her shoulder purse and slid the purse behind the driver's seat. She got in and said briskly, "All right. Since we're going to be friends, do I call you James or Jim?"

"I'm usually Jim. What makes it so important that we be friends all of a sudden?"

A swinging headlight beam from another car turning to leave the garage flashed across her wide lenses. I caught the hint of another smile. Then a sigh.

"We did get off on the wrong foot, didn't we? I'm sure it was my fault, but I thought we stopped all that on the stairs this afternoon. In the office, well, I could hardly offer you a ride if Dave thought we had daggers drawn. He's amazingly considerate and protective of me, you know, for which I love him dearly, and he's quite suspicious of your involvement in all this."

"Was it my ex-wife who told you I beat up women?"

She turned the key in the ignition. The car started at once. Then she tilted her head back and laughed, light silvery slivers of sound a lot like Felicia's but genuinely amused. She started backing out of her parking place.

"First Lucy Scanlon did. Tim's wife. Felicia told me later."

"'I didn't know Felicia even knew Tim's wife."

"I don't think she did, but she knew Jennifer Kendall. Lucy got it from Jennifer when they were having a hen party to celebrate the sale of the Scanlons' old home."

The guard at the exit waved us through.

"I didn't realize Felicia and I were a topic of general interest."

We turned up to Sixth then turned right. It was quite dark now.

"Of course you were. Felicia was gorgeous and obviously used to money. She made quite an impression, though to be frank some people thought her a rich-bitch snob. The few times I met her she was playing the silent martyr to the hilt. Of course she was talked about. I'm not having much luck getting you to talk, am I?"

"Talk about what?"

"Well, our big murder case. Your involvement with so many of the cast of characters."

"That all just happened because Helen Pavlik lived not far from me. Of course, I've known Aunt Kate and Charles for quite a while."

The light at the Manzanita intersection turned red. June braked to a smooth stop, then eased around the corner, heading for Fourth.

She said slowly, and quite unexpectedly, "I think it was a blow to Dave, learning that Helen had had a baby and he wasn't the father. Oh yes, I knew all about that. Always did, because Dave told me. I didn't mind, really. I wasn't much fun in those days, in and out of the hospital, and I remember her as young and quite attractive. But that was all over long ago. . . ."

Her voice trailed off. When I didn't say anything she went on after a moment in a different voice, "Why was Dave so cagey about this witness he's expecting? Though from what he said it has to be someone in our own circle."

The light at Fourth was with us. She turned left and headed for the Pollock Highway.

I said, "Doesn't want rumors buzzing around, I guess."

"I don't start rumors," she said sharply, "though I admit I like to listen to them."

"Like the one about Scanlon's daughter."

"Believe me, I heard that one from an unimpeachable source!"

"Have you got Megan Kendall fully plugged into your gossip network? Yesterday, when you were taking her home, my name came up because I'd picked up Kate Cromwell when you were all in the committee office. You quite innocently told Megan I was a notorious sadist. Just a little something she ought to know. Jesus, June, what do you people do when you talk about someone you have a good reason to dislike?"

"Are you saying the accusation isn't true?"

"Of course it isn't true."

"It originated with your wife. Why would she lie about you?"

"I don't know."

"Is she crazy?"

"I don't know."

"No wonder you're in a custody fight."

What did she know about that? There didn't seem to be much privacy in Dos Cruces.

I asked, "Was it Dave who told you Helen was back in town?"

Her face was serene in profile. "No, I told Dave." The corner of her mouth tilted upward. "Lucy Scanlon told me."

"Just a little something she thought you ought to know, huh?"

"Something like that."

Traffic was thin. I let some time drift by as downtown tapered off into a few semi-residential blocks of apartment buildings and small businesses and neighborhood-type shops.

"Look," she said suddenly, "I know I've done this all wrong."

"Done what?"

"Tried to get you to talk. I thought I might learn something useful to Dave. . . . We've never had anything like this happen before. Anything that's, well, horrible, and touches so many of us. And then of course poor Clint this afternoon."

We passed the illuminated Alpha Beta sign at the corner of Palmetto. Beyond it, Fourth reached into the night with no traffic and few lights before the flashing red signal above the T-intersection with the Pollock Highway.

"There are things I can't tell you because I learned them in confidence," I said. "I don't even know which of them, if any, have anything to do with the murder. Clint told me he guessed he had seen someone he shouldn't have seen at the Osterreicher house, and that maybe that was why he couldn't remember rather than the fact that he was blacking-out drunk."

"He was still quite lucid when you talked to him, then."

"He seemed to be."

"What sort of woman do you suppose Helen was, actually? I mean I've always gathered she was, well, promiscuous poor white trash and not very smart."

"She had dyslexia, which was probably why she dropped out of school. She made it with a lot of guys but had friends who weren't lovers who remember her warmly. Charles doesn't, of course. He's quite convinced she came back to Dos Cruces as part of a plot directed against him personally."

"And you don't think so?"

"No evidence for it. She was an attractive widow of thirty-nine whose husband had left her financially very comfortable and who was trying to find the daughter she'd given up for adoption over twenty years ago. She'd never had any other children and now never could. I think she just quietly moved back to town and leased a house and looked up a few old friends and then somebody came through the front door and shot her."

"Why couldn't she have another child? She wasn't too old."

"It's in the autopsy report. She'd had a hysterectomy."

MacAndie had told me of June's repeated failure to bring a child to term. Would that evoke a twinge of sympathy for her husband's old girlfriend and her attempt to find the baby she'd surrendered? Or would it provoke a flood of abuse?

I looked at her to gauge her reaction. She sat behind the wheel as responsive as a cardboard cutout, staring at the flashing red light and the line of red reflectors running along the fenced shoulder on the other side of the Pollock.

Staring, but apparently not seeing.

I said sharply, "Red light!"

No response. By the time I'd figured out everything I couldn't do about it we were shooting across the intersection.

The front end hit the shoulder. The seat belt harness dug into my waist and ribs, my head bounced on my neck like a ball on a rubber band. The Mustang hit the red reflectors squarely. Wood tore. Fencing flew and I got a sickening sense of being airborne. We only sailed a couple of feet but hit with an appalling crunch. One of the tires burst and the upholstered seat came up to meet me like a granite ledge. The jolt went up my spine and slammed my jaws shut hard enough to fuse my molars and turn my brain to yogurt.

Somewhere in all this the engine died. The car ran a few feet downhill, slewing sideways, and finally stopped. Dust swirled in the headlight beams and for a while no one said a word.

Then I drew a breath of profound relief and let it out through loose lips. I leaned back in my seat. The molars weren't quite fused after all.

"Lucky traffic's so light on the Pollock these days," I said inconsequentially. "Did you have to kill Clint too?"

$\triangledown$

Chapter 31

A DETATCHED CORNER OF my brain was immediately appalled at what I had said. The rest of me, more shaken up by running the red light and crashing through the fence than perhaps I'd realized, didn't have that much sense.

June fumbled a handkerchief to her mouth, dabbed briefly, and examined it.

"I bit inside my lip," she said in a voice of dull bewilderment, pressing the handkerchief to her mouth again. And then, a few moments later, she turned to me and said in the same dull voice, "What?"

"Did you have to kill Clint too?"

"Why on earth would I . . . ?"

She couldn't even be bothered to finish the thought.

"You were afraid he might remember seeing you at the Osterreicher house Wednesday night."

"You said he couldn't remember who he saw."

"Maybe he didn't see anyone. But you were afraid he *had* seen you, and might remember, and might tell Dave. When you called Dave from the public phone this afternoon, you were hoping he wouldn't have anyone to send out to Clint's place, so you could volunteer. But he had Mo Vurpillat, so you had to wait a couple more hours, doing your thing for the festival committee, until Dave actually asked you to go. By then Clint had drunk himself unconscious. What did you do, find a plastic sack and put it over his head and keep it there till he stopped breathing? It might not have taken long. Who knows what kind of shape his heart was in?"

Still sounding vague and unfocused, she said around the handkerchief, "This is absurd."

"Not really." I was dealing off the top, talking to release tension and not hearing what a small wild voice at the back of my mind was trying to tell me. "When Lucy Scanlon told you Helen was back I'll bet she made sure you got the implications. Neither of you knew about the hysterectomy, so you immediately thought of Helen in terms of your one big failure. You'd never been able to give Dave a kid, and here was his old girl friend back, still young enough to do just that. Your husband might dump you for a piece of promiscuous poor white trash. That possibility threw you into a panic. Helen threatened your status, your sense of worth, everything. Who would think of checking the police chief's wife's gun? Or even know she had one? So you took it to Helen's and shot her and drove home. Simple as that."

She lowered the handkerchief, looked at it, then refolded it carefully.

"What nonsense. I was home before 8:00 Wednesday night and stayed there."

"You were seen getting home at 8:30." No need to explain that it was Megan who had seen her. "Clint probably saw you leave the Osterreicher house. Just your luck there's a streetlight in front of it."

"I wasn't there," she said in the same listless tone.

All she had to do was keep saying that. She didn't have to prove she was innocent; the state, the prosecution, *someone* had to prove her guilty. And now finally that frantic voice managed to make itself heard, giving me the advice I had given Clint. *Go with the evidence.* There wasn't any. Neither for the gun my imagination had given June, nor that she was the woman Clint thought he had seen.

"I wasn't there," she said again without force.

She unbuckled her seat belt and turned off the ignition. The dash and headlights went out. She opened her door and the dome light came on. She slid out of the car, dragged her purse out from behind the seat, and slid the strap onto her shoulder.

I was ready to apologize and repudiate everything I had said.

June stuffed her keys and hanky into her handbag. Her hand came out holding a slim little purse gun.

Before she got it leveled I had thrown my door open and was diving out. There was a vicious *snap!* Who knows where the bullet went. I stopped thinking, hit the downslope on automatic pilot, and kept rolling, scrambling to escape the light spilling out of the car. She had to move to the back of the car even to see me over it. By then I was running in darkness over uneven ground parallel to the highway with only the sound of panic in my ears.

My hearing came back when the gun snapped twice again. One of the bullets hit something at the proper angle and spun away in a thin diminishing whine—and then, astonishing in its outraged normalcy, a man's voice yelled, "Hey, lady! Put that gun down! What d'you think you're doing?"

I risked a look. I had to be forty yards from the Mustang. Not many people could hit the back of a barn with a handgun at that range. I dropped to a crouch. I hadn't heard him ride up, but now I heard the crunch of his footsteps. A motorcycle cop, dark uniform, white helmet, came through the gap in the fence dragging a big revolver out of his holster.

June stood by the rear of the car, behind the driver's open door. The gun in her hand looked as inconsequential as a toy squirt gun.

He said it again. "Put the gun down, lady."

June said quietly, "I'm June Hostetler, your boss's wife."

"Yes, ma'am, you could be, but let's do this my way. First put the gun down."

"All right, you take it," June said, and held out the gun to him. It went *snap!* again. The motorcycle cop couldn't have been four yards away. He took a step back, grabbing his gut with his free hand. He sat down heavily.

June still stood there, gun leveled.

The cop said in a thinner, gritty voice, "Drop it, lady!"

June adjusted her aim.

The big gun went off once. June slammed backward onto the rear of the Mustang and damn near over it, then slid off as limp as an empty dress.

Chapter 32

THEY QUESTIONED ME in another of those cramped little rooms.

The wounded cop's name was Hal Hoffman. I had almost met him yesterday, when Mac had made me stop at the scene of the accident. Hoffman had talked briefly to the cops who chased out to the scene, closely followed by an ambulance, when I called in on his motorcycle radio. Even so, I had to tell my story to successive teams of cops till my throat was raw. Their faces were all harder to read than *Finnegan's Wake*. They wanted to suspect I had pulled one of the triggers myself, if not both of them, but Hoffman's story backed mine up. Mrs. Hostetler had fired at Officer Hoffman without provocation. Yes, I saw her adjust her aim as though to fire again after the officer fell. Yes, his action was justified. Yes, I was getting tired—and bored. Of course I appreciated they had a job to do. I just wasn't sure what it was.

Then Hostetler came in with Ray Gallardo. Dave's face was slack with shock, the color of wet putty. Ray did the talking, running me through the whole thing one more time.

When I was through Dave said nothing. After a while he nodded to no one in particular. The look he gave me said I had done him an incomprehensibly malicious injury. He left without saying a word.

Ray chewed his lip.

I said, "June was in no danger from Helen. He wouldn't have traded her, even if Helen could have made him a father. I guess her failures that way left her a bit unbalanced."

"Yeah. Or something."

"You think he suspected?"

"If he had, he'd never have sent June out to check on Clint. Seeing June might have triggered Clint's memory and blown everything. Look, don't blame him too much. The murder rattled his cage pretty bad. It stirred up memories and mean junk—and people kept leaning on him. He'd forgotten about the gun. He said he gave it to her before they were married. She wanted to learn to shoot and be a good cop's wife but never could hit anything. She probably shot Helen from inches away."

"She never came near me. Hoffman was no farther away than you are."

"Her gun better come up guilty or you're in deep shit."

"It will. Otherwise, why'd she try to kill me?"

"How would I know? Come on, I'll take you home."

His car was an old Chevy Nova in need of new seat covers. We took the West Eleventh route. Ray told me Tim Scanlon had taken Charles Cromwell home.

"In a good mood, I bet."

"He was so mad he wanted to accuse the Chief of trying to cover for June by making him the fall guy. We had to restrain him physically. He told us all about you, too. He says you're a lousy meddling shyster son of a bitch. He's going to have you investigated for disbarment."

"It's good to have friends."

"What made her think she could get away with killing you?"

"I don't think she thought. About any of it. She saw Helen as a threat, went into a panic, dug out the gun. Got to Helen's just ahead of the traffic. No planning, just luck. Tonight she came unglued when I told her about Helen's hysterectomy. She'd taken the big chance for nothing. If I'd been thinking straight I'd have kept my mouth shut. Who'd have thought the silly woman would be carrying the gun with her? Anyway, she'd given herself away, so I had to go. Hoffman saw her try, so he had to go too."

We came to Fox Hollow and turned past the darkened shopping center.

"You think she really killed Farrell?"

"I don't know," I admitted. "The autopsy should tell you."

"I wish there didn't have to be one. An unstable woman who led an empty life, or thought she did, commits an impulse murder and gets out of her depth two days later. Bang, bang, end of report. Bad enough without dragging in another murder."

"Yes."

"Jesus," Ray said. "It's real shit when these things hit so close to home."

"They're always close to someone's home."

"Did anyone tell you? We found Helen's will. Left everything to her daughter, Frances Mary Rowan Fairland. Sounds like your little friend from Santa Barbara."

"Shouldn't be hard to establish."

"She won't have to work anymore. Unless she wants to. I guess these arts and crafts people aren't just in it for the money."

He swung the Chevy onto my track and stopped in front of the house.

I got out feeling worn and unathletic. I should have felt great. I'd survived a car wreck and being shot at, and Katy was home with me. The D.A. would have to prosecute Felicia or the *Chronicle* would declare open season on the whole Gang of Three, accusing Ed Hammond's financial involvement in their development scheme of diverting the course of justice. But prosecuting Felicia would itself be a mockery of justice. Maybe I'd get to keep Katy for good, and that was the most marvelous and pitiless and unforgivable thing of all. It made me feel like a bandit, tired and mean, with a bad conscience.

"Thanks, Ray."

He raised a hand and said, "No sweat," but not as though we were buddies or anything. He turned the car and headed back toward town.

The night was warm and still. I should've been able to smell the desert. All I could smell was my own fatigue and sweat. I needed time in a steam room. I needed ten two-hundred yard repeats. I needed a clear path into my own future. Things beyond my control were going to happen in the next few days, and until they did, and a few details sorted themselves out, I couldn't even start thinking straight.

The porch light glared like an unfocused eye. The front door opened.

Jennifer murmured from the opening, "You okay?"

"Thanks, I'm fine." I went inside. "How about you?"

"Oh, fine." She closed the door, took my hand. "The phone's been ringing—Kate Cromwell, Megan."

"I'll call them. Charles, too, I guess. And Fran Rowan. Katy give you any trouble?"

"I got her bathed and tooth-scrubbed and into her jammies right after you left. She fell asleep in my lap watching a Jerry Lewis movie on Channel Five."

Katy's door was ajar. I pushed it open. The Mickey Mouse nightlight glowed softly from the baseboard.

Katy was sprawled on her tummy under the sheet, the yellow Pooh Bear within reach. Her breathing was miraculously free, soft, steady. I bent over and kissed her on the temple and said goodnight. She took one breath that was a little slower and deeper than the others, reached out a hand until it closed on a yellow fabric wrist, then buried the side of her face deeper into the pillow.

I led Jennifer out of the room and pulled the door almost shut. We wandered into the kitchen. She had washed and dried and put away the dishes.

"Thank you, Jennifer."

"Are you going to get to keep her?"

"For now."

"So you'll keep the house and won't have to move to L.A."

"For now."

"Sounds good to me."

"To me, too. Guess what?"

"You're nice to go to bed with, but you lead a complicated life. What are we doing in the kitchen?"

"I was thinking coffee, but what I need most is a shower."

"Goody. Want some company? Or is that out, with Katy here?"

"God, no! You still haven't guessed what."

"What sort of what? Animal, vegetable, heterosexual?"

"Felicia's dad and the family doctor want to get her to a shrink, but she won't go. Now Ed wants me to help convince her she should."

She said, "What does he think you—" and stopped. Her face went blank, then began to look disbelieving. She backed away, her hands making fists, the skin pulled tight across her nose and cheekbones. Her eyes blazed.

"He came to you and you're *flattered*?" Her voice had found a rough steel edge. "My God, that old bastard wants you to help him keep Katy! To talk Felicia into going to a shrink who'll fix her up so she can beat you!"

"She wouldn't let me get close enough. I wouldn't know how anyway."

"You'll find a way, you're the guy who adopts orphans. You've started seeing her as a victim—you're ready to adopt *her*. Thanks, but no thanks. It's been lovely playing house, but this is real time in the real world. I'm not going to hang around and watch them take you apart."

I was suddenly exhausted. I couldn't manage the placating gesture, the disarming grin, any of the usual routines. I couldn't summon the energy.

I heard myself say, "You've got the car key."

"If that's what you want."

My shoulders twitched indifferently. In front of me was a dark-haired slender woman I hardly knew. She had mood swings and problems and responsibilities of her own, and I had no claim on her at all. She had striking eyes and petal-soft lips and tits like flowers. My kid liked her kid. It came to me without urgency, like an echo from an almost forgotten past, that letting her go away mad would be a very dumb move.

I said, "Hell, no, that's not what I want."

I thought for a moment she was going to make some biting retort, but she didn't. I stared at her and she stared at me and for a while we just stood there under the overhead kitchen light, stiff and awkward as a pair of store-window dummies.

She closed her eyes. When she opened them again the fury had left them, and her hands were unclenching.

The stiffness left her shoulders.

"Hey." The ends of her lips quirked uncertainly. "This is getting pretty heavy."

"Heavy stuff on the agenda," I said.

"Yes, but . . . why rush it?"

"No reason to. How about that coffee?"

She said, "How about that shower?"